The Names
of the Moons
# of Mars

The Names of the Moons of Mars

Short Fiction
by

Patricia Roth Schwartz

New Victoria Publishers
Norwich, Vermont

The following stories have been published previously, some of them in slightly different form: "Feather" (entitled"Friends") in *Harpies Quarterly*; "Rosalie" in *The Lau-
rel Review*; "Endangered Species" in *The Creative Woman*; "The Unveiling" and
"Winter Apples" in *Focus, the Literary Journal of the Daughters of Bilitis*; "Sunspots"
in *Unholy Alliances: New Fiction by Women* (Cleis Press); "Bodies" in *Sojourner*;
"The Names of the Moons of Mars" in *Beloit Fiction Journal*.

Typeset in ITC Garamond.
Printed in the United States of America

Library of Congress Cataloging-in-Publication Data
Schwartz, Patricia Roth, 1946–
     The Names of the Moons of Mars : short fiction/ by Patricia Roth
Schwartz
          p.   cm.
     ISBN 0-934678-19-7 : $8.95
     I. Title
PS3569. C5673N36   1989
813' .54—dc19

                                                                    89-3090
                                                                    CIP

ISBN 0-934678-19-7

Acknowledgements

My deepest thanks to the following:

Ellen Frye who first showed Claudia Lamperti my stories and without whose support and tireless editing this book would not have come to pass; the members of Fly-by-Night Writers, my incredible writers' group, with heartfelt appreciation for their love, support, constructive criticism, friendship, and great pot-lucks: Athena Andreadis, Ellen Frye, Amanda Powell, and Susan Stinson; Joan Larkin for her brilliant writers' workshop at Blueberry Cove, Maine, where most of Fly-by-Night originally met each other and at which the title story of this book was written as a free writing exercise in 90 minutes and never substantially changed.

Also to Katharyn Machan Aal, former director of the Feminist Women's Writing Workshops, for her support and inspiration; Vivien "Vee" Sandlund for reading my stories and for being the other "wild desperado"; Margaret Hackman for computer assistance; Claudia Lamperti of New Victoria for believing in me and my writing and for all her hard work, patience, and skill as an editor; Marcie Pleasants for her excellent proof reading; Ginger Brown for the magic I found in her portfolio—images of what I write about even though she did not know my work.

And finally to Suzanna Nolte for entering most of this manuscript into the word processor—and for the love and care that shapes my life as it is now in all its joy and possibility.

Contents

for Suzanna

and

for Ellen

I. Spinsters

Feather

"You've got another letter from that wild desperado person," Anne flings out, tossing me the envelope that contains the Chatham Place reunion invitation. "Over my dead body am I going with you back there. And what kind of a weird name is that for a grown-up? Boo! And the one she's got for you is even worse. Pooh! Paula is a perfectly fine name. I have no intention of calling a lover of mine Pooh. I don't even know what that means."

"A bear of very little brain," I say. This cuts no mustard with her. Anne had been read to, I believe, in her salad days, from the Encyclopedia Britannica. It shows. She's a professor of political science at a prestigious college, the only woman in her department slated for tenure in a few years.

I am a lawyer. Of course, a three-piece suit to me is a shirt, jeans, and underwear. Some days I only manage two of the pieces. I work for a small firm that deals mainly with sex discrimination and gay rights cases. Some weeks we even get paid.

At receptions with other feminist academics, Anne loves to tell people I'm an attorney; after that she usually mumbles into her Ritz cracker and changes the subject. Recently, we've been under a great strain because a colleague of Anne's had found out about a partner-track opening at a snooty law firm called Berkeley, Hubbard, Berkeley and Smith dealing with family relations cases for which I might apply. Anne's pressuring for it.

"Listen, Pooh, I don't mean to interfere, but are you sure Anne is really for you?" Boo, lounging with her feet in her size ten Nikes up on the arm of her goodwill couch, had just gotten back from hitching around Nicaragua the week I fell in love. Boo's a double Sag—tact isn't her strong point.

We'd spent four years together, my best friend Barbara and I, as quasi-roommates in two funky apartments in an old house on Chatham Place in which we shared an entry and a front hall and often a great deal of our lives. Every day after she'd spent a hard day at school (she was apprenticing to become a master carpenter), she'd strip and soak in the tub, taking the phone and a beer in with her. She had an extra long cord that stretched from the jack in the kitchen. It's a miracle she was never electrocuted. I was a law student then, hating every minute of it, dreaming of the day when I could duck into the nearest phone booth and emerge, suited up and ready to fight for truth, justice and the feminist way. When I knew Boo was in the tub, I'd come on down from studying upstairs and scrunch down beside her, fully dressed, we'd gossip in between her calls to her many other friends, lovers, and ex-lovers all over the continent and beyond.

"But you're my best buddy, Pooh," she'd say. "Who else would help me roll my socks at the laundromat? Who else would teach me how to make potato salad? We're desperadoes, you and I," she'd go on, referring in part to how both of us had gotten ourselves out of dead-end jobs and into school, managing on slim resources, "the wild desperadoes of Chatham Place, Boo and Pooh! We answer to no man; we create our own destiny."

"I don't know *what* you see in that woman," Anne would often remark crossly, both when we all lived in the same town and later, after my defection in Anne's footsteps to a bigger metropolis where her plum new job had taken her. Since at that time I was merely a poorly-paid Legal Aid employee and had, as Anne saw it, nothing to lose, I quit my job, pulled up stakes and played wife until I found something else.

"She's my buddy," I'd say. "She's Boo, the other wild desperado."

"Desperate is right—but I don't know why you want to glorify it. What will *she* ever have—becoming a carpenter, for god's sake?"

"A lot of bookshelves," I'd reply. Anne refuses to dignify that kind of talk, so she always goes to sit up late over the page proofs of her book that's coming out soon, *Comparative Political Systems in Borneo*. Of course, we don't have sex.

"Sex." That's what I told Boo about why I was getting together with Anne. I'd never known anyone so passionately clear about what she wanted—from her own body and from mine. Now that we find plenty of differences between our minds, our hearts and souls—something that the torrid interval of our courtship had not allowed us to discover—things have cooled down a lot. Still, I know that I love her. The way our cold toes find each other's in the bed, the vague dreamy look of her eyes when her glasses slip down her nose, the strange lumpy sandwiches she packs for me when I have to work late, all speak of something deeper and perhaps unspoken that we have created between us yet all too rarely tap.

"All you're going to do at that stupid party is talk about old times, people I don't know and things that happened that never involved me," Anne insists, yet, when I offer to go alone, she packs her briefcase, cancels a faculty reception and travels with me, grumbling all the while, to Chatham Place, back to Boo and our motley crew of yore.

I promise her we won't leave her out of the conversation, yet the minute we're in the door, Boo gets me going. The only other people there so far are Zia and Lou, two secondary buddies, apprentice desperadoes, Boo used to call them.

"Where's everybody else?" Anne looks nervous.

"Oh, you know how we are." Boo's opening a beer, letting the creamy foam froth out over the top. "They'll ramble in when they want to; they're all on LST."

"Lesbian Standard Time," I whisper in Anne's ear, trying to fulfill my promise.

We all settle on the floor leaning against the Goodwill couch, lounging on some big cushions I had once helped Boo shop for at Bradlee's. Boo's mother died when she was very young; I'd always attributed her equanimical approach to life to her utter lack of female socialization. She often wore neither jacket nor boots, she was not afraid of spiders and could neither cook, sew nor decorate. For all that, she relied on me, the well-bred daughter of an earnest family. "I never have people over for dinner, Pooh," Boo would often wail, having perhaps read *New Woman* magazine or some such at the dentist's.

"You have me over all the time."

"Yes, but you bring your own dinner!" And, true enough, often, 6 P.M. would find us often on her couch, each with a plate of something—Stouffer's or boil-in-the-bag we'd each cooked in our own separate kitchens—to watch Mary Tyler Moore reruns. This, I see now, has always been my ideal for a relationship—Mary and Rhoda. Anne was more like Phyllis. No accounting for lust.

"So who's still in town? Who've you heard from?" Zia and Lou burst out, and then follows an hour of solid gossip, nothing malicious, just catching up, the stuff lesbian gatherings are made of. Anne, having come out after an intense seminar on "Woman-Identified Sexual Politics" at a major feminist conference, was often lost at times like this.

We go on about a few people—Liz's breakdown, Ellen's becoming born-again, Brandy's flight into the arms of a man, their baby, Karla's baby (via a turkey baster), Jo's move to Arizona and subsequent election to head of the Battered Women's Services for the state, Andrea's novel in which she exposed all five of her ex-lovers, Margie's arrest for destroying property (her cheating lover's window, smashed with rocks), Bonnie's daughter's drug problem, Nesta and Carol's house, Cora's new romance with a gorgeous acupuncturist from Big Sur, Joanne and Sally's new business doing paint and wallpaper, Ricki's multiple lovers....

"You know who I wonder about?" Zia says, lounging back against her cushion. "Feather."

"Who?" Anne's brow by now looks permanently creased. She's worn much too nice an outfit, was trying without any success to keep it from crease or stain, impossible in Boo's environment.

"Feather," I echoed...and it was as if I were back there that New Year's Eve in the frigid cottage by the river so many years ago.

Born Faye Esther Stein in 1952 in South Jersey, Feather came to our small New England city as part of a lesbian/feminist country commune, Emma Goldman house. The collective were four city women, outspoken, political, flamboyant, thrust among us like the carnival come to town; all of it felt exotic, dangerous, alluring. Our first introduction was an ad placed in our women's center newsletter inviting all lesbians to a potluck at the farm. Many of us carpooled the forty-five minutes to the country location. For a while we just wandered around the rambling, shabby, sparsely furnished house, gorged on hummus and pitas and enormous platters of veggies, then finally huddled after dark in the living room where a fire failed to start in the ancient grate as the house filled with smoke. The price of our meal was having then to listen to our hostesses deliver a lecture on feminism, Marxism, classism, separatism and several other "isms" most of us had never heard of.

Feather was the youngest by far of the group, somehow not as tightly connected as Marta, Pat, and Bev, all seasoned veterans of the New Left and, after that, Radicalesbians. They'd picketed together, been arrested together, had heads busted together, been each other's lovers in turn for years. Somewhere along the way, as one would a stray puppy, they'd picked up Feather, needing a fourth for rent.

Marta had inherited the farmhouse and land from her grandmother, the only member of a dwindled family who hadn't lived in "The City," as all of them called it.

Our community, apolitical, provincial, and insular as it was, remained a bit cowed by Marta, Pat, and Bev. Feather was easier to adopt. She got work at a daycare center where she was fabulously inventive with the kids, whom she resembled in baggy overalls, rainbow suspenders, squashy hats adorned with the feather of her chosen name, and in her elfin stature, enormous brown eyes and tilted smile. Once the director figured out what "Out of the Closets, Into the Streets" on the button on her backpack meant, she was sacked. She waited table then at The Edible Mushroom where she got to know most of our community, particularly Lou, the cook.

Feather's parents, Lou is remembering now, were blue-collar workers, City College night students, passionate social activists. Feather called herself a Red Diaper baby. Her father was accidentally killed in a demo. Her mother was later accused, within their particular political group, of being an informer. She was tried and convicted, Feather always maintained, by rumor mill. When all of their former friends deserted her, the young mother had to raise her child alone on next to nothing. Feather told Lou that sometimes her mother would hit her, but now she understood how the hard times must have provoked her to it.

"So what happened to Emma Goldman House?" Anne's getting interested in spite of herself, I can tell.

"Oh God, you wouldn't believe it," Zia takes up the story. "The whole shebang crashed in flames one month after the big opening."

"Yeah," says Boo, "some kind of huge conflict over money and class. All the chickens died. The three Honchos split and the house was put back on the market. Feather got a job pumping gas—remember—beside the restaurant. She found that great place to live down by the river, some artist's cottage or something. I think the artist had a grant to go to Italy, and she let Feather have it for peanuts for watching her stuff."

"Then she got really active," Zia goes on. "She joined everything—the coffeehouse collective, the women and violence group, the newsletter committee. I used to see her at every meeting."

"Her and her dog!" Lou is laughing.

"Remember that mangy mutt?" Boo's reaching for another beer, practically wiping the tears of laughter from her eyes.

"She didn't believe in flea powder!"

"She used some organic remedy—little flannel pouches—hanging around its neck on a string!"

"God! That dog stank of garlic but it kept on scratching all day!"

"Whatever was it's name?"

"Naibsel."

"What?" Anne's incredulous. She's even hunkered down on the floor, which is going to be curtains for her new slacks.

"Naibsel. Lesbian spelled backwards," I tell her.

"Oh God, yes," Lou says, "and she claimed that was Sanskrit—some ancient temple inscription to some goddess."

"I slept with her once," I tell them.

"You did? You slept with Feather?" Anne can't decide whether she's horrified or outraged.

"No, no." Boo and I are leaning on each other now, clutching our ribs. "She only slept with Naibsel—not Feather. Her virtue's intact, Anne! Honest! I swear! She told me all about it the next day," Boo promises her.

"Yeah—you fink," I shoot at her. "You hitched a ride with whatever cutie you were shacking up with that night and left me. My car wouldn't start. It was New Year's Eve," I explain to Anne, "ten below and a party at Feather's for the whole community. Were you there?" I turn to Zia.

"Sure. I'll never forget how cold it was. She kept the windows wide open so the animals could come and go at will. She had two cats—Sappho and Mata Hari."

"What *was* her reason for never turning the heat on?" Lou asks me. "I forget."

"Because," Boo supplies, "she believed that women could generate our own body heat by psychic means."

"My God," says Anne.

"Well," I defend Feather, "it *was* in the *The Wanderground*. Anyway, the animals waltzed in and out all night. Feather felt they had a right to a natural life—she didn't want to restrict them."

"That's all well and good, but personally I drew the line at letting them tiptoe through the refreshments," says Lou. "That's why I didn't stay. I just couldn't bear to eat anything once I saw those little footprints snaking through the tofu."

"But, Paula, you slept there." Anne really wants to know the rest of the story, not quite sure if she can trust Boo's assurances.

"I *told* you, it was ten below and my battery couldn't take it. I had no choice. But I didn't get any sleep. Naibsel was on the spare room mattress and she was a big dog. There wasn't room for me. Feather wouldn't make her leave the bed. She said that dogs shouldn't have to be second-class citizens and sleep on the floor. She said we had to learn to love animals because, in the case of nuclear war, we'd have to evacuate with them to the hills."

"Incredible! Remember when we held the meeting to start a women's restaurant?" Lou asks.

"Yes," Zia goes on, "and she said it should be a free soup kitchen—that women shouldn't have to pay for food."

"Dogs and cats, either." Boo's laughing.

"Right. She said no woman had the right to exploit another woman financially—you know, like feminist musicians charging admission to concerts."

"Yes, she called them 'star trippers,' and she thought that women's bookstores shouldn't charge, and in fact, they shouldn't even sell books because only middle-class women got taught how to read well enough to really use books."

"So what happened?" Anne keeps on pushing.

"The restaurant group broke up," Lou said. "It just splintered and died out. No one could agree after she started hassling us."

"Were you still in town after she was arrested?" Zia asks me.

"Yes, and I still have copies of the women's center newsletter with all those letters to the editor, pro and con. Most of them con."

"Yeah, it was pretty cruel," says Boo, "trashing her and what she had done. Personally, I think it was pretty brave. Not that I condone violence or destruction of property, but...."

"What on earth did she do?" Anne asks.

"She and an old friend from the city—a straight woman, actually—staged a sit-in in that adult bookstore that used to be over on Prentiss Street—you know, by the bus station. Her partner in the action was a nurse, and they drew blood from their arms and threw it all over that stuff in the back room. Feather said all those books and magazines showed kids and everything. I guess it was pretty vile. That store was notoriously disgusting. Real hard core."

" So did she go to jail?"

"Yes. She got out in ten days, though. She had a superb lawyer—the son of a lawyer her parents used to work with in the old days. I guess he scared up the money for her fine some way or other."

"I thought she wouldn't speak to men."

"Mostly she didn't, but eventually she was saying that after the nuclear holocaust we'll have to evacuate with them, too, so we'd better start getting friendly."

"My God—men and dogs!" Boo said. "I'd rather sustain a direct hit!"

"But she had an awful time in jail, anyway," Lou went on. "She said she was raped there—not by the guards, but by women, for being a lesbian. She said they...."

"No, Lou—don't go into detail. I believe you. I know it happens. I just can't take it." I begin to feel overwhelmed with feelings I'd long suppressed. Anne knew all about me and Boo—the wild desperados and all our escapades. There was a grimmer side, too. One I'd just as soon keep buried.

"Well, I for one never believed she made those calls," Boo jumps in, as if to my rescue.

"What calls?"

"Well, no one really knows. Jessica—she's a therapist—she started getting a lot of weird obscene calls...from a woman...."

"But a therapist works with disturbed people. It must've been one of her clients...."

"No...Jessica said that she worked with normal people, that none of them could've done it. But, I must say, she never actually claimed that Feather did it, either."

"Then who did implicate Feather?"

"Anybody. Nobody. It was pretty terrible."

"I did visit Feather once, after she left for New York," Lou says. "I looked her up when I was down visiting my cousins in the Bronx. I never believed she made the calls, but we didn't talk about it. Naibsel had been injured by a car, and Feather couldn't find a job. I gave her what I had for the vet bills, but there really wasn't anything else I could say or do."

Hearing all this, I feel ashamed. What no one here knows, not even Boo, is that Feather came to me right after Emma Goldman folded, Naibsel trailing behind on a piece of tattered rope, necessity having forced Feather to break her rule about freeing animals from second-class citizenship. She knew that my apartment had an extra bedroom that most of her friends' didn't have. I sent her away. "The landlord won't allow pets," I said. This happened to be true. It was some time after that that I turned down an internship with a private firm in order to work with Legal Aid.

It was all so long ago, yet I see her eyes, sometimes—Feather's—at night, before I go to sleep. They're huge, like the ones on those horrid gift shop posters of little kids with giant cowlicks standing up on the tops of their heads. Feather found a place to stay that same night with Brandy and Ricki, who were lovers at the time; she stayed for several weeks until she found the house-sitting job. That was when she planned the action. After she got out of jail and all those rumors about the phone calls started, she split for the city. After Lou's visit, no one in our community ever heard from her again.

Now. all of us just sit, pulled back into the present in sudden silence, one of those moments that happen in group conversation, a
lull as if on cue. "A ghost walking on your grave," we used to say as
kids. We can't seem to get up any more steam for talk. We'd been
laughing about Feather. Now, I see that we wish, in some clumsy
way, to honor her—even if only with our awkward silence.

The door bell rings. Rowdy voices call out. Boo jumps up. The
party has begun.

"That's a pretty sad story about Feather," Anne murmurs into my
neck as we snuggle down—it must have been 3 A.M. The party had
finally wound down—in Boo's double bed. She was either out on
the couch, as she'd said she would be, or, as I really suspected, off a
few blocks away in Zia's bed.

Anne's hand cups my breast. My nipple tingles alive. Her tongue
flicks my ear lobe, her thigh eases its way between mine. It's clear
what she wants; visits to or from my old gang always do that to her,
as if passion between us would erase those bonds, tie me only to
her. My hand slides down to take in the curve of her firm bottom—a
pleasure I haven't enjoyed in a long while—to draw her to me.

"I know. I think about Feather sometimes. Annie...I don't want to
take the new job." I feel her stiffen, begin to pull away, all that melting softness gone rigid.

"Why, Paula? Don't you want to get ahead? Don't you want to
succeed?"

"Don't I want your version of success, you mean? Don't I want to
let you be proud of me?" I pull away, too.

Anne is completely disengaged. Now she sits up, pulling the
sheets over her bare breasts. Even in the extremity of the moment,
my fear and rage, I hate for the lovely sight of them, in the faint light
of the sinking moon through Boo's tattered shade, to vanish. It
seems that all that warmth and pleasure might move forever past my
holding. I wrap myself in the rough blanket, then stand up, almost
reeling from fatigue yet with a cold resolve seeping through my
body.

"I'm sorry, Anne, but I have to do what's right for me." The cli-
ché almost sticks in my throat, but I know now, from long experi-

ence, that nothing of greater brilliance is going to come to me.

"It's being here again," she says, "with Barbara.... (She refused to say Boo.) "...and all of those other losers, that's influencing you,"

"My friends are NOT losers!" I glare at her, my face hot with anger, my stomach knotted with fear.

After a long pause, she speaks. "I'm sorry," She looks sheepish; her eyes drop. "That was unkind. They aren't. They're good women—and they love you. I guess I...well...." Her hand twitches on the sheets. "You know what it really is?" she seems to let out a long, scary breath.

"What?"

"I really feel like a fool admitting this, but I feel left out...jealous. Barbara and those others—they have a place in your heart where I can't ever be. I'm not like them. I'm not funny and zany. I only know how to work hard." While she's talking, I remember the story she told me once about her father holding up her straight-A report card and asking, "Where are the A-plusses?" She had told me this to illustrate how well he'd motivated her toward success.

Anne, without her horn-rims, always looks vulnerable. This moment, this night, she looks utterly lost, a small, abandoned child. It's a side of her I've yet to fully encounter. She pulls the sheet tighter, seems to curl inward, as if herself alone were her only buffer against a cruel world. I know where I've seen those eyes before, that lost look.

Draping the blanket over me, I shuffle off to the kitchen to put on tea, not very easy in a kitchen belonging to Boo. Between three bottles of A-1 steak sauce—"Well, you *told* me a good shopper takes advantage of sales!" I could almost hear Boo screeching—, a package of Hamburger Helper and a box of saltines, lies one sticky, crumpled Lipton's tea bag. I pry it off the shelf and begin to boil water in a blackened saucepan. Then I scour out two heavily encrusted mugs. One says "Bob's Auto Lube" on the side.

All this activity helps me to calm and settle. What can I do? My life isn't working and I don't have a clue. Maybe Anne's all wrong for me. Maybe I should dump her and start all over. Maybe I should move back here with Boo and the gang. On the other hand, maybe I should take the job with Berkeley, Hubbard, Berkeley and Smith, buy a lot of gray flannel, get a pair of pumps with small stacked heels and start going to women's power breakfasts.

I realize then that any one of us can only run so far so long. Eventually we've got to turn and face what we're running from. I've never believed in second chances. Maybe, though, I decide now, I could start to imagine new beginnings.

Behind me I can hear Anne crying. This has never happened before. Bearing the tea, I turn and go in.

"Do you want to leave me?" she says. "Do you want to move back here with your friends?"

Moonlight, soft and lustrous, floods the room. Anne's face is pale, her tears gleam on her cheeks.

I know then what has to happen, what I have to do. I sit down heavily on the bed, hand Anne her mug, and take a gulp of tea. It tastes like old gym shoes. "No," I say, "No. I want to go back home with you and talk about a lot of things. I want to see my friends here sometimes. I want to find some friends at home we both like. I don't want to go to those receptions with the Ritz crackers. I do not want to change my job. Some of us have to do what there is to be done— no matter what the cost. I like me and the way I am. I guess you and I need to find out if we can work out our differences, but I'm willing to try if you'll just let me be."

She wipes her nose on the sheet. She looks up at me and we look at each other for a long time. It's as if I were seeing her face for the first time, letting her see me. I feel something stir deep inside, different from lust, from the careless passion we'd once known, yet it pulls me.

"Okay," she says, finally. Her voice is small. "Okay...Pooh."

Intensive Care

Six years I've lived at Bradford Court with Madeleine for a neighbor. Her window boxes, wired to the railing of her balcony porch, groan each summer under the weight of marigolds, petunias, geraniums. This year Madeleine's taking no chances; the flowers are plastic, garish, perpetual. Beside them she's planted a little statue, plastic, with a fabulous crown and stretched-out arms. Madeleine tells me it's the Infant Jesus and he prays for all of us.

Every time I cross the courtyard to my entryway, I have to pass Madeleine and the Infant. She always sits, plump legs white as grubs, propped on a folding canvas stool, ample bottom cradled in a canvas sling chair, a straw hat with "Miami Beach" lettered on the brim tilted over her blue-white curls.

Jack, her husband—shorter and just as plump, but without the curls, only a few strands of hair combed over his shiny pate—used to occupy the sling beside her. For weeks now, mysteriously, he hasn't appeared.

I'd like to stop to chat and ask. A foreboding deep in my gut pushes me onward with just a wave and the kind of smile that happens with the mouth, not the eyes. From May to October every year for six years, Jack and Madeleine have served as a kind of audience before which I appear every time I walk past. Jack's absence has coincided exactly with the appearance of the flowers and the Infant. I'm no dummy. I know when I'm well off pretending nothing's up.

It's just that there's been too much, I'm thinking. Everything's been just too much. First off, Artemis, my black cat, disappears. Next, I'm out of work, laid off by the law firm where I was a paralegal. Mother and Father are off again as usual, this time Sri Lanka—

or is it the Kashmir? I forget. They did Kenya and Johannesburg last season, I do remember. I have a shelf dedicated to the gifts they send me, little figurines and vases and things, each more useless than the last. "I know this isn't much, dear, but I really don't know your size, dear," Mother will say, over the phone, each time. I don't like to remind her that she never did.

To fill the hours I'm thinking of volunteering at Children's Hospital where my friend Vicki works as a nurse. "Intensive care," she says when asked. "It'll kill ya every time." Vicki chain smokes and has the foulest mouth on a female I've ever encountered. I always liked her because I knew I could never bring her home.

My ex-boyfriend, Virgil, the civil rights lawyer, got himself arrested in a demo about U.S. aid to the Contras, and, since I can't knit or bake, I really have nothing to offer him now. Besides, there's the little matter of the other woman he got himself chained to the fence with....

Except for Madeleine's insatiable curiosity—she asks more questions than the Census—there's nothing now for me to take care of.

Actually, come to think of it, that's not true. Peaches, my new room-mate, puts her furry claws up against the glass in her magnificent glass-walled garden-court condominium, scrabbles a bit toward me in greeting, seems even to know her name, as I dribble water into her dish. Only Vicki would have a tarantula named Peaches for a pet. Only Vicki would decide to strip and varnish the floors of her entire apartment herself using a toothbrush to apply five coats of varnish one after the other. "Peaches'll die if she smells this shit. You'll have to take her."

I agreed, but only until feeding time rolls around again. This requires live crickets every six weeks. I never liked that dumb Disney movie about the wooden puppet, don't mind crickets being consumed, yet I can't quite feature watching while their little limbs telescope into Peaches' mouth.

So I come and go, structureless now except for Peaches' watering schedule and the usual mundanes like laundry and food shopping, which seem to stretch out endlessly now, instead of being jammed into odd extra moments, or, more often, not getting done at all. I've even started folding the underpants neatly, rolling the ankle socks into little balls made out of turning matching pairs inside out and over each other. I've also started standing in front of the rows of breakfast cereal at the Star Market, reading the labels for nutritional content, assessing the unit price. How much worse can it get?

Actually, this evening there's plenty on the agenda besides underpants and cereal. Vicki's invited me to a Tupperware party at the home of Nancy-Ann, another nurse. Vicki abhors these events, goes only to shock with her assessments of the stud potential of all the new doctors, and afterward, to gossip unmercifully to me about the sex life of all her friends. Since I have none myself, I'm safe.

My other possibility is a meeting at the Somerville Town Hall about tenants' rights. We all got a flyer to attend. I'm not sure who passed out these missives, but I think I recognize the style of Arthur Demetri, my upstairs neighbor, who lives there with his wife and kid, the one who was born with a heart defect and was supposed to have some risky surgery. In order to distract himself from this hideous reality, Arthur buries himself in causes. He's always circulating petitions about things like whales, dolphins, the rights of trees.

This one's a little closer to home. Bradford Court's an ancient structure, a red brick monstrosity, risen L-shaped around a square of dirt and weeds. In the center stands a chipped granite birdbath inside of which a chubby cupid with a fig leaf over his little crotch ("Much like my last lover's," Vicki always says, as she passes) lifts a dimpled arm.

I wonder now, when I pass by clutching a heavy grocery bag full of Quaker Oats'n Honey All Natural Granola, what Madeleine's Infant thinks of this rival. Here on this neglected and dislocated piece of earth, Pagan and Christian seem to intersect, under the shade of a droopy catalpa and a few measley azaleas whose blooms wither as soon as they emerge.

I don't blame Madeleine a bit for going plastic. Miles Management Corporation took over the building last winter after Mrs. Forman, the building's owner, was shunted off to a nursing home in Bradenton, Florida. Recently, they've sent us all letters trying to jack up the modest rent to a sum that none of us can possibly afford.

Bunny, her son, who owns a lot of other property, mostly tenements in Roxbury, Arthur Demetri found out, was the one who
packed her off after she fell in her top-floor apartment. Rumor has it
he's got power-of-attorney, and no one knows where his daughter
Kath is. She used to work here summers while she was at Northeast-
ern's engineering program. She'd help out Mr. Webb, the maintenance man, as well as take a lot of the older tenants shopping in her
rusty Rabbit. Arthur said he'd heard she was working now on an oil
rig in Greenland.

I used to want to do stuff like that, too, but Mother thought a job
at a law firm would always provide security— not to mention a lawyer husband. If Mother had ever gotten a load of Hollowell, Hollowell, Gonzalez and Fink, she'd understand why, at pushing thirty-
three, I haven't exactly managed either.

Bradford Court's a colony of leftovers and left-behinds, I realize
now, as I shuffle across the courtyard, praying that Madeleine won't
be out on the porch. Because of her prime location, she doesn't miss
a trick, found out the names of everyone in my life by just asking
them on their way to my door. She loves to pepper me with questions, too. "Haven't seen Virgil lately, dear. You haven't had a fight
now, have you?" "You look nice today, Marty—a job interview, I
hope?" "Where's that nice friend of yours, the nurse? She's really got
to cut out that smoking, not good for the complexion."

On the other hand, I'm almost praying she will be out, Jack beside her, because that would be a good sign. On the third hand—
it's always seemed to me that only two hands are definitely insuffi-
cient—I haven't had a good sign now in more time than I can remember. In fact, I probably wouldn't know one if it came up and bit
me on the nose. When I start stopping in front of the ol' Infant and
genuflecting, then I'll know I'm really far gone.

Better go water Peaches, have a little Honey'n Nuts granola, and
call Roger—a friend of Virgil's and mine from Hollowell, Hollowell,
Gonzalez, and Fink—to see what I can find out about Miles and our
imminent evictions.

"Those bastards! Haven't got a leg to stand on," Roger spews
out, after ascertaining for sure that I haven't been in contact with Vir-

gil. Then follows a huge amount of legalese which I ought to know about but can't seem to grasp. His reassurance doesn't help. All I know is that in thirty days I could be out on the street—Peaches with me, if Vicki's floors haven't dried. And what about Madeleine and Jack? I know those plastic flowers'll take root anywhere, but what about them? They've been here thirty years. So have Brigid and Bill, the couple who live underneath me.

Until I found out his nickname, I never used to call Bill anything, because Ulysses, his real name, seemed too formidable. He and Jack used to work at MIT as maintenance supervisors. Now they draw their pensions. Brigid gets one, too, from the Food Service and Cafeteria Workers' Local. What Madeleine used to do, I don't know. She asks more questions than she answers. I imagine she was a switchboard operator who listened in on all the calls—or a postal employee who steamed open the letters.

Down the hall from Madeleine lives Mr. Bronski. I don't know him very well, but he used to love my cat Artemis. He called her Blackie because he didn't know her name, fed her chicken livers behind my back, and wept when he learned of her disappearance. I had to tell him about it when we met in the laundry room one week after his wife's death.

He was smoking that cigar he always has jammed in his mouth, below his black-rimmed glasses and pitted nose, trying in vain to stuff what looked like an army blanket into the washer. He was using something to push the blanket down that resembled a sawed-off broom handle.

Before, his wife, who went to the same hairdresser as Madeleine, (except that she favored the lavender rinse) always did the laundry for the two of them. "Sophie just keeled over in the bank," he told me, "just keeled over, just like that. They called the paramedics. She never woke up. Just keeled over." He kept chewing on the end of the cigar, all the while pushing the army blanket down into the soapy water.

"So where's Blackie?" he said valiantly, trying to change the subject.

"Sorry, Mr. Bronski," I've finally begun to learn that the subject isn't that easily changed. "She's gone. I guess she died, too."

We stood there crying, both of us, until the washer started to overflow and I had to go call Nick. Now Nick is another story. He has a beer belly and carbuncles on his neck. None of us like him. When Mr. Webb, the former maintenance man, was declared brain-dead on arrival at Somerville Hospital after a massive stroke, Vicki said to me, "How could they tell?" Even though she was right, all of us missed him nevertheless. At least he'd amble over several days after your request to unplug the sink or free up the toilet and fumble around with a wrench or something. Nick just fumbled—with his hands. The last time I'd had occasion to call him, when I couldn't get any hot water, he'd snuck up behind me in the hallway after replacing the faucet, and put his revolting hand on my shoulder. I know he doesn't have carbuncles on his hands, but I could feel them as if he did, feel cold pus oozing onto my shirt.

I hated myself for weeks afterward for doing nothing, saying nothing, for just walking fast out of his reach when I saw him heading for the courtyard. "I would've surgically removed his balls and stuffed them where the sun don't shine," said Vicki, who always carries a disposable scalpel in her rucksack. "What's the matter with you?"

It occurred to me then, starting to put my Quaker Oats away onto the high shelves in my pantry, hurrying up so I could do another load of laundry and then maybe reorganize my closets again, that everyone here in Bradford Court was not only a leftover but a loser—at least what I mean is that we've all lost something. And now Miles was trying to take us away from each other.

Roger could help if I'd let him. He's a real brick, the kind of man who has a telephone directory for every major city in the U.S. and every suburb of Boston and town in Massachusetts arranged alphabetically on the shelves in his den. I know this because Virgil and I went to a party there once. He also has maps of every possible location you can think of in cardboard map boxes arranged also alphabetically on some other shelves. When you go out driving with him, which we did once up to Singing Beach, he likes to use a magnifying glass and a little ruler and he likes to calculate the speed of travel between points. He has a rolodex full of all the people he has ever known since kindergarten and he calls each one of them on their birthdays using his AT&T credit card. He used to call me, too, when I was dating Virgil, but now he's not sure if it's okay.

A burning desire comes over me suddenly, either to get ahold of Vicki and get to the Tupperware party quick (this is because I'm starting to fantasize about all the things I can encase in airtight, watertight plastic, even things I don't own yet, but could acquire in order to have that experience) or to see Jack.

I rush out into the courtyard and run smack into Peggy and Joe. They're a couple, too, although Peggy is much younger than Brigid and Madeleine, and she and Joe aren't married. At least they don't have the same last names. No one ever asks what's the scoop, although I know that whatever it is, Madeleine knows.

"Where's Jack?" I ask, not bothering with preliminaries. I never do with Peggy and Joe. They're both blind. They always know it's me, and exactly what's up, and how I'm feeling. Joe gestures with his white cane, asks me again a few times about Artemis whom he, too, dearly loved. She used to come up and rub around his cane and his ankles, purring to beat the band.

"Back now," they say. "Been having some tests."

"Tests? Tests for what?"

"Nothing good," they say. Their eyes speak volumes. I don't press further and wish them a good day. Off they go, arm-in-arm as always, Joe's cane tap-tap-tapping down the walk, past the catalpa, past the cupid, past the Infant Jesus whose head does not incline a bit.

"Tupperware!" my mind screams again. This, I realize, has come up in direct opposition to a bunch of other thoughts such as a compulsion to contact my parent's travel agent or else the warden of the Danbury prison. Tupperware seems imminently more sensible. I calm myself, as I trot back inside, with soothing fantasies of women.

I have always loved women—the lines and lines of secretaries and paralegals at Hollowell, Hollowell, Gonzalez and Fink, all with chubby china mugs out on their desk-tops, philodendrons, pictures of kids and grandkids, catalogues whipped out at break (along with homemade cinnamon rolls and Sara Lee and Dunkin Donuts) for Avon and Popular Club and other things you could dream over and get on layaway. All that learning how not to live in the moment because the moment was so unbearable, all that salvaging of the future for themselves, in the form of rosy tints for the flesh, relaxing scents for the bath and indestrucible vessels for perishables that would let you sleep at night knowing the egg salad couldn't go bad.

I want in on this sisterhood in which even Madeleine could be a patron saint. Madeleine cares—I see that now. What would I do without her or Jack, whom she refers to like this: "When I first moved to this building, they wouldn't let you have any pets, except your husband." All this is directed toward me who can't catch a husband and whose cat attracts male strays who spray around Madeleine's porch, stinking up the air.

A chorus of wild grieving wails wells up in my chest—for my lost job, my lost cat, for Virgil, for my mother who thinks I am still a legal secretary and who doesn't know that my cat is lost or even her name.

Just as I am about to rend my garments or something equally annoying—as later I would have to mend them, and I don't sew—there comes a knock at the door. Fearing Nick, I'm cautious, sticking only my nose around the chain lock.

It's only Bill, in his undershirt, arm hairs tufting out under the scoop sleeves. Since I'm out of work, he's taking to making little surprise visits to ask me if I saw *Jeopardy*, or to bring me a supermarket flyer left at the door.

This time he wants to know if I've heard about the tenants' rights meeting tonight. I can smell the homely scent of hamburger and onion wafting up from their kitchen.

"Are you going?" I ask.

"Well, years ago, you know, there was something like this. People were afraid to go. There was a reporter there. People were ashamed to be seen. They covered their faces with their pocketbooks." Bill shows me how that's done, making a pocketbook out of his hands.

"Well, I'll be up the creek, then. I don't own a pocketbook."

"But what can we do? We can't pay what they're asking. Not on our checks."

Not on mine either. Unemployment now just covers the basics and job openings are few. "My friend, Roger, the lawyer, says we'll be okay. He says they don't have a leg to stand on. Bill, how's Jack?" I ask him abruptly. We never refer to each other's misfortunes here. Even Madeleine keeps assuming Virgil will be back, Vicki will quit smoking.

Bill is silent, just shakes his head gravely. Downstairs Brigid shrieks for him. Upstairs in the Demetri's apartment, the vacuum cleaner begins to roar just as the baby begins to howl.

I close the door, sit down and begin to make my list: bacon, dried apples, pins, stamps, leftover cottage cheese, leftover deli potato salad, leftover canned soup. These are all things that can be stored in Tupperware. I get up. I water Peaches. I sit back down. I begin to write a letter to the Miles Management Company telling them about the incident with Nick. When I get to the part about what I am going to do with Nick's surgically removed balls, I crumble the letter up, pitch it across the room. Eventually, I tip over onto the couch pillows and drift off, sleeping like a stone through the tenants' meeting, through the party at Nancy-Ann's, through perhaps the rest of the tattered remnant of my poor excuse for a life.

Suddenly, a hideous noise splits the night—and my skull. It rips through the silence and dark, a torpedo cutting a ship like butter. It pulses in my head like a scream from an expressionist painting. My heart races—yet I can't seem to move. Finally, I realize where I am and what has happened—it's nighttime and I am on my couch and this is the fire alarm.

A frantic knock at my door, a voice, which I eventually recognize as Bill's with Brigid's behind him as a counterpoint, calls out, "Marty, wake up, wake up, Marty, there's a fire!"

"Yeah—I hear it. I'm coming." But I don't move. I don't care. I think of my parents receiving a telegram in Sri Lanka, turning to the discreetly deferential dark-skinned waiter on the palm-fringed veranda with expressions as if a mosquito were bothering them. I think of Virgil being led to the electric chair calling out my name. I think of

Vicki weeping all over her nice new floors and of Jack somewhere in there across the courtyard, languishing, coughing feebly, swathed in a ratty old bathrobe.

I stand up, my legs gone to sleep under me screeching now with new blood, and I stagger over to where Peaches lives. The door won't open easily with the terrarium in my arms, just about buckling my back under its weight. Luckily, I'd never locked it after Bill came up. I kick it open, descend the stairs, perilous since I can't see. Bill and Brigid have left the entry propped open. They're out here in their pajamas and slippers and pink sponge rollers. Brigid, gesturing wildly with Peggy and Joe, similarily clad, who, although they can't see, have certainly caught their drift. They're gesturing wildly, too. Fire sirens can be heard far down the street.

We, the tenants of Bradford Court are making a fuss, causing a ruckus, waking up the nighttime. Lights blaze in every apartment all along the rows of windows that line the building. The Demetris emerge, having pulled on jeans and sweat-shirts. They probably sleep in the nude, my mind registers for telling Vicki later. Their sweat-shirts are inside out and the jeans aren't zipped. They 're carrying the baby between them. I notice he's pink and plumped-up since I saw him last. Guess he's had his surgery. I realize I'd never tried before to find out.

I'm still clutching Peaches in her home. I don't want to put the terrarium down, even though my arms have long since ceased to have any sensation and I can feel deep ridges forming in the palms of my hands. Peaches is scrabbling wildly. I'm speaking to her soothingly while tears course down my cheeks. She shouldn't have to stay in Vicki's empty apartment all day long, at least not while I'm home and could give her the care she needs. Maybe I can find crickets in some kind of freeze-dried form or something.

A young woman, slim, athletic, highly-tanned, with a huge bunch of keys clipped to her khaki work pants, comes striding into the courtyard. "Calm down, everyone, calm down. The firemen will be here shortly. Who can determine the source of the smoke?" My God—I realize suddenly—it's Kath, back from the oil rigs.

"It's up by Mr. Bronski's place," Bill volunteers at the same moment Brigid begins to scream for Madeleine and Jack.

"Okay, okay," Kath annouces. I am amazed by her presence, authoritative yet gentle. Greenland must be quite the place. I wonder how much it costs to get there from here.

"Where's Nick?" somebody asks. Kath pauses, looks around at all the sleep-smeared faces. "Hernia surgery." As she speaks, almost imperceptibly, the corner of her mouth twitches. "Any problems from now on, call me. I'm up in Grandma's place."

"What about Miles Management?" I manange to squeeze out. The terrarium's now collapsing my diaphragm.

"My lips are sealed," she says. "You'd better hold a tenants' meeting. You didn't hear me say that." And she plunges into the smoking building. A few minutes later, out troops Madeleine, Jack, and Mr. Bronski in a little line with Kath shepherding them. "Mr. Bronski's smoke alarm," she shouts out, just as a burly troop of firemen in out-sized boots and ridiculously flapping rubber coats galumph into the courtyard trailing a snaking hose, bumping into each other as they run.

Everything's okay. Not to worry, folks. Go back to bed. Everything's okay. We've got everything under control," Kath keeps saying.

"I couldn't sleep," says Mr. Bronski. He is wearing fraying pajamas, gray from lack of washing, and a pair of scuffed dress shoes, untied, with no socks. For once, he's forgotten his cigar. "I was cooking chicken in the broiler. I'm sorry. I didn't mean anything by it. My wife used to cook, not me. I can't ever get to sleep now."

Kath comes up and takes the terrarium out of my arms. I flex my elbows. The absence of the heavy weight makes me giddy. I feel like I could hold the whole world in that empty space between my outstretched hands. My back straightens.

"Tenants' meeting tomorrow night!" Arthur Demetri's shouting, passing amongst everyone with some flyers he's remembered to rescue out of the ostensibly burning building.

"I'll get my friend, Roger, the lawyer, to come advise us," I burst out.

"I'll bring the chicken," Mr Bronski says.

Then I remember to look over to Madeleine and Jack. She's all neat and put together in a ruffled blue robe with a hot pink nylon gown flowing beneath it, fluffy slippers, too, like the kind we wore to slumber parties in fifth grade. Jack's hanging onto her. He's got on a corduroy jacket over brand-new gray and maroon striped pajamas, not a ratty bathrobe after all. His bald pate is shining in the lights from the windows above. He's pasty-colored and looks like hell, but he's smiling, Madeleine propping him up as if showing him off.

The Infant's still there by Madeleine's plastic black-eyed susans. He seems to have shrunk a bit. The cupid looms larger than life, half-shadowed, half-lit; as if caught in the gestures of dance, the flicker of a smile moves over his lips.

I stretch my arms again, raise my chin, and walk over to reach out my hand, "Hey, Jack, don't be a stranger."

Command Performance

When the invitation arrived—green paper, thick and dark as velvet, gold-edged, so much like her—I knew at once who it was from. I stared at the looping, flourished handwriting, seeing instead her face. Barbara, on a hot July day, supple, tanned, grinning, lying upside down on the grass, squinting up at me through sunlight and leaf and shadow, green and gold, reaching for me, laughing. Barbara....

Now in winter in the foyer of her apartment as someone else takes my coat, I stand smiling, projecting a brittle ease to mask my terror. In the lamplight I see her, face still framed by those angel-wings of hair I used to sweep back with my hands, my mouth, the better to caress the softness of her face....

From across the room I see her, not yet aware that I have arrived. She is pregnant, as the brief note on the invitation had kindly prepared me for, and radiant, as I knew she would be.

Secretly I wish to detect some scrap of evidence that she's sorry, hurting inside, longing for me still. But no, in reality all I can do is appreciate her, now as always. Nothing about her has changed save the shape of her belly. She is so easily full, not swollen or bloated, a woman truly "with child"—filled, fulfilled. Yet she looks as stylish as ever in her candy-cane-striped, crisp, polished cotton gown.

I wince remembering that effortless ability she always had, even in turtleneck and jeans, to look elegant and sleek. Unlike me, Barbara always knows what to wear and how to behave. My own clumsy and laughable attempts to imitate other s in hopes of fitting in never succeeded. I'm not surprised that I became an actress; that way I could pick anyone to be, anyone at all, just as long as it wasn't me.

Barbara now plays the madonna, her long-fingered hand settles on her belly, her head turns....

She sees me. My heart lurches. My upper lip bursts into beads of sweat. I smile. I smile.

"Maggie!" Her voice, the voice of an actress, carrying, without rise or strain across the room, over the music, the party voices, the sounds of festive crockery and glass.... For an instant, if we dared, across all that space, we could exchange a spark. It doesn't happen.

All graciousness and ease, she approaches. This woman is an actress, born an actress.... I am swept into the room, the party, her life as she lives it now.

No longer do we meet in the time-out-of-time that our summer together had been; now I am but a guest invited into her chosen world. Why had she done it—addressed the invitation, precisely sealed the envelope, dripped the hot red wax onto the flap, stamped the curly 'B' into its molten heart? And why did I come? Never mind. Here we are.

On the surface, I am willing. I glide along with her, cream in coffee, constructing my role. Interloper, misfit, I become someone else. I fool neither of us, yet I carry on.

"Maggie! I'm *so* happy to see you!" Her kiss on my cheek, her hand on my arm, are stage-gestures only. "Maggie, I'd like you to meet...Roger, this is Maggie.... We were in a piece together this summer.... Elizabeth, this is Maggie...yes, a women's piece.... Maggie, you remember Neil...."

All the faces in the lamplight, candlelight, firelight are soft and glowing with holiday cheer, both bottled and real, turn toward me, gentle, urbane, accepting, nice, above all, nice....

I nod, respond. I turn from one to the other, mouthing the correct phrases. I smile. Most of all I smile. We converse, all open, charming, nice people—our words like the ice in our drinks, tinkling.... As far as they know, I'm one of them, the pampered children of the affluent, dressed, fed, doctored, therapied.... These are the survivors of a generation of dissent and disillusion, the ones who didn't drop out. Most of them can't imagine those of us who had nowhere further to drop.

I balance a canapé between two fingers as the conversation ripples around me, actually bite it in half, ridiculous since it's small enough to be swallowed whole. The theatre, names, places, titles, and people, all fall easily from our lips. Even the women's piece of the summer, my entrée to this world—where and how I met their darling, their Barbara—has become safe and respectable. In this sheltered, well-lit living room—fireplace, candlesticks, blocks of colored ice idly drifting in the punch-bowl lagoon—feminism in the theatre may be lightly touched upon, as long as it remains aloof and removed from their real lives.

Diamonds and gold bands on manicured fingers, wifely touches on husbandly arms, lingering glances toward Barbara's belly, reveal to me the same conventional shackles behind those counter-culture exteriors, beards and boutique clothing....

Suddenly, I want to turn—from the anchovies on crackers, from the bland, blank, totally unaware face of Charles, Barbara's lawyer husband and father of her accidently conceived, yet now-so-cherished baby—and scream: "I am not who you think I am. None of this is as it seems to be. I am not nice. I am queer. I am a dyke. I am your worst nightmare apparition come to claim you and your precious Barbara, who loved me, loved me I tell you—all summer, in the daylight, in the nightime, in our cabin, in the woods, on the grass. Despite how she looks to you, your dear sweet Barbara is just as queer as me!"

Instead, I take another cashew, another sip.... Barbara is now conducting a tour. Eagerly, the docile guests follow. The kitchen, with its rows of little jars, all labelled and filled, the baskets on the walls, a glossy scene from a magazine.... Next, Charles' study, so obviously his, law books heavy on shelves, dark leather, wooden ducks, uncompromisingly masculine. I risk a slit-eyed smirk. The bedroom follows.... Quietly, I fade back, the wide bed with its neat, expensive spread just at the corner of my eye.... I needn't look, can't bear to imagine Barbara and Charles coming together in their matrimonial nest with any amount of passion.

That summer we rarely used, didn't need a bed. Once the spark between us was ignited, claimed for what it was, we took each other in laughter and in tears whenever, wherever, we could. Clothes peeled off that long, thin, tanned body as easily as tissue paper from a rare, delightful gift whose beauty and worth never diminished no matter how often it was given.

We found each other at the Women's School in Vermont, studying feminist theatre. I was one of the grass-roots originators of the program, living in the city on waitress wages, doing political theatre at night. She was a polished, professional actress—children's theatre in an affluent suburb, funded and secure—dabbling a bit to increase her range.

I was the confirmed dyke, gay from the age of three, falling in love with kindergarten teachers and Sears catalogue models, all the way through the now-classic, tragic adolescence. The loneliness and fear that led me to the furtive affair I fell into with an older girl was overshadowed only by the horror of having my parents find out. Forced into the grasp of both priest and shrink, I almost sank under waves of shame. Only in the last few years, having seized the lifeline of the women's movement, the safety net of a few strong friends, had I found myself afloat at last in my own waters. Alone as I was, still I claimed the word—*lesbian*—as an incantation.

And then there had been Barbara, the nice, straight, married woman, angel-haired, so delicate in contrast to my own shorn and rough facade. Even now I hold in my mind the image of those sessions at the Women's School. All of us would sit in a ring talking, making the risky but exhilarating attempts as a collective to create the piece we would produce for the last week of the school. Barbara, in her Indian shirt heavy with cotton lace beneath which her nipples were full-circled shadows, would sit quietly amidst the others. When the group began warily to deal with lesbianism as a theme, suddenly, surprising us all, Barbara came alive, turning the radiance of her face, hair swinging at each gesture of her head—which I longed even then to cradle in my hands—to the whole group, and confessed that she was married. This took courage since present were several heavy-duty dykes; all the other seasoned feminists were at least 'bisexual.' She told us she'd never had a woman lover but thought that women together must be (I remember—how I remember!) "sweet."

Fast, so fast—everything happened. I didn't have time to stop— as was my custom before plunging headlong across the minefield that seemed to be my life—to talk myself into some semblance of caution.

Everywhere—for me—was Barbara. We'd linger too long after powerful rehearsals unwilling to let go of how it felt to let our energy meet and soar. She'd say good-night, then creep into my cabin by the river much later, to giggle and whisper like a twelve-year-old over her latest idea for an improv. One late night found her leaning back in my doorway, holding her lean, electric body under its thin cotton gown in my arms much longer than an obligatory goodnight; her mouth, in the scented summer dark, heavy with longing, found mine—just a brush of the lips at first, then, again, longer—so delicate, so tender, I could have wept....

All of that has brought us now, not to where I'd dreamed we'd be—together—but rather to this place and time, just before Christmas, each of us starring in a separate script. The plump little tree, so Barbara-like with its gingham bows and wooden ornaments, miniature soldiers, musicians, angels carved in Switzerland, stands by the hearth where the fire begins to collapse now into glowing coals; sherry sinks to little amber pools just over the stems of the glasses, as one by one the lovely guests pay their respects and leave, at least half of them to go on home to turn to their partners—of course of the opposite sex—to say, "They were *so* perfect—let's...."

What a way to overpopulate the earth!

Away from them all, I turn, in the only gesture of the evening that isn't an act, crumple my holly-motif cocktail napkin and hardball it into the fire. From across the candle-shadowed room as she stands just so by the side of Charles, her arm on his, Barbara looks up in response to the spit of sparks my gesture provokes. I take in the full measure of her eyes. It is the only moment of the evening in which she, too, ceases to perform.

Neither of us has ever been better.

With the last jolly burst of leave-takers, I see myself out, using camaraderie over the mistletoe as a vehicle for my exit. Behind me, the sweet smell of wood-smoke rises as I walk to catch the last bus into the city. Pin-pricks of stars begin to mix, in the dark bowl of the sky, with tiny, fast-falling flakes of snow....

The house, I imagine, glows from every window. There lives inside me a small bank of embers and not from the wine. I don't look back.

Bread

En route between Marmee in Beckley and Michael in Brattleboro, the day after Thanksgiving, snow holds down my plane. As I sit here—marooned in La Guardia, perched on a suitcase full of pork chops—I realize why I hate airports. For me, they seem always to reek of profound ennui, everything suspended, yet constantly dislocated, all that purpose centered on moving between one place and another, yet so little action. When I was a child back in West Virginia, we did so little traveling; getting ready to go was something else. I suppose, if it comes to it, the real truth is that airports remind me of my life.

For years, Marmee sewed me outfits, for "later," tucked nice things away in a drawer for "good," never had anything special for herself—only the frugal and the everyday, the habits of her childhood she'd hoped to outlive for me. Calico—like the squares, faded now and frayed, that lay stitched into the quilts her aunts and cousins and mother had made—seemed to me almost holy cloth, the stuff of which queens' robes and priestesses' might be made. Marmee wouldn't have it.

Instead, we bought new, at Kresge's. Later, with the insurance settlement from Dad's death, we bought from Sears: nylon, rayon, sateen. Even the sounds of those names I hated. They glided down the throat like those vile colored liquids in the little wax bottles we'd beg and beg a nickel for, then gag on later, too sweet and too bright.

That's why so many years later when I met Michael in the aisles of The Karmic Carrot in Brattleboro—I'd picked Vermont for college;

I'd wanted to leave Marmee, but not the mountains—I thought he was. Real that is—buying stone-ground whole wheat flour for his bread, wheat-berries to sprout, baking powder without aluminum. After all, what had I to compare?

For Marmee, storebought v̄as status, homemade meant poor. On our table, always, was Jane Parker—white, thin-sliced. For our school sandwiches she cut off the crusts. To save myself ridicule in the lunchroom, I'd feed mine to Socrates, my friend Jennie's Airdale, on my way to school every morning. Six years I spent eating only a Hostess Ding-Dong for lunch.

Back then my only ally was Jennie—a friendship Marmee tried desperately to discourage; her disapproval of Jennie's family bordered on the violent. Jennie's father, a retired classical Greek scholar, was highly suspect; her mother, a pianist who wore antique floating gowns, even at ten in the morning, was worse.

For lunch Jennie often took cucumber sandwiches, crustless like mine, on white bread circles, or slices of something called paté, which her parents, although impoverished, ordered from Richmond. Jennie, who started winning scholarships early and had no dolls, only books, was clearly destined for greatness. She often talked about taking me with her—to the Vienna Woods, or, at least, Picadilly Circus, which we imagined was full of bears jumping through hoops.

Twenty-five years later, instead, here I am with my meaty cargo, wishing I could spot another Socrates to feed. Piedmont Airlines, chancy at best, has not yet provided us with another flight. The journey to Brattleboro could be days away. I'm praying the chops—rock-solid in their wrappers of aluminum foil when Marmee forced them in between my L. L. Bean all-cotton sweaters—haven't started to putrefy. There are no Socrates; all of them lie tranquilized in boxes in the luggage bay, dreaming of dinners like this.

"All that vegetarian stuff." Marmee's tone, as I had prepared to leave, had been too wistful to embody a full reproach. "No wonder you look so anemic. Take these." The visit had been such a letdown, she was bucking up so bravely—none of this was new, but I pretended it was; none of that was new, either—I had to let her stuff the chops in. I held off, though, at the all-beef jumbo franks. One must draw a line somewhere.

"They give Michael gas," I protested.

"That Michael, he's such a good teacher. Lulu, you're such a good teacher. Why can't the two of you look for jobs and settle down. Why can't you...."

She meant to say "reproduce," push out four little women or little men or any combination thereof. She stopped herself. She fingered the skirts of the storybook dolls she'd dressed for me over the years of my childhood—Anne of Green Gables, Rebecca of Sunnybrook Farm, Rose. She'd probably have gone on to all eight of the cousins, too, except that finally I begged her instead for a bike with a shiny horn and a headlight for night. The last doll Marmee gave me was Beth March. Beth died, I know—but we never spoke of it. I have her still, along with all the rest of them, just the same: waxen-faced, flaxen-curled, sateen-skirted.

"We are—settled down."

"You call that settled."

"Ma, it's just like the place Grandma Lucinda had, and Grandpa Roy...."

Her face told me—that's why it's not all right. She bustled purposefully around the range then, snapping on and off all the burners, opening the big and little ovens, just to show me, then rummaging in the Amana freezer. The carbon in Grandpa Roy's lungs bought this, the carbon in my father's sent me off to Vermont to meet the real thing I had longed for. I am not to forget it. She took a box of Hostess donuts out of the metal bread box, the one with the enamelled chickens on the side. She poured me milk in a tall Kresge's tumbler. She placed the donuts on a flowered china plate of which she has a set. "Eat. You need your calcium."

"Cynda, you have got to be kidding," Michael shrieked when I brought home Hostess donuts, the chocolate-covered kind, one day after we'd been married a year or so. He'd been baking the whole time, waiting for a call to sub. The area in which we chose to go back to the land is one of dwindling young people, decreasing school enrollment. We couldn't get teaching jobs no matter how hard we looked, which we did despite what Ma seems to believe. With unemployment, savings, subbing, a little tutoring, selling honey, goats' milk, firewood, and growing just about everything we eat, we manage—barely. Grandma Lucinda had never complained. I didn't see that we should either.

"Don't you know what that white flour is going to do to your intestines—not to mention that white refined sugar?" Tufts of flour splayed over Michael's eyebrows. He looked like a villain in a silent flick. Silently, I took the donuts out to the compost and threw them in. The cardboard box, of course, I put in the paper-trash barrel.

Waiting—I think, as I reached, first for the chamomile I gathered and dried myself, then for the china cup that was part of the collection Marmee had made against my wedding day—how much longer?

"Five hours," Piedmont tells us, five hours longer for the next flight to Brattleboro. Our alternatives are Bradley and Logan. I hunch down on my bag, sure I can smell the pungency of rotting meat. Everyone around me seems just as torpid. Children slump against mothers' shoulders, drooling onto parkas. Fathers cram hands in back pockets, pull out crumpled cigarette packs, let their eyes flash furtively around, the only sign of motion. Reservation agents, behind their desks, keep on working their jaws, despite eyes that died hours ago.

If I were home now, in the log cabin we built during that buggy summer of our wedding from a pre-fab kit, there'd be a sweet applewood fire in the woodstove, lentil soup simmering in the cast-iron pot. I'd be settled in the bentwood rocker, Grandma Lucinda's quilt over my knee, Michael at my feet leaning against my legs, my fingers in the hair Marmee finds shockingly long, having no way to know that all the radical fringe she fears us to be part of have skull cuts now.

Why does this domestic image fail to move me? Why does it feel so static? Is it because I've lived inside it too long?

In my mind's eye, as I huddle in the plastic airport chair, I rise and go to my kitchen. Smooth pine-wood shelves, rows and rows of them, clean, open, varnished—hours of our lives gone into those shelves. I run my hand over the smooth glass surfaces of the jars that line them: seeds, nuts, berries, beans, grains, all the subtle textures and colors of earth and the things that the earth grows.

I realize now, finally, after so much pretense otherwise, that this is not what I want at all—any more than I want what Marmee's got yellowing for me between aging sheets of tissue in her dresser drawers. No wonder, month after month, my blood spills out, bright and cruel; Michael swears when he learns of it, stomps out to the woodpile to channel anger into clean steel. Nothing can root, no matter how fertile the soil, if the life-wish the seed needs to hold in its heart is not there.

Michael, like Marmee, wants progeny. As I hunker down now, in the airport, watching the results of haphazard proliferation stroll by, I know what I want. I know that I want to be out—out of the whole messy, teeming, heartbreaking process of life producing life.

"But, honey! Look here! It's so amazing! Look at the head crowning! Read here about how the husband and wife bond during the coaching."

I am repulsed by the color photos in the book on home birthing Michael has bought me. The blood, the placenta, the white cheesy stuff the baby comes out covered with are part and parcel of our life here at the farm—too basic, too elemental. Real, after all, is not for me. I cannot imagine enduring all that only to bring an innocent creature into the world, to keep it tied to you for life, no matter how far it tries to travel.

As for that fabled bonding between husband and wife the birthing books wax on about so glowingly—all I remember is frigid mornings under our pile of Hudson's Bay blankets in our sleeping loft, Michael curled on his side, sunk deep in dreamless slumber, me watching the frost flowers on the skylight pane as the deathly light of dawn seeps through, feeling my warm breath rise only to crystallize above my face, feeling a desolation, a loneliness, so deep and acute I want only to rise and walk out into the snow to sleep again—a sleep from from which I would not have to wake.

When I force myself to envision babies, all I see are waxen faces, frozen eyes, immovable curls.

Now I rise, swiftly, from my airport chair, ask a kindly lady next to me to watch my suitcase, hoping her nose isn't too keen, and begin to pace the long concourse. Its ceiling is vast, so is its length. It looks like it goes on forever, and if I keep walking it, so can I.

I think of Jennie studying harpsichord now in Montmartre, of the snapshot she sent me of herself standing in an outdoor market so full of bustle and smells they fairly burst out of their Kodak trap to claim me, too.

The breads on the stall beside her, as she mugs for the camera in her characteristically weird, lovable Jennie way, are shaped like works of art—hoops, loops, glazed and glistening, some twisted into thick braids or spun out into long thin fingers, vari-colored, light and dark, the grains of many regions mixed together.

Suddenly, I find myself desperately hungry, eager to sink my teeth into something crunchy on the outside, light on the inside, but just chewy enough, with a warm, yeasty fragrance, maybe dripping with rich, fresh butter....

Back at my seat—the lady has guarded my suitcase well—I rifle through my wallet to make sure I have my American Express card. I'd gotten it back when I had a full-time job, just to use for flights to Marmee, just in case—it comforted her—of emergencies en route. How much for a ticket to Paris? I imagine that I can almost see the red-and-blue logo of Air France beckoning down the long concourse....

I sit and run my finger around the sharp edges of the card, over and over, my legs draped over the suitcase full of rotting pork chops, and I wait....

Power Failure

On the fourth day of Ellen's flu, the lights went out at 4:20 P. M. It was March, twilight had not quite begun. Sheila cursed. The M.A.S.H. re-run they had been watching, both propped up in their double bed, was abruptly interrupted; still, she expected the power to flow back on immediately, Hawkeye and Hot Lips and Radar to continue to fill the tiny screen with the semblance of life. When this did not happen, when, for a long series of unnumbered minutes, the digital bedside clock did not register the advance of time, Sheila rose and flung her sweater on against the chill, of silence, of suddenly threatening nightfall.

"Oh, God! Now this, too! Jesus! What's the matter with me? I think I must be cursed." Ellen sank deeper into the sweated, crumpled sheets, phlegm rattling in her throat, tissues wadded under her nose. She whined at the best of times; now was not one of them.

"Merely a coincidence, dear," Sheila spoke coolly, almost mechanically, as she gathered crumpled tissues, dirty glasses, crumb-filled plates from the bedside table. Deep inside, another emotion, hotter and more dangerous, started to swell, yet found itself pushed back.

"Hey, stop!" Ellen hurled at her back as she headed for the small apartment kitchen to ditch her cargo. "You took my juice! I wasn't finished!"

Tough luck, Sheila spit back—silently. At the sink she poured the half-inch of sour juice down the drain, stood looking out at the air shaft, at the window opposite—all dark, all blank.

"Oooh!" Back in the bedroom, Ellen was moaning again, thrashing in the sheets, trying to get comfortable, punctuating her misery with a few hacking coughs.

"Are you sure you shouldn't call a doctor?" Sheila loomed back in the doorway, almost swallowed by the darkness behind her. The bedroom windows still bled with bluish daylight as full dusk gathered just past the vacant lot by the funeral parlor next door.

"What doctor? You know I don't have one. Listen, do we have any batteries for that radio of mine? We've got to find out what's happening."

"It's only something temporary." Sheila's tone resumed, metallic, even. "I told you to call that doctor Barbara told us about. The woman. The one near here. You could get an appointment for tomorrow."

Ellen just coughed.

Sheila moved into the living room where the windows facing onto the same view as the bedroom's stood up in the darkness, pale tombstones. Night outside was dropping fast. There was just a narrow strip of sunset, crimson below a whole bowl of twilight three or four blocks away. "The power failure's only around here, I think," she called back to Ellen.

"Figures. This lousy town." Ellen had not wanted this working-class suburb with its ratty blocks of paint-peeling 'three families', but had wanted to live in an area with more brick and lawns and a good delicatessen.

Funds had not permitted. Besides, here, in this neighborhood, Sheila felt comfortable, a known quantity, as she walked to the seedy laundromat, past the Elks' Club, the Table Talk Pie Thrift Shop, the little drugstore whose fly-specked cardboard Easter Bunnies lingered on into June.

Ellen had grumbled but moved in anyway; she talked a lot about sculpting, acting lessons, all the while rapidly spending up her grandmother's bequest, while Sheila went out daily to work at a keypunch machine.

"I'm sure Les would've done something if it was just in our building."

"Don't bet on it. He can't be bothered. Oh, God, I'm dying.... Where's my aspirin? Hon, can you get it for me? Could you look for those batteries now?"

As Sheila brought the bottle of aspirins, the water glass—smooth gestures, practiced—the heat inside her burned its way up an inch closer to the surface. "Don't bad-mouth Les. He's pretty damn good. Remember when he came over during his own supper when our pilot light blew?"

"Cheap cruddy stove."

"If you think Les's a lousy landlord you should've grown up where I did." Sheila yanked the sheets straight, adjusted the blankets, plumped a pillow. Ellen settled down in the bed, reached for more tissues. Sheila continued, "You cross the Greca brothers, you end up trying on cement booties.... Why, once my mother didn't have the rent and the...."

"Yeah, yeah," Ellen's tones were relentlessly nasal; the hacking cough persisted. "I've already heard about your sainted origins in the slums. Must we constantly elaborate?"

"So-ree!" Sheila aped an insulted ten-year-old. She took back the aspirin.

"Hey...listen, hon...could you heat up some more of that soup? And better get those candles out and look for those batteries? In case you haven't noticed, we really are blacked out. I'll bet it's sabotage." Ellen sounded as if that fact would please her heartily.

"You're crazy." Sheila replied again, not loudly enough to be heard. She'd learned that one years ago in the Greca brothers' tenement: how to give and give and yet keep some secret part that was herself—bitter but intact.

Pantherlike she moved through the small rooms, now totally dark. Outside, the town was equally without illumination. Cold and blue, the gas jet flamed under the pot of soup. By its eerie glow she could see her way to the drawer where the candles were found. Five slender ones, all with hair-like cracks that had saved them from dinner-party use, went into the coronet-holder which was Sheila's only reminder of her mother. Only, that is, besides memories of too much make-up for too-puffy eyes, a voice that could cajole like no other, the many devious hiding places for whatever could comfort her for an afternoon, a night....

One by one, the candles spurted into flame in the living room's dark cave, until the whole room glowed softly, a haven of warm light. Sheila clicked the batteries into place; the little radio began to purr. The evening newscaster had everything to say—about the wide world and the city their town leaned against—except about the circle of dark-light-dark in which they found themselves.

"Is the soup ready yet?" Wrapped in the blanket Sheila had so carefully tucked in only a few minutes before, Ellen came into the living room trailing crumpled tissues. "Nothing on the news about the power failure, huh? What if it goes on for days?"

"Sit down, Ellie. Don't chill yourself. I'll get the soup." Sheila gestured to the alcove where she had placed the candle holder on the small table where they ate. She left the room to bring soup bowls, spoons, and good napkins on a tray.

"Yuk. I'm tired of this." Ellen clanked her spoon in the bowl. "Listen—Sheila?

"Yes, dear?" Her own soup stood untouched, grease filming the surface.

"This could go on all night, even tomorrow. Let's call my mother and go on over there. Color TV and everything. She could thaw out some steaks. We could sleep over. It's going to be awful here." Her tone was dulcet with the effort to convince, all the whine squeezed out of it. "Oh, by the way, Sheil, could you get rid of all these candles? They suck the oxygen out of the room."

Silently, Sheila rose, cleared the table. Pouring soup down the drain by the light of the one candle she'd lit in the kitchen, she watched the limp, swollen macaroni catch in the drain and puddle together. What was around her seemed to have no limits. Yet beyond, she knew, was Ellen's mother's apartment, a high-rise with a view. Were they there now, they'd sit in semi-darkness also, as usual, elegant tapers in crystal globes, meat sizzling in the broiler. Floor-to-ceiling picture windows would be full—full of lights, points of light, windows of skyscrapers, other apartment buildings, airplanes rising and gliding down, the harbor lights and once, on the fourth of July, fireworks, bursting, like cotton candy, green and pink.

Sheila shivered, reached for a dish towel, wondered idly how on earth people had ever lived in olden times. "Sure, Ellie," she called out finally, watching from the doorway as Ellen, with wetted fingers, snuffed out, one by one, her slender candles. "Go on to your mother's. But not me. I'll drop you off. I'd better stay."

After Ellen was gone, she sat in the dark a long time. Finally, rising, alone, she paced, letting the darkness fill her skull, giving her a clear, clean place in which to begin to reconstruct her reality as if inventing language for the first time. It seemed to her that the night was like a starving wild thing crouched at every window and door waiting for the sun to slip down past the edge of the earth. Dryness and vacuum seemed to be what lived inside her skin. Dawn, she realized, had never been in her vocabulary.

The hours passed. Sheila's rhythm settled, steady and measured. Toward morning, everything came back on—lights, clock, TV, refrigerator. The surge of power that was flowing now felt like it came from her will alone.

She moved to gather her things to leave, to find pen and paper to write the letter she would post on her way.

The Names of the Moons of Mars

When my second husband, Bradford up and left us penniless after allowing his sporting goods shop, "Balls to Play," to fail, I had no
choice but to rent out our house and move, with my two kids, home
with Ma and Daddy, not an easy adjustment to make when you're
thirty-eight.

Right now the kids are at camp, luckily—paid for well in advance
out of my earnings since Bradford declared bankruptcy, grew a
beard, bought a rusted, dented, stripped-down van, and took off to
Alaska with Sheila, my jogging partner. I may never jog again. Without the store discount, I can't afford the shoes.

Today it's a balmy, light-hearted Saturday afternoon in late June,
and we're out in the garage, Daddy and I. The door's wide open to
the driveway and the green brilliance of suburbia beyond. Daddy
calls the garage Piazza Giorgio, after his name, George, and his lifelong dream of escape to the Tuscan Hills.

As a retired insurance agent of Yankee-German stock, this is as
far as he's got. The car he keeps out in the driveway. The garage itself he's decked out in a fresh coat of floor paint, a few folding lawn
chairs, and a yard-sale TV. He's patched together a ship-shape kitchenette down there, too—hooking up Ma's old stove to a wall outlet,
adding a miniature fridge, the kind college kids keep beer in, and a
few wooden shelves. All this gives him a cozy refuge, a den in
which to outlast the long winter of his marriage to Ma.

She's upstairs, of course, in her lair, the master—or should we
say mistress—bathroom, the one with the built-in vanity. She's got a
TV in there, too, an eight-incher on a metal tray table. In fact, my
parents own five TVs, usually play them all at once, so that it's possi-

ble to move from room to room all over their split-level ranch and never miss a flicker on Merv Griffin's face. Ma likes to keep everything she might need right in there—Revlon lipsticks, especially a shade called "Love That Pink" which she buys three tubes at a time in case they stop making it, hair rollers, eyebrow tweezers, eyelash curlers, lots and lots of earrings, and her sneakers with Velcro tabs which you can't buy anymore. She's got a lot of closet space elsewhere, but most of it's taken up by back issues of magazines and every Sunday paper since 1952, plus piles of clippings from the Living section all gleaned for me, stuff like "How to Make Your Marriage Last," "Hassle-Free Child-Rearing," "Two Thousand Christmas Gifts You Can Make from Old Coat Hangers," "Cream Cheese—the Versatile Ingredient." What this means is that her wardrobe hangs from all the coat hangers I never used for Christmas gifts from the top of the shower stall door, the towel racks, and the hook on the inside back of the door.

Most days she finally manages to leave bed about eleven, disappears inside the bathroom with the TV, 'getting ready,' as she calls it, although for who or what, one is never quite sure, and emerges about 4 P. M. looking for my father who's been down in the Piazza since 6 A. M. It's a life.

Anyway, now I see my opening, settle into a lawn chair opposite Daddy. "Daddy, how are you?" I ask right to his face. We haven't talked at all since I moved back a few weeks ago. I know he's got to be upset about Clara, his mother, ninety-three, in a nursing home in a town called Seminole, Florida, and about my repeated marital disasters (Bradford's my second), and the fact that he spends all day in the Piazza Giorgio and my mother the same up in the bathroom...

He looks at me. "Oh, well, Anna...." he starts off, serious but bland. He's got a stainless steel bowl of popcorn in his lap. He likes to do these little cooking projects down here in the Piazza, using the electric popper he got at a yard sale, or the teflon fry pan, perfectly good, he found in a junk shop. "...did you ever realize that every single kernel of popcorn is different from all the others?" He fingers one, holding it up to look at it with reverence before popping it into his mouth. "Just like snowflakes."

Just this minute I love this man. His lifelong faith in the scientific method is truly awesome. When I was little, he taught me all about things, like how the pupa releases the butterfly, what sun-dogs are, how to make baking soda explode, the names of the moons of Mars—which, I remember now, are Deimos and Phobos—panic and fear.

"Gee, Daddy, I never thought of that. You'll have to tell Eric and Susan."

These are my kids, six and ten, who dress in sneakers held together with safety pins, not velcro, and stretched-out polo shirts upon which no animal fetishes reside, but who find in every refrigerator container an adventure in microbiology, in every rainbow a poem, in every sky a rainbow. No wonder Bradford left. I think we were just too much for him.

My business, Wreath of Life—a cottage industry done out of the spare room—was more successful than his. I sell homemade bread and handmade wreaths and arrangements made out of dried weeds and grasses.

Right after Susan was born, I learned how to do the wreaths—with coat hangers under the weeds—from one of Ma's clippings and just took it from there. Bradford sold lacrosse sticks and polo mallets but never played.

"Yes, I'll tell them," Daddy says now. The kids love him, too, but we're all leery as well. His humor can turn like a summer sky from brilliant to angry, his benign musings to wounding cuts.

Funny how Emilio, my first husband—the drifter-turned-inventor, the one I set up with a workshop in the cellar of our seedy rented three-family walk-up in New Haven—resembled Daddy, or one-half of him, anyway. Emilio was sweet, amusing, in love with the way the world smells and feels and works. He took in what love was but could no more construct of it a durable home than hold a handful of water.

Bradford is more like Daddy's other side, a scorpion when roused. He always felt less familiar with tenderness and care than he did with his athletic supporters, all arranged on the shelves of his shop is ascending sizes. Squash rackets and fencing masks he could understand, but never the fruit of his loins.

How we kept sane, Eric and Susan and I, I can't imagine, except for making baking powder explode in the bathroom and staying up till 4 A. M. together—winding grapevines and kneading dough.

Now Daddy takes some more popcorn, leans back in his lawn chair, and tells me, "I'm keeping the door open, Anna, because of the radon gas."

"Oh?"

"That's right. It's been identified as a serious problem in many homes in the New England states. Didn't you know about it?" His tone, as he crunches another handful of kernels, has begun to veer. Knowing the signs all too well—I spent my childhood disguised as a table-tennis ball—I straighten my spine, look humble and alert. One reason the kids are still at camp, although we desperately need the refund of their fees so we can eat till Christmas, is that I can't bear to see them acting like me in front of Daddy.

"Well, it's in this month's *Scientific American*. The gas is radioactive. It's a natural phenomenon released into the atmosphere by certain formations of granite. I'm surprised you haven't read about it. You do still have your subscription?"

I mumble something. Daddy used to give me one every year for Christmas until I married. The only sign that he minded Emilio was that that year there was no magazine, only a ruffled housecoat picked out by Ma.

Now, he sets aside the steel bowl, picks up his copy, begins to read aloud about the half-life of the isotopes of plutonium called, astonishingly enough, 'daughters.' It appears that some of the radon comes through television sets. Most of it seeps up from the ground, right through the concrete foundations of houses. The only hope is energy-efficient homes that minimize the exchange of indoor/outdoor air. Suction fans appear to be of some use, yet it's hard to tell because the gas is utterly undetectable, can't be seen, tasted, or smelt.

Can all this be true? Absently, while he reads, I've been scarfing the popcorn. Between the Piazza Giorgio and not jogging, pretty soon I'm going to look like a house. Fine by me. Bradford hates zoftig women.

"In twenty years of taking the *American,* I've only found one error." Daddy's tone is stiff. Abruptly, he snaps on the yard-sale TV and turns it to face me while he continues to talk. The voice of the third party, someone on "Agronsky and Company," not Agronsky, but one of the others, seems to fill up the space between us, which, as I've been sitting here with the sunlight outside slanting down sideways more and more, has grown uncomfortably close.

"Where's your mother?" Daddy bursts out, knowing perfectly well. I am praying she isn't planning on brisket and boiled potatoes and carrots for supper. She claims it was a recipe of Clara's who always said how much Daddy loved it as a boy. He says he hates it. He always refuses to have any, makes himself a peanut-butter-and-grape jelly sandwich on one piece of folded-over Sunbeam bread and sits at the table and eats it in front of her while she cries. I take another handful of popcorn. It's always wise to buffer against a ruined appetite later.

"Same as usual," I reply. "What's this show about, anyway?" I ask, pointing to Agronsky, not caring, just trying to divert. "They all talk funny."

"I know," Daddy replies, a hint of wickedness gleaming through his severity. "I think they might've been affected by radon gas."

We grin together, then laugh outright. The sun's back high in the sky. Suddenly, I don't feel thirty-eight with stretch marks, cellulite, no husband and nothing in the bank.

"Yesterday I went out." Daddy's more expansive now; we seem to have squeezed together through some tight place. "I had a beer with Herb Watson."

"Where did you go?" Daddy never has social engagements except for a twice-yearly jaunt with Herb, whose wife, Edna, president of The Milford Women's Club, knows my mother.

"Frenchy's—like we always do. We get a small pizza and a large pitcher of beer. Do you know how big that is? Four or five glasses." He shapes it for me in the air.

The thought pleases me. For my parent's peer group, Frenchy's is really slumming. French Canadians hang out there, and Daddy likes to impress Herb with his French, learned originally from his mother who was from the Alsace.

Herb's mother was a charter member of the D. A. R. Herb is a retired banker. He and Edna live in a house that looks like it belongs in *Art and Antiques* magazine, which is one of the ones my mother gets and stores the back issues of in her closets. Frenchy's and beer must be a rare treat for Herb who spends most of his spare time in his workroom in the lower level—they don't have anything as vulgar as a cellar—making miniature Chippendale furniture out of kits.

I've always envied the Watsons. They live with such neatness, taste, order, and polish—none of which I've ever been able to bring into my life—yet I wonder how different, really, are they from Daddy and Ma? Herb always wears clean chinos with creases and mink-oiled topsiders, but Edna still won't let him out of the workroom to tread on her Persians upstairs in case they show the wear.

Now I can tell by the sound of footsteps coming through the ceiling that Ma's finally left the bathroom for the kitchen. It's 4 P.M., time to start the brisket, which will be served, partially burnt, partially cooked, at 7:30. Nobody can ever figure out how I learned to bake such good bread. I never want to tell them it's from another clipping. "Just a mutation," I murmur.

The sound of the TV's a good guide to where Ma is in the house. She's got a hearing aid now, at seventy, ten years before any of her friends in the Women's Club, and the volume has to blare.

Suddenly the phone rings. My heart lurches. Maybe it's the camp saying that Eric drowned when a canoe developed a hole in the bottom or that Susan got stung by two thousand wasps. Maybe it's Bradford. Maybe it's not. The possibilities are endless. I wonder, do they have radon gas in upstate New York?

"Don't answer it." Daddy leaps up. "It's just Clara. She's been calling all day."

This is news to me. I've been out in a vacant lot gathering milkweed and cow parsley. I've got to wind more wreaths, even without the kids' help. What I've got in the bank won't cover the mortgage on my old house and groceries for the kids and me for two weeks.

I guess I'll have to put the house up for sale and relocate my business into one side of the Piazza Giorgio. I figure Daddy'll like that, schmoozing all day with the potential customers. He could tell them all about radon gas and the names of the moons of Mars. In fact, I've been waiting for just the right moment to ask him if I can use his stove to do the bread in.

I can't use Ma's new kitchen upstairs. She's got too many rules involving which implement is appropriate for the job at hand and what dire consequence will result if the exact procedures she requires aren't followed. She's got special knives for cutting bananas and certain ways to lay sandwich meat on bread and how to thaw out frozen juice. No wonder she never comes out of the bathroom.

I tried to ask her once about her mother who came from a ruined family in Charleston and took in boarders to make a go of it and still send Ma and her sisters to a school where they learned elocution and posture and wore white gloves to the dances. All I found out is that they had to take Grandmother off to a sanitarium once, where they gave her some kind of electro-shock. "Was it depression?" I remember asking in a hushed tone.

"Oh, no. It couldn't have been anything serious. They only kept her for a week. Please never mention this to Edna Watson. Promise me." Worry lines pulled between Ma's eyebrows. I promised.

Right now, though, Ma's great worry is the squirrel problem. Out in the back yard she's stuck up a huge bird feeder, loaded it with sunflower seeds and popcorn kernels from the Piazza, all of which get eaten all day long by fat, rapacious squirrels who can scale up the pole despite the slicking of Crisco she's applied. The article on bird feeders in the Sunday "Living" swore that this method was infallible. Now that it's proven a bust, she's gone to her last resort, a plastic inflatable owl. (The owl, apparently, is the squirrels' natural enemy.) She got Daddy to get it for her at a garden center.

Right now, Ma's mad at Daddy because he won't blow up the owl. I guess this means we're definitely having brisket. Frantically, I scour the bottom of the popcorn bowl with my knuckles to scoop up the last tiny burnt salty bits.

"Why on earth was Clara calling all day? Is she okay?"

"No." Daddy looks panicked. He reaches for the *Scientific Ameri-*

can and the *TV Guide* simultaneously." She doesn't like the Home. She says they leave her standing by the commode with her pants down. She keeps telling me she's going to shoot herself."

"Daddy! Shouldn't you do something? Talk to her? Call a counselor—a minister?"

"Pigswill!"

As soon as the words were out of my mouth, I realized my folly. No such persons have ever entered my father's universe.

In fact, the reason Bradford gave for leaving me was that I started going to Bob, an ex-Unitarian clergyman who's now a Gestalt therapist. Bradford said he wouldn't submit to the humiliation of being talked to behind his back in the guise of a chair. I tried to tell him it was Daddy in that chair but he didn't believe me. "Underdog, huh?" Bradford had snorted, as he stuffed his belongings into a knapsack from his store that night. "I'll show you from underdog!"

"But Daddy, what should we do? If Clara's being mistreated, we can't just leave her there!" I've forgotten how stubborn Clara is—how, after my grandfather died, she refused to come up north—how she always complains about wherever she is, as well as about how mean she claims everybody always is to her.

I still remember her stories about how she first came to this country from the Alsace, and had to make her living in a hat shop. All the ladies of Charleston flocked around her because she had a way with egret feathers and because she read their tea leaves. Still, she liked to tell us how they mocked her accent and never left her a tip.

Daddy flew into a rage the one time I asked him more about the tea leaves. "That's old wives' tales! That's just pigswill... superstition!" His eyes were so wild I never asked again.

"There's nothing we can do," he says now. "Don't answer. She'll stop calling. When she calls tomorrow, I'll just pretend she never said it. That always works fine."

I have to concede. The thought that comforts me is that Clara probably can't get bullets in the nursing home, unless she bribes an aide. Still, although Seminole's pretty far from Miami, you can probably get anything you want on the black market. Maybe later I'd better sneak up to the upstairs phone and call her anyway.

Right now the ringing's stopped. Ma never heard it. Daddy's grubbing through a drawer in his kitchenette to find a magnifying glass to read the *TV Guide*.

"Damn fool of a doctor told me I have a cataract coming on," he tells me with his back turned. "Pigswill! All a ploy to get me under the knife."

"Laser, Daddy. It was in *Scientific American*."

"... under the knife," he repeats, ignoring me. "All he wants is a fat insurance payment for himself. Just like that dentist who told me I needed my gums cut up. Cured it myself with baking soda and warm water."

Successful, he whips the magnifier out from under the rubble of church keys, bottle stoppers, greasy string, and little clippings of recipes that stuff the drawer. He starts to peer into the afternoon's listing when the phone starts up again.

Unable to shake visions of bears eating my children—they do have those in upstate New York, I know—or over-sexed counselors, or ptomaine poisoning, I yank it off the receiver.

"Hello." It's not the camp. It's not Clara. It's not even Bradford. It's Sheila.

"Hi, Anna. We're in Pierre, South Dakota." She pronounces it "Peer." "I called to tell you I can't stand him either. I'm flying back tonight. Bradford's going to live at the convent here. The nuns took him in. They gave him a cross to wear around his neck made out of nails—real nails. That's what they do at the convent, make these little crosses. Bradford told them he could market them mail order and make them a bunch of money. "I really need to talk to you—it's about this great idea I got to expand Wreath of Life. We get a loan for a second-hand van, see. I know how to drive one now. We could set it up down at the New Haven green where all the hot dog wagons are. Only, listen to this, instead of hot dogs we sell chemical-free pitas all stuffed with organic fillings. You know, falafel and baba ganoush and everything. Your mother's got a bunch of recipes in her closet, doesn't she? So listen, do you want to go jogging on Friday?"

"Fine," I say. "I'll see you then." As a jogging partner, Sheila was always a weak starter but strong in the sprint. Whistling, I leave the Piazza, carefully lowering the garage door behind me. Daddy's absorbed in the Bob Hope Classic broadcast live from Pebble Beach. He's leaning in real close to the set, not only to see but also to hear the sacred-hush tones of the commentary.

I make for the backyard. The inflatable owl's languishing on the back stoop. I puff the owl full and hang it jauntily from the feeder. I'm wondering idly if I couldn't get Emilio's number from one of his old buddies down at the electrical supply store or the junk yard. With all this radon gas around I'd love to tip him off to the possibilities of the household window suction fan game. I know he could invent a really spiffy one.

Tonight I wonder, looking up, will Mars be visible from this latitude? As I turn to go back inside, a squirrel approaches the feeder. The owl sways in the wind. From the bathroom window, I hear the rise and fall of voices coming from Ma's TV. I hold my breath. I'm rooting for the squirrel.

Spinsters

Amanda Archer became my first friend in New York City. For an actress relocating as I was from Seattle, from suburban rep to the big time, the transition was gut-wrenching. My hands shook for six months, my dreams could've sold to Spielberg. Amanda saved my life. We met in line for an audition. I was drawn at once to her willowy height and intense coloring. As a professional, I had a cold assessment of my own good points (huge, velvety, long-lashed eyes) and bad ones (short, stocky body, coloring too beige). Amanda had auburn hair—few knew how henna had helped—and milk-pale skin. Allergies to the sun kept her in white cotton stockings, billowing floral skirts and a wide-brimmed hat although it was September. She seemed to float within a cloud of perfumed talc. When I told her I was surprised to learn she wasn't from the South, she said that many made that assumption. The air she cultivated seemed positively antebellum, yet I soon discovered (for I had begun to study this woman as one would a part, my own role—recently divorced, pushing thirty-five, out of work, out of luck—having reached the end of its run) that what she really was was Yankee, a similar condition.

She'd grown up in New London, Connecticut with her widowed mother in genteel near-poverty in an old paint-peeling white house with a wide veranda a few blocks from the beach. Her father, until his death when she was ten, had managed the Ocean Beach Amusement Park in town. Perhaps it had been there—amidst mirrors in which you couldn't recognize yourself, in the spinning lights of every color, the constant jangle of the carousel—that her penchant for the theatre began. My own had ignited during endless Saturday afternoons at the twenty-five-cent double features my aunt and grandmother, who had raised me, sent me to while they cleaned house.

New York, Amanda told me, when she finally got there, had struck her as much the same as her father's park—only real. I knew what she meant. Both of us grew up on sounds—the mists and drizzle of my girlhood on the Puget, the timid winters and suffocating summers of hers on the Long Island had not prepared us for the Great White Way we'd rehearsed all of our young lives for, pursing illicitly lipsticked lips in front of bathroom mirrors, secreting copies of *Stage and Screen* deep in our underwear drawers. Now that we were here, each of us at last in the vale of her dreams, the only question was, could we survive it?

The day we met, we had six hours in line to see if we'd be called—and all for the dubious privilege of serving as a shoulder in a Zest commercial. We had plenty of time to talk. After neither of us made it, bedraggled and weary, we headed down to the Bowery to Amanda's loft where I was all too eager to take up her invitation to dinner.

My own housing, the top floor of an old brownstone in Chelsea, was exquisite—wide ancient varnished floorboards, leaded, many-paned dormer windows that cranked outward, a foyer as big as the rest of the apartment in which I hung the lone reminder of the mother who had left me shortly after my out-of-wedlock birth—a four-foot-high Art Deco mirror in front of which I always kept a vase of the best flowers of the season: iris, calla lilies, Fuji mums. The only problem was the landpeople who inhabited the bottom two floors. I had met them through church, to the bosom of which I had flown after the move. (Familiar rituals of the Christian Science faith of my aunt and grandmother provided my only ballast, before Amanda, on alien seas.) The landpeople, a devout older couple, neither went out nor entertained past eight at night. Of course, I might do as I pleased, yet because we shared the same entry and front hall, the constraint that I couldn't somehow left me paralyzed. I liked to be home as little as possible; in New York, that could be dangerous.

Amanda's loft, however, was worse than the streets: the stairs leading up to the two precariously tiny rooms stank of human misery. How such a creature as my new friend could remain fresh and scented while traversing daily such a terrain baffled me. The loft it-self smelled only of overcooked cabbage—this was a relief—although the steam radiators, which hissed relentlessly for an hour every other hour, caused the smell to deepen. In the alternate hours one froze. Amanda merely flung on and off a variety of thrift-shop shawls and thus neither sweated nor shivered. The bars on the win-dows frightened me, as did the bathroom which was worse than the hall and in which one could only just sit on the toilet, knees touch-ing the opposite wall. There was no shower or tub. Amanda bathed at the Y where she also took daily exercise.

"Meet the gang!" Entering the room as if it were a capacious par-lor, she made a sweeping gesture which included two animals who appeared to be cats and another youngish woman, plain, bespecta-cled, who crouched in an old chair out of which stuffing sprung, knitting a sweater. "Hi, I'm Betty. Welcome to Bedlam." On the tiny, ancient black-and-white TV, an old Ginger Rogers/Fred Astaire mo-vie was playing.

"This is Eliot," said Amanda. "We found him and his lady love here in the alley." Amanda swooped to stroke the more slender of the two feline creatures. "We named him Eliot because he looks like J. Alfred Prufrock." Staring down the whiskered mug of the gray-and-tan narrow-nosed fellow, I had to agree. "This is Lola."

"So named," Betty chimed in, "because whatever she wants she gets!"

"So I see." The animal resembled a small footstool with eyes. Try-ing to avoid plunking right down on some part of Lola's huge ex-panse, I case about for somewhere to sit. My Burberry could not possibly accept any of the alternatives I might choose. Finally I just took the coat off, turned it inside out as casually as I could and placed it, lining-side down, as a throw over the only other chair, whose original color could not be determined. Lola purred like a ce-ment mixer when I ventured to pet her marmalade fur. She did not move. I doubted that she could.

"Hate to tell you, Mandy dear," Betty was saying, "but they were up to it again."

"Oh, blueballs!" For such a delicate creature, Amanda swore like a sailor. She flung herself backward onto the chaise which was really two mattresses stacked together under the window with an old Turkish spread thrown artfully over them. She arranged her skirts as if she were at tea under the magnolias. "You see, Helene," she launched into what was obviously a much-favored tale, "these two operate as a second-story team. We think that's how they survived in the alley as well. Our refrigerator doesn't close all the way, so we put a bungee cord around it and then a fifty-pound bag of dry cat food against it."

"They won't touch the cat food," Betty took up the narrative, "and after Ricardo—that's my boyfriend—went to all the trouble to buy it for them at a wholesale place in Jersey and haul it all the way up here, too."

"Ingrates!" Amanda interjected, then plunged on. "You see, Lola flings her body against the bag and knocks it over. At that exact moment, Eliot leaps for the cord and pulls it down. The door opens and voila! my meal ticket for the week is devoured."

"You cook a week ahead?" I was baffled; out where I came from, cats knew their place. In fact, in the hygienic home of my aunt and grandmother, they had none at all.

"No, no!" By now Amanda and Betty were weak with laughter. "How I earn a living is I cook for other people—like couples who are both doctors, or catering lunches for small businesses. I keep a lot of the stuff in the fridge; if the cats eat it, I'm in big trouble. What did they get tonight, Bets?"

"You don't even want to know," her roommate intoned somberly. She rose, stuffing the sweater—which looked like it was large enough for a man although wildly striped in vivid purples and reds—into a plastic bag. "I have to go call Ricardo now. They let them go to the phone between seven and eight."

"Where is he this week?" Amanda asked.

"Bellevue, but he'll be getting out soon."

She vanished out the front door.

"Going to call down at Dave and Larry's, our neighbors. She has the key because of watering their plants. She'll have more privacy. She's been obsessed for years with Ricardo; he's always in and out of locked wards—suicidal. He's originally from Bolivia," Amanda finished as if there were a connection.

"Dave and Larry?"

"Actors, too—only they work. They're gay, of course. Do you mind?"

I sighed deeply. My ex-husband Andy had just come out. "Not in the slightest—just as long as I'm not married to them."

"Yes, I know what you mean. Well, New York is the best place to maintain celibacy I've ever heard of. All the nice guys are married—to each other. Oops, sorry! Maybe you're gay." She said it completely without censure.

Flustered, I replied, "Uh, no...I mean, well, I never thought about it."

"I have." Amanda stretched back on the chaise like the graceful cat her own real ones would never be, flinging her shawl aside as the radiators started to rise up. "Worse luck, I'm not. All my lesbian friends are married off, too—summer homes in Cherry Grove, the whole bit.

"So what do you do for a love life?" I emboldened myself to ask. The demise of my marriage had left me less than anxious to pursue one again for myself, yet I was still studying the part of my new friend.

"That's what my shrink's always trying to find out," Amanda replied cryptically. "Shall we go search for some dinner? I do believe I promised you a repast."

Chastened, I followed her into the cooking alcove where the infamous refrigerator sported its bungee cord; indeed, a giant bag of dry cat food lay against its door as well.

"Have you seen a psychiatrist long?" I ventured timidly. Having obviously laid a bomb with the love-life question, I hesitated to pry, yet my relentless fascination with this exotic creature—now beginning to rummage in her cupboards on my behalf—compelled me to ask.

"Centuries," Amanda replied extravagantly. "Eureka! Yes, we have coriander!" She whipped a little bottle off the highest shelf. "Actually, that's what the Biddlemans are for."

"Pardon me?"

"The Biddlemans." She began to slice onion, then to clarify butter. "The doctor couple I cook for on Tuesdays and Thursdays. What I charge them pays for Dr. Frobisher. You'd love the Biddlemans. She's a dermatologist. He's an opthamologist. Their BMWs have license plates that say EYESDR and SKINDR. That's in Connecticut, of course, at their country house. New York license plates have too many letters. You'd have to be a gall bladder doctor. I cooked there once, for the weekend—at their country house."

"Is Betty in the theatre?" I flung out, eager not to hear further about this peculiar pair.

"Lord, no—bless her soul, she's sane. She works in a jewelry store in the village." In just a few minutes more, Amanda presented us with a meal—created from the odds and ends that Lola and Eliot had not devoured—the likes of which I had never eaten. I cannot remember exactly what it was, only that it was stir-fried and exquisitely seasoned. So began a friendship that became central to my life, flowering like I remember the moonflower vines at home on summer evenings.

We tried hard together, Amanda and I, to become famous. She became a pair of legs in "General Hospital," a pair of hands in an Ivory Snow commercial and, finally, a scream in a particularly vile horror flick in which women's dismembered corpses figured prominently. "I draw the line," she said, "after that one." I, working temp and using my savings, became broke.

All of our rehearsed speeches from *The Belle of Amherst* and *Summer and Smoke* and *Saint Joan*—I had also prepared Viola and Miranda, although deep in my heart I knew I no longer possessed the body of an ingenue—served for nothing. We never got called to speak them to anyone, even though we haunted the Papp regularly.

Week after week passed in this fashion, long lines at calls, sore feet, aching facial muscles from forced smiling.

"I hear that beauty queens put vaseline on their teeth," Amanda told me one day in line. Jane Fonda breezed by. We were trying to get to be extras in her latest flick to be shot on the streets of our far-from-fair city. She wasn't nice, snarling at reporters and well-wishers as she passed. "Another illusion bombed to hell," Amanda interjected, reaching for the perfume atomizer with the crocheted bulb she kept buried deep in her capacious straw bag.

"Whatever for?" I asked, perplexed.

"Well, I used to worship her work. You know, *They Shoot Horses...*, *Klute*, stuff like that."

"No, no. I mean the vaseline!"

"Oh, yes...well, it makes your lips slide up off of your teeth."

"Oh, Amanda!" I groaned as if I had a toothache.

"Ye-es, my dear?" She clutched my arm and leaned in close. The perfume was Shalimar.

"Listen, Amanda, I need to tell you something. I don't think I can take this anymore."

"Buck up, babycakes. After the fourth hour, the feet feel disassociated from the body."

"No, no...I mean the whole shebang. I have an interview tomorrow...."

"You do? You vixen! Where? You didn't tell me! I know, it's something you think I'm too jejune to qualify for, something meaty—like a Sam Shepard or a Tom Stoppard."

"No, no, you fruitcake! I mean an interview for a real job. It's with an international oil cartel."

"My God—Arabs! Helene, they execute women!"

"Amanda!" I pinched her, hard. "No, it's Yalies!"

"That's worse!"

"Amanda Archer!" I was speaking now, tightly, between clenched teeth. "It's real money. It's regular hours. Health benefits. Life insurance. I am too old for all of this. I do not have enough talent. I have crow's feet. I have love handles and no one to grab them. I am practically menopausal. I must get my life in order."

"As you wish!" Her nose went up, her eyebrows soared. She drew the deeply fringed shawl of the day around her, narrowed her exquisite shoulders and glanced at her Mickey Mouse watch. "Enough of all this. I must hit that little market on Third for mussels before they close. The Biddlemans adore mussels. I may be needing extra sessions with Frobisher." She flounced off, renouncing forever her chance to rush out into a street screaming while Jane Fonda hovered over a bloody body. Back over her shoulder she tossed, "I cannot imagine what on earth you need life insurance for—unless you plan to endow Eliot and Lola."

A week went by and Amanda didn't call. During that time I prayed a lot and cried. I would have shopped a lot, too, but there was no capital. The best thing about getting a real-world job, I felt, was that I would be able to buy something again. To calm myself, I began to visualize trips down the aisles in Bloomingdale's and Saks, arms dripping with garments to be tried on. I imagined, even, shiny new French enamel cookware I could buy for my alcove kitchen, Waterford crystal vases for the foyer, presents for Amanda and Betty and Eliot and Lola, maybe even Ricardo, who was at that very moment sunning himself in Florida. Every winter, it seemed, he hitched down and got himself admitted till spring to the St. Petersburg V. A.

When the phone finally rang, Amanda pretended as if nothing had happened, didn't ask how the interview had gone, therefore never found out that I had a second one scheduled, virtually had the job in the bag. I'd be a research associate on international oil prices. The Yalies had been in top form. They all went about as if they were in a Noel Coward piece. I knew I was going to say yes to them, goodbye to days on line, nights mending panty hose.

"Dinner Saturday? Your place? I'll cook." This was how, often, we spent our Saturday evenings. Her place was too depressing for me; she knew how I felt though we never spoke of it. My cooking was equally depressingfor her, and that, too, went unmentioned. It occurred to me, as I agreed to purchase the brie, that we had the perfect marriage of a sort, a harmonious blend of talents and liabilities designed to enhance the former, defuse the latter. Like a wealthy Victorian couple, we kept to our separate dwelling spaces. The fact that we were not lovers, nor ever would be, meant that we could co-exist forever as dear companions, much as I imagine Harold Nicholson and Vita Sackville-West had done. I only hoped that what we had could transcend my defection from the stage.

The whole issue immediately became subsumed under an even more burning one. During the year and a half that Amanda and I had known each other, neither of us had dated. I was grieving over Andy, still reeling from transplant shock, as well as the daily bombardments of the city, to even consider whether or nor my body had needs that a close encountered might satisfy. Amanda seemed content enough with her little family in the loft, her cooking jobs, her endless auditions, and her trips to the good Dr. Frobisher.

One afternoon, on the way back from a committee meeting at my church, with which I remained respectably involved as befitted a single woman of gathering years, a presentable young man fell in step beside me. Clean-shaven, neatly pressed, he had a look about him of the midwest. In New York, this was so reassuring as to be bizarre. I found my gait slowing as well as my tentative smile meeting his. The whole thing was like something out of a women's magazine in the fifties. "Hello," he said. "I'm new in town."

"Yes?"

"Would you be so kind as to tell me where the public library is?"

I directed him, found out his name was Bill Baxter, that indeed he was from Sioux Falls, South Dakota, here on a training program for the New York Mutual Life Insurance Company. He was slated to return to Sioux Falls after some weeks, at which time a promotion would be offered. Yet his dream, he said with a slight mist of the eyes, was to someday live permanently here, where, he seemed to feel, all possibility lay open to a person who possessed both drive and will.

"What line are you in?" he asked, his face as clear and ingenuous as a Boy Scout's.

"Oh, international oil," I said sincerely, so glad I did not have to perseverate on my life upon the wicked stage. Already I was imagining him and Amanda and Betty and maybe even the elusive Ricardo together for a dinner party. It wouldn't wash. Resolutely, nonetheless, I pushed on. "Well, I do hope you enjoy your stay in the Big Apple."

This last made him beam like a cherub. "I'd enjoy it so much more if you'd do me the honor of joining me for lunch tomorrow. Your choice of restaurant."

Since even my proposal from Andy—"Hey, wanna get

hitched?"—had been nothing like this, I accepted. Of course we went to Schraffts.

Soon after we were dating regularly. Because he was staying with his sister and brother-in-law in Queens, we always went to my place or out. I took him on the Staten Island ferry, to Radio City Music Hall, up the Statue of Liberty. He always called me. "My brother-in-law works nights, he's always sleeping" and "They don't like us to get personal calls while we're at the seminar" were the reasons he gave for not sharing any phone numbers. Entranced as I was by the solidity of his presence, the way he'd tip big and say, "Have a nice day, now, you hear," to surly cab drivers and vicious street people alike, I thought nothing of it. He called regularly, bought tickets to *Cats*, gave me bunches of red and pink carnations (which I had to bring to the secretaries at work since I couldn't possibly deface my foyer with them), and always kissed me chastely at the door.

About that I had begun to wonder. The body I had so long ignored began to rumble alive again. Perhaps because my grandmother and aunt had always made it plain that to search for my lost mother would kill them, I found that as I aged I had begun to idealize family. I realized that all of a sudden I was imagining life under a double goosedown puff in Sioux Falls with adorable little Bills and Billettes tumbling in their nurseries. We were going to have to do a lot more than those chaste pecks for that to happen. Amanda I had seen less frequently, and then, gradually, not at all, during this period. After her repeated invitations to get us all together had met with continuous flimsy excuses from me, she began to get the message. Her answering machine, with a tape using Mae West's voice—"What a dump!"—was always on when I did try to reach her for the occasional chat. I even drifted by the jewelry store where Betty worked to learn that she had taken a six-month leave of absence and flown to Bolivia with Ricardo who was going to pursue some sort of herbal cure for depression administered by the local Indians. Imagining Amanda alone with only Eliot and Lola was more than I could bear. The only picking up that loft ever suffered was at Betty's hands. It must be thigh-deep now in cat hair and empty coriander bottles.

My new job was going nicely. I found that as long as I read neither the theatre review section of the *Times* nor *Variety* I was fine. I began to pursue the accretion of my serious corporate wardrobe. I missed what would have been all the fun of Amanda helping me pick it out; Bill accompanied me docilely enough through the stores but wasn't mischievious enough to camp it up as Amanda and I had done. We'd admire each other in the dressing room, deliberately within earshot of the salesgirls—"Oh, darlin', if the chemo doesn't work, I think this will look so nicely on me for the wake, don't you think?" The Yalies loved me, invited me constantly to fern bars for lunch and promised I could go next year to the international oil conference in Cologne. "Is that where perfume comes from?" Bill asked, quite seriously.

"Isn't it almost time for you to be heading back to Sioux Falls?" I began to query him one night over Sanka at my place, trying gently to warm up to the inevitable, that we hop in the sack, buy the ring and head out for the Heartland together.

"Uh...well...uh...yeah..., well, the seminar's been extended." He got red, had to run a finger in around his white collar which, I noticed, was finally showing some city grime. His face was a little blemished now, too—the rich food, no doubt, and the filth in the air. He left my place earlier than usual that night, and the peck was more peckish than usual.

That was when I first began to get suspicious. Bill didn't call for a week. When I tried New York Mutual Life there was no seminar and no such person. After that, in one desperate evening, I tried every Baxter in Queens on the insane presumption that his sister had kept her maiden name or that there were other local relatives. No one had ever heard of him. I found myself stumbling around in a daze. I kept drifting to the phone to dial Amanda—somehow my fingers wouldn't fit into the little holes. I felt ashamed, guilty, bad, for forsaking her and a friendship that really mattered. I deserved, instead, just what I had gotten: Bill—and then no Bill. I couldn't decide which was worse.

Then, finally, I received the call at work. It was from a young woman named Roseanne Penney. She said she worked for the public library. She told me she had cajoled my number out of the pastor of my church. She had claimed to be a long-lost college roommate who didn't know my married name. (I remember explaining to Reverend Woods that, for professional reasons I'd kept my married name because I'd used it for the stage.)

She told me that Bill had only ever mentioned my first name and that I went to the First Church of Christ, Scientist in Chelsea. She told me that he was a dangerous psychopath and sexual deviant, that she had a restraining order out on him after he had broken her nose after they first had sex. "He can handle everything else," she told me. "Then, as soon as you do it, he tells you you're a haridan from hell and hits you with a frying pan." She told me that she didn't want to frighten me or interfere in my life, but that he had mentioned me the last week or so he had been seeing her, trying to tell her that she was a trollop and I as chaste as newly fallen snow. She had had to change her phone number, her locks, and move in for two weeks with a girlfriend from the library. "Is there someone you can stay with?"

"No," I said and hung up. The only shred of truth in anything Bill had told me was that he really was from Sioux Falls where the chief of police had told Roseanne there was an outstanding warrant for his arrest on the charge of assaulting a rental car saleswoman as well as suspicion that he was involved in numerous other unsolved crimes of this sort perpetrated upon secretaries, nurses, kindergarten teachers, all single. His real name was Elwood Peavey and he had never worked for an insurance company.

Because my doorbell was my landpeople's and they were away on an extended tour of the Holy Land, I could not tell if my doorbell rang in the following days. I could not tell if my phone rang because I unplugged it. No calls came in at work, yet I recalled now that Bill, or Elwood, had never liked to call me there. He had always seemed overly suspicious, now that I reflected, about the intentions of the Yalies and of what went on in the fern bars at lunch. Two weeks passed. I slept at night, or rather did not sleep, with a lot of the lights on and a rolling pin by my bed. My boss suggested that I begin to take dessicated liver pills for my anemia, which must be the cause of the blue bags under my eyes, he said, and begin to go for steam treatments and hot mud packs at the health spa he recommended. My other boss, the one who had been converted by Muktananda after beginning to acquire an ulcer, recommended chanting and meditation and various dishes concocted out of seaweed or fermented soy.

After I began to have heart palpitations on the subway while it was stopped between stations for indeterminable periods of time, which it frequently was, I finally gave in and left Mae West a desperate message for her to have Amanda call me at once.

Amanda was chipper, did not tell me "I told you so" or even try to razz me about having left the theatre. In fact, it was as if no time had passed. She planned a date for us the following Sunday afternoon at one of our favorites, Rumplemeyers on the park. The afternoon turn out exceptionally balmy for March—a generous dollop of early spring, a day of grace for the winter-creased denizens of our metropolis who seemed to crawl up, in record numbers, out of the stinking tubes that propel us to our destinations, to worship the sun and the air even on this blighted scrap of earth.

Amanda and I settled as of old into the ice cream parlor which always felt to me like the inside of a box of expensive chocolates, intensely pink and ruffled. We ordered our usual, a single Coupe Romanoff—Grand Marni`er, strawberries and vanilla ice cream nestled into meringue—and two spoons. I poured out my whole hairy tale, which Amanda listened to impassively with only one lovely eyebrow arched. All she said when I had finished was, "Well, Betty's had a few episodes like that with Ricardo."

"What? I thought he only hurt himself."

"'Tis but a slip from the self to the love object," she said with grim affect.

We addressed ourselves to the Coupe then, in silence for a few moments, until finally I felt compelled to burst out, "I know it was crazy, but Amanda, haven't you ever felt desperate to get married or at least to get serious with a man?

"Well...not really...not anymore...not for years and years. I mean, what are my choices? Ricardo? Bill? What does being on stage teach us? Romeo? Cyrano? Dr. Frobisher thinks it's because I never found a man like my father. You know, no one else had the key to the amusement park."

"Do you think you'll ever stop seeing that shrink?"

"Do you think you'll ever stop going to church?"

There was no rebuttal to that one. I simple spooned up another strawberry that had died in bliss and smoothed my Burberry around me.

"What it is, really, I think," Amanda leaned way back, flinging her arms wide, then fluffing her glorious hair and adjusting her flounces, "is that some of us were meant to be spinsters, plain and simple. Why fight it?"

"But..." I started to fluster, the teachings I had had all of my life from the women of my family—none of whom, I suddenly realized, had ever managed marriage, except my grandmother and her husband who had died young in Ardenne—rising up around me to rebuke me...and then I felt them all begin to collapse like so many houses of cards. I let out a great gusty breath. I saw my gleaming apartment. I saw my serious corporate wardrobe lined up in my closet. I saw Amanda and the feline felons chummily ensconced in layer after layer of disorder on the Bowery, contentedly eating out of pots and pans and serving bowls, licking their fingers and paws and chops. I saw my friend and me floating gracefully into old age on each other's arms, meeting again and again for dinner, for tea, concerts, exhibits, performances in Bloomingdale's fitting rooms.

I saw myself at last here in this city, at home, taking root. My life was not what I had ever dreamed or imagined or even, at the moment, what I would have chosen out of all my fantasy choices, but simply, where I was.

"There are worse fates," I said, as I scooped up the last bite of meringue dripping in sauce. Reaching across the table, I spooned it into Amanda's mouth, letting little raspberry dribbles cruise down her chin. "Shall we waltz on over to Bloomingdale's when we're done? I just can't imagine how those salesgirls are managing without us."

II. Underwater Women

Rosalie

In the year of the flood we moved to Wheeling. In our house, set up from the cobbled brick street on a narrow hillside lot, we stayed dry and safe. Still, the newspaper and radio reports were grisly. I saw filthy rising water in my troubled dreams, the surprised eyes of people about to swallow their own deaths while all their worldly goods swept by.

My first new friend in our neighborhood, Jeanette Bingley—twelve like me, staying next door with her aunt—had been flooded out. Crouched together on our porch inside the giant cardboard packing box we'd claimed as a clubhouse, I'd make her tell me again and again the hair-raising tale of her family's evacuation into the night, sleeping on Red Cross cots, eating off tin plates. To me the most courageous part of it all was when she got the tetanus shot and didn't cry.

Jeanette felt like the best friend I'd ever had, even better than Mary Jane and Ellie back home in Charleston. My mother took me to children's art classes sponsored by the city, held downtown in a drafty studio in an old warehouse above the dirty brick streets; I scorned the studies of bottles and pears and began a huge charcoal mural of the flood to give to Jeanette.

The day before school started I ran next door to find her gone; the family's house had been pumped out and she hadn't even said good-bye. Gone, too, of course were Ellie and Mary Jane and our numerous secret societies—Three Knights of the Bicycle and The Sign of the Skull and Crossbones. All that was left was Wheeling Creek, thick with mosquitos, and the winter to come. Jeanette's aunt had told us the coal furnaces turned the snow black with soot. I had to start sixth grade, back on square one, everything riding on who I could get to be my friends.

The next day I collected the new Crayolas—sixty-four colors, sharpened to a razor point—and the scissors and the jar of paste my mother had bought, and trooped like Jeanette on her way to the tetanus shot down the aisle of a classroom full of unfamiliar, staring faces. Everyone else—girls, anyway—had pink and green-lined notebook paper in binder notebooks; no one had crayolas and paste.

"This is Patty from Charleston," announced Mr. Royce, the first male teacher I'd ever had; his very presence gave me the creeps. "She had straight A's in her old school—so let her be an example to you boys and girls." A faint murmur rippled the rows of seated children. Glances were exchanged. The gaze on me was murderous. My fate was sealed. At recess I walked alone, shoulders hunched, kicking the playground gravel.

I sat in the back row making cootie catchers out of folded paper under my desk, trying to decide how to survive. If only I could somehow dissolve my wrong start and attach myself to two or three girls who would sit with me at lunch, invite me over after school, pass notes to me in class, gossip in the girls' lav.

Over the next few weeks I got it all figured out. It was easy to rule out who wouldn't do. The Girl Scout crowd revolved around Billie Lou Olsen whose grandmother slept in their dining room in a hospital bed and who earned her cat-and-dog badge on a rabbit she kept in a smelly hutch her father had built. Her sidekick, Dotty Brown, had hair sort of accordion-pleated from a Toni home permanent and wore things to school like her older sister's cast-off blue chiffon formal because her family was too poor to buy new clothes.

Madge Tyler was another loser. She had a dog named Jeff which, she claimed, would say "Mama" when fed a piece of bologna; she wanted a dime to exhibit him doing this for you after school. Madge herself always ate a piece of toast with mustard on it for breakfast, was always late for school, and forgot everything, including all her assignments. She palled around a lot with Margaret and Martha Hawthorne. Margaret was doughy and puffy and wore rimless spectacles; Martha was slender with delicate features. Despite my immediate assumption that the opposite would be true, Margaret had a D average, and Martha, who was always reading advanced library books, got called a brain. I would have chosen them as friends but the injustice of it all overwhelmed me.

Instead, I continued on alone, writing plays on my new pink and green notebook paper during study hours, and, at home, hiding out on the glider on the porch with *Great Tales of Terror and the Supernatural* which I had stolen from my father's bookshelf. As time passed, it became clear to me that my only antidote to this life would be Joan and Leslie, two sleek, inseparable, dark-haired girls with stylish clothes who managed to be terribly brilliant without being bookworms. Joan's father was an executive of Stone-Thompson's, the best department store in town. Besides brains and beauty, they exuded glamour and class. Leslie's father was head of the major radio station. Every Saturday Joan and Leslie were featured on the "Little Theatre of the Air" on which they read child parts like Pollyanna or Rebecca of Sunnybrook Farm.

Their only friend was Lynda Rooking whose father worked at Wheeling Steel and whose grandfather had died of black lung disease. Despite these liabilities, Lynda was included in their circle because she was tall and developed and wore straight skirts and carried a huge clutch purse which was rumored to contain sanitary napkins which none of the rest of us needed yet. Lynda had the advantage of being the only student in the class whom Mr. Royce would excuse to go to the bathroom whenever she raised her hand. As she left the room his eyes seemed to fixate on the purse.

Joan and Leslie permitted Lynda to sit with them at lunch and then to stroll with them around the playground disdaining the crude and childish boys who hurled themselves about trying to impress.

I would have killed to be included.

After several sleepless nights, I hit upon the way. My play! Featuring Sgt. Joe Tuesday and his sidekick, Frank Furter, it detailed the solving of a multiple murder case in which a dastardly criminal (who turns out to be a monkey) spikes bottles of soda with poison in a factory which reach the homes of unsuspecting victims. It was entitled *Horror in the Soda Pop Factory.*

How simple it would be! Leslie would show her father the play and all of us would take parts for the radio. Friends and stardom!

I could hardly stop shaking as I approached the three of them in the girls' lav which smelled of excrement and lysol in equal parts and in which we would all rather spend all of our recess instead of on the playground with the sun and the air and the boys. I was just about to break into my rehearsed speech when I realized we were not alone. Under the nearest cubicle door feet were visible. Distinctive feet. Rosalie's feet.

Dotty Brown was poor and oddly dressed—that everyone knew—but she did crimp her hair and was twelve years old and got good grades and did not smell. She also sold more Girl Scout cookies every year than anyone. She was tolerated.

Rosalie was none of these things and she was not.

Rosalie—whose last name was Nice which gave everyone a lot to laugh about since it was assumed she was anything but—was fourteen and still in the sixth grade and could barely read and had hair like a rat's nest and smelled of B. O. The stories about her—fantastic and endless—always circulated here in the girls' lav or on the playground. She lived in a shack by the railroad tracks (someone said it was actually an abandoned railroad car); her parents had thirteen kids; her father was a drunk and her mother worse....

Some people felt sorry for Dotty Brown since she was poor because her father had been killed at Wheeling Steel in an accident, and people's mothers tried to find subtle ways to pass things on to her ("Oh, this just shrunk right up in the wash and doesn't fit Sissy now, but you're so small, and it's your color....") But not for Rosalie. Her color was mud-brown.

Her very despair and odor roused in her peers a killer instinct.

The shoes I saw beneath the cubicle door had once been white buck. They were big as boats. The socks above them were rolled down. The ankles were bony, the legs like a chicken's and perched far apart. The stream of urine between them was loud and seemed never to end. My coveted group of three didn't seem to notice. They actually turned on my approach to include me. I was still shaking and tried to smile.

"What size bra do you wear, Patty?" Joan, who was buxom and actually overweight but incurred no scorn because she was rich and handsome enough with perfect skin and thick, shiny, dark hair and a wardrobe from Stone-Thompson's, spoke to me first.

"I...uh...well...ah...my mother won't let me wear a bra." Actually, it was more like what on earth would I hang it on? My chest measured 28 AA, but I didn't want to say.

"I wear 32 A," said Leslie, sticking out her chest in her lambs' wool sweater, just like Joan's but a different color.

"I wear 36 B." Joan was smug, smoothing her hands over her upholstered front. Lynda said nothing, but it was clear she could compete.

I was desperate with fear. Obviously I didn't stand a chance in this group. Still—my play! There were parts for us all, counting the soda pop factory owner and the grieved housewife whose husband had drunk the poisoned pop (the monkey didn't count as he had no lines). I was just screwing up my courage again to tell them about it when Joan began to talk, as she so often did, about Rosalie. "Did you see her today? Who does she think she's kidding? Those falsies!"

I didn't know what that meant, but I kept my mouth shut. With a 28 AA chest, I couldn't afford to take chances. "Yeah," Leslie went on, "it's really disgusting—they look like Sno-Cone cups under her sweater." Everybody laughed, and I caught on. "And that sweater and skirt! I think they came from the Salvation Army...."

Suddenly I realized, though I was standing now with what felt like real friends, their shared laughter wrapping me with a warm glow, that I could no longer hear pee from the cubicle and that I knew whose feet and whose listening ears were behind that door, though the others—since I had only heard them speak this way behind Rosalie's back—apparently did not.

The next moment in time is not one I can make up for no matter how long I live. That I know. The fact that later in the year I cast the decisive vote making Dotty Brown Cookie Queen of the Girl Scout Dance, and that I even made her crown, myself, out of silver-painted cardboard and plastic jewels, makes no matter.

That I invited only Madge and Martha and Margaret to my birthday party (Madge forgot to come), that I joined Girl Scouts and became best friends with Billie Lou and and fussed a lot over her rabbit, that I went carolling for hours with only thin boots on to nursing homes and other frightening places with the troop and never complained—cannot redeem me.

I knew, and said nothing. I stood and knew that Rosalie heard, and said nothing. A grotesque smile hung on my face, breath stuck in windpipe. The smell of the toilets rose up about me, thick and suffocating. "Yeah, and she never even takes a bath! She really stinks!" They all laughed. I tried to join in though no real sound would come from my throat.

"I DO NOT STINK!" Rosalie flung back the door; it reverberated against the wall. She strode into the middle of the room, her pointed breasts the armaments of an Amazon. Her eyes flashed. Usually she talked to no one, ate her meager bag lunch alone,—we all paid for our hot dishes on trays—and entered and left the lav quickly, eyes downcast.

Today she stood her ground. She said nothing further, merely looked from one of us to the other—it seemed her fierce gaze lingered longest on me—slowly, in turn. Then she stormed out of the room. We remained, crumpled together like discarded Kleenex, giggling weakly. "Phew, boy, does she ever stink," Leslie tried—but there was no power left in her words.

I began to tell them about Victor and Eddie and George in my school in Charleston. Victor always smelt like he had just pooped in his pants, and Mrs. Fletcher, the fourth grade teacher, had broken a ping-pong paddle on Eddie's backside trying to spank him in front of the whole class, and yet we had all contributed to paying for a Halloween pumpkin for each of them that contained pencils and sharpeners and erasers and rulers and candy because they were too poor to buy their own. "Eddie used to eat the paste, though," I tried to laugh as I told them.

"We could get Rosalie a pumpkin," Lynda said. She was serious. Leslie and Joan nodded gravely. "My father could get us the stuff wholesale," Joan said.

"Mrs. Fletcher told us that Eddie and Victor and George went with their families every winter down south to pick oranges and stuff to earn money. That's why they always missed school and got bad grades and had to be in the fifth grade when they were fourteen."

"Yeah, I think Rosalie's family does that," Leslie said lamely. The bell rang. In silence we filed back to class. Mr. Royce was punishing Tommy Hall for talking. Tommy had to bend over the desk and be beaten with a belt. His whole face screwed up, but he wouldn't cry or yell out. I thought his face looked like Rosalie's. I fell in love with him and began to plan a Valentine's Mail Box for our sixth grade party. I could make it myself and decorate it with red crepe paper and doilies and cupids, and that way would be able to send Tommy Hall a Valentine....

Rosalie had dragged her desk all the way from the front row back to the last, across the room from me, so she wouldn't have to sit by Leslie and Joan. Mr. Royce didn't even try to stop her. She never spoke to any of us again, but she never looked down again either, and she stopped wearing the Sno-Cone bra.

I won a Blue Ribbon at the City of Wheeling Recreation Department Children's Art Show for my mural of the flood. Leslie and Joan and Lynda asked me over for a slumber party on a Friday and then to go to the radio station on Saturday and play Phronsie in *Five Little Peppers*.... I said no. I stayed home and read Little Lulu comics to my younger sister and wrote to my grandmother and scratched my father's back as he watched Sid Caesar and tried to get my mother to let me help her in the kitchen.

None of it helped.

Winter Apples

How I got to be so hungry is a longer story. The one of the affair is shorter, though no less desperate. Mid-winter, I found myself in a middle-sized, nondescript city of mediocre opportunity.

Some eleven months earlier I had debarked at this stop because the price of the ticket coincided almost exactly with the amount of money I had. Easing travel-stiff limbs I had gotten down from a littered train into a dim and airless station located in a part of town that was, like myself, fallen from once-promising to rock-bottom times.

I stood on a corner mired in gritty slush, hunched against a raw wind, knowing no one, belly rumbling. I re-wrapped my fraying muffler around my neck as I ducked inside a dangerous-looking café that was alive with the zap and dazzle of pinballs to spend my remaining quarters on food that tasted of grease and papier maché.

Those pinball machines, the first signs of life the city had offered me, somehow could not be denied; the first job ad I saw led me to the work I did to meet my meager rent and grocery bill. Days my fingers pranced on the terminal of a word processor, fingers that had once midwived dreams and visions of my own conception on a Smith-Coronamatic that belonged to me.

Things soon looked up. I found a boxy, plain apartment three blocks from the nearest (and only) gay bar in town. Since I saw myself as a woman possessed of A Past—having had two classically disastrous former lovers, The Teenage Crush and The Married Woman—I soon developed a set of unchallenging cronies from amongst the pool-table spectator set. They led me eventually to the local women's center where my talents for sublimation and denial through hard work were quickly appreciated.

The myriad of lowly duties to be performed at every social function the dyke community threw that year multiplied with my eagerness to serve and thus survive. I plugged speaker wires, sloshed
cranberry juice into makeshift punch bowls, applied under-
developed muscles to rows of folding chairs—month after month, all
the while cultivating my image as The Lone Wolf, scarred and sad-
dened by A Nameless Tragedy none dared ask about, yet chastened
and humble from the Wisdom suffering imparts. It passed the time.

A small dyke press had once published five hundred copies of
my book, just before a group of local punks and tight-lipped house-
wives (really agents of a clandestine government organization) had
vandalized the presses and burnt the books, all in order to save the
genitals of America's children from same-sex caresses. The few remaining copies of my work lingered almost unremembered at the
bottom of a dresser drawer in my new apartment. The feminist Literature and Poetry Group I had once astounded with razor-sharp in-
sights and revolutionary profundities—where I had first met The
Married Woman, where I had begun to meet the death's head in the
glass that was my own—seemed also long forgotten.

Now my local library, which smelled of damp sweaters and the
hair oil of elderly men, dispensed just enough pulpy sci-fi and het-
ero romance to keep me from the terminal stages of anorexia of the
soul. I spoke to no one save of coffee breaks, overdue fines, or
where to plug speaker wires.

Finally, one day, in the temporary euphoria of a sweet, mid-
December thaw, something seemed to break. A small ad in the
women's center monthly newspaper, the most advanced literary attempt to be found within a two-hundred mile radius, led me to a lesbian poetry reading in a clammy but Liberal church's basement. A
bravery born of desperation—I hadn't known either to possess me to
that degree—pushed me to speak to two young, open-faced, obvi-
ously-in-love dykelets, whose lavender-tinged cloud of barely post-
adolescent romance was sufficient to screen out the more blood-
chilling aspects of lean, hard-bitten me.

Becka and Ceil, students who lived above a general store in a university town an hour's ride from the city, were both women's studies majors as well as volunteers for the local rape crisis hot-line, gay switchboard, and community food co-op; they became my first and only real friends. Feeding me baked Lentil Loaf with Sunflower Seed Sauce and other delicacies born of their tight budgets rather than any form of political correctness, served on a rickety thrift shop table, these two listened to my rantings, Saturday after Saturday. As I complained, they'd just hug me, ply me with more carob brownies and ginger-root tea, and drag me off to coffeehouses, potlucks, and benefits for battered wives, seals, whales, and faculty women who had had the audacity to sue department heads who had asked them to suck their cocks in return for tenure.

Finally—as if bringing me the first snowdrop, or the song of an oriole in February— they offered Suzanne.

Awkward as 14-year olds we sat at a table, the four of us, nursing cups of cranberry juice and trying to think of something to say. The occasion chosen to bring me together with Becka's and Ceil's friend and former teacher was The Women's Center Annual Susan B. Anthony Birthday Dance, currently in full swing around us: That is to say, four couples gyrated to the strains of our imported, live band in the cavernous, shit-brown auditorium of the local YWCA whose gawky program director, immediately after taking our check for the inflated amount demanded for rental, had run around in a homophobic frenzy ripping our posters off the bulletin boards.

Prior to The Fateful Meeting, I had been eagerly advised, "Sandie, she's just what you need." Indeed. Suzanne wore—it took me a few moments to convince myself I wasn't hallucinating—a velvet bow tie. Her voice was low and clear. The intensity with which she expressed herself opened for me vistas of memory I had feared forever walled off. I yearned to respond in kind—to sweep her into my arms on the currents of my brilliance and sensitivity.

Instead, crumpling styrofoam, I sat, mugging through a limp story about how we'd rented the band—which was just now making a brave but futile attempt at a Holly Near tune, all the while revealing exactly how dreadful it was. So much for entertainment first heard at an all-nude, matriarchal festival in the woods.

"I guess non-monogamy must be where they come from.... Every time I called one of them to fix the date, she was sleeping at a different woman's house...."

"Oh, Sandie, who cares about them? Tell Suzanne about your book!"

"Yes," Suzanne said, looking straight at me, "do." Her eyes were speckled, gray-blue, holding only a hint of green.

And from that moment on, the evening tumbled past me like the vivid blur a child's eye takes in, rolling down a hill on the last day of school....

We left the dance in two cars, myself, of course, in Suzanne's. I remember now what she told me—about the lover-who-had-left, to New Jersey, to a job at another university, to another lover—about the book manuscript she needed to publish to gain tenure lingering unfinished in the cold, no-longer shared house while her savings dwindled as oil costs rose.

I took in none of what the story could have told me about what was to follow for her and me. I heard only the voice, saw only the eyes. As I sat beside her, the back of my jaw began to ache.

Our excursion to The Bar was brief; the room smelled of beer, leather, and sweat; the disco pulsed mercilessly. No wonder the dance was hanging itself from the rafters that very instant; lukewarm cranberry and a band called the Sassafras Sisters could never compete with this.

The three blocks to my place had never been shorter, its no-color walls and Early Yard Sale decor never more inviting. A book from my bottom drawer—from under a silky gown now yellowing with disuse that The Married Woman had particularly liked—was easily produced; so was a notepad on which to write my number for Suzanne so that, of course, she could return the book to me.

Which was how, the very next Saturday night, after a week of forcing myself to swallow hard constantly, I ended up at her place for dinner.

The house was cold. So were my hands. I held them around the exquisitely glazed pottery mug filled with fragrant mulled cider Suzanne had brought me as we sat at the table—polished mahogany, very Victorian, her Great-Aunt's—waiting for the chicken to poach.

"I'm sorry there isn't rosemary." She spoke in the way I remembered. The bow-tie, of course, was not in evidence, but her eyes—greener yet in the candlelight—most certainly were. "That went to New Jersey, too. I just haven't replaced it."

I took a deep swallow from my cup; the spices, the heat, the sweetness coursed through me, chest, belly, swelling with sensation.

We'd spent the afternoon exploring the town's oldest graveyard, searching for fragments of women's lives. Suzanne had taken my hand—at her touch my breath almost left me—in order to steer us toward her favorite headstone deep under the sweep of an ancient pine, where a mother and all the babes she's lost in infancy lay.

Later, by a still, dark pond along a wooded trail with sunlight filtering only dimly through the welter of branches above, Suzanne told me this was the special spot where she came to be alone, to think, to remember....

The lover was not the only one who had left. In a way her mother had always been lost to her, wrapped in a kind of flour-and-crisco efficiency that pushed away a girl's musings, killed the spirit. Her older sister, an artist, had filled the gap until suddenly last year, in her forties, breast cancer had taken her.

"After my sister died, I couldn't even watch a TV game show," Suzanne told me over lemon mousse, as the candles guttered low throwing shadows across the plump curves of winter apples nestled in a pewter bowl, "without weeping uncontrollably for the loser."

"But isn't there always a winner as well?" I set down my thin handled dessert spoon, looked up at her through flame and shadow.

"Perhaps...I never noticed." She rose and cleared the table.

A little later, Suzanne settled into a chair in her living room. It had a tapestry fabric and wide wooden arms. I stood in the center of the room.

"I'm sorry, there's no couch. It..."

"Yes, I know, '"...went to New Jersey.'" We did not laugh. My face grew as grave as hers; I crossed the polished, hardwood floor, sat on the arm of the chair.

Her hair, a gentle brown catching the lamplight, was soft under my hand. Her mouth, under mine, was soft, as was the down of her cheek, her earlobe faintly pink....

In the bedroom, her Great-Aunt's handmade quilt, six floor-to-ceiling bookshelves, full, all full—Woolf, Dickinson, Plath, Austen, Brontes, Sand, Lessing...

...Senses reeling, raw need surfacing at last, I hardly knew which deeper hunger first to slake.... Deciding for me, Suzanne drew me down to her bed.....

Slowly, slowly as I eased them one by one from their holes, the buttons of her shirt stung my fingers like fire; opening her to me was an act of reverence. The beauty we were together seemed to expand into all the void that had been myself.

Despite my need, and hers, we paced ourselves, touch on touch, until, finally, after what seemed a time out of time, the flood of our feelings, coursing as a river between green banks, as the blood itself through the waterways of the miracle of the body, burst, in loins, throat, heart, first from her, then me....

"What an amazing woman you are!" Her words nestled in my ear. Against the night, the mounting cold, we held each other under her Great-Aunt's quilt, tight, arms wrapped binding as a child's around each other's sweetness and sweet relief, until morning flushed the white church spire across the country roads.

The bells pealed out the day, white and cold. She went to church.

I waited. With my fingertips, I caressed the books on her shelf as I had her body. I rehearsed in my mind not only more nights like the one just passed, but other nights when we would share even more secret recesses of the spirit—words, ideas, poetry.... Until that moment, I had not known just what it was I was starving for.

After church, which was attended largely by townspeople whose ancestors lay in the graveyard where we had first touched, Suzanne explained why she went each week—the need for ordering, pageantry, the feeling of a stout-walled space into which she could safely release her sorrow and her pain. She told me how the music, the flowers, the harmonious voices of the well-schooled congregation, all gave her the sense of protection and nurturing she needed now that she was alone.

I dropped my eyes to my tea-cup—white porcelain, delicately flowered—and hopelessly mumbled something about the reading my old Group had done on Mary Daly, about the full moon ritual to celebrate our menstrual blood we'd held in an attempt to dismantle patriarchal structures, the cycle of poems I'd stopped working on but hoped to start again soon, using woman-oriented spiritual images....

"Yes," said Suzanne. She was wrapped in distance. Last night seemed to have fallen into a deep crevasse that had split open between us. Sweeping crumbs into her hands, she gathered the linen napkins, moved into the kitchen.

All my many words rattled back at me from this space that was hers...alone. My stomach, despite the popovers and the chocolate in a little silver pot, gave a crude rumble.

The cold within the room opened around me, filling every nook and corner. The sky outside the high, uncurtained windows rose full of the bare branches of trees—gaunt, bony arms yearning into an emptiness as vast as the human heart can contain.

The Unveiling

Those girls! Eleanor Barnett crossed the parking lot this early New England April morning, about to allow her day to be spoiled.

She found herself raising her head to more fully take in the pale rose flush of the sky, the tender scent of earth and water on the breeze, in a gesture rare to her—sensual, almost animal. On a morning like this it was easy to realize that her years numbered nearly sixty, deeply satisfying to appreciate that yet another winter had been survived.

Such peace and now this! Her neighbors—college girls, she supposed, three of them, roommates, subletting from the middle-aged owners who were abroad—had begun, as usual, to fling themselves out of the front door with a highly inappropriate burst of noise in the still sleeping condominium community. An then they began—also as usual—to hug and kiss each other goodbye.

Eleanor hoisted her leather briefcase and turned abruptly away. *One would think they were departing to trek in Nepal, or Tierra del Fuego, never to return!*

Head down and shoulders tight with disapproval, she reached her sedate dark-blue compact, its windows pearled with dew, and dug in her bag for the keys.

Such a display in public! In the course of thirty-four years as a teacher of one sort or another, Eleanor had been confronted with youth in its every aspect, yet the sights and sounds that bombarded her almost daily from across the way struck her much as a sojourn in a foreign city would—headlines, announcements in a train station, all in a language utterly alien.

The three young women spilled in and out of the place at all hours, doors banging, a large rangy dog yelping, recorded music rising and falling—much too loud. These things in and of themselves did not distress Eleanor. On the university campus where Eleanor taught such flamboyance was common. What caused her heart to constrict in her breast was the openness with which these young women, variously attired in workboots, overalls, T-shirts (bra-less, of course), Indian blouses, and filmy, floaty long skirts, embraced each other and their friends, all of whom—save two skinny boys with gold hoops in their left ears—were female.

It had taken Eleanor several weeks to realize who and what was living next to her. Her immediate response to the situation was one of silence.

Her life with Charlotte—the safe, ordered, dear and ordinary routine of days, weeks, years—cloaked and veiled her like the garments of women in faraway middle east states. Eleanor was just beginning to admit that what was usually 'protected' in this way was the self itself from the full exercise of faculties: sight, insight, speech.

Finally one evening—ritual martinis on a tray, soft-music station tuned finely in the background, the last of the winter's sweet applewood was spitting on the hearth—she turned to her companion of twenty years. "What do you make of our neighbors across the way?"

Charlotte waited. When she finally spoke, it was, as always, crisp and to the point. "Obvious, I should think."

Accounting, Charlotte's life-long field, had taught her accuracy and precision with numbers; it had never occurred to her that one might use words, either, in another way. "Discretion has not generally been a strong point of the young."

Disapproval stitched Eleanor's mouth. "Yes, but...." She found an urgency she could neither explain nor contain welling up behind her words making a lapse back into silence now impossible. "Times...ways...how people think...all these are subject to change."

Always the historian, the keen detector of what lies deep underneath the daily chronicle of human lives—wars, revolution, natural disasters—melding them together to form pattern and sense, Eleanor was suffused suddenly with a sensation the drink alone had not caused: vertigo, warmth.

"About some things, change doesn't happen," Charlotte replied. An ample woman, solid, in contrast to Eleanor's delicate frame, her firmness seemed to close off dialogue. "Time to look in on the chicken." She moved into the kitchen where lemon and tarragon absorbed her fully, leaving Eleanor with her drink, her unanswered questions and her vertigo.

Nor did they speak again of the matter. Between them the unspoken—the unspeakable?—for almost more winters and springs than one could count, had become an indestructible bond.

Or—Eleanor had lately found pause to wonder as she lay awake beside her deeply sleeping, peacefully breathing companion—a chasm of unbridgeable width? So much need not, could not be spoken—would be sullied, dirtied, cheapened, were it to be. Even so— Eleanor wondered, wrung with bewilderment—what was the language one might use?

Yet—her thoughts floated backwards—they had managed, in the beginning and in all the years in between, using what language lovers have always used. She could remember now, far more vividly than had a surfeit of spoken words been free for the taking, a certain glance as light fell across a room, the caress of palm on a cheek, the body's own need, insistent, undeniable. For them, there had been no proclamations, declarations, promises.

Only now, in these still, sleepless dawns as winter, inch by inch, gave itself up to the lengthening light of spring, did Eleanor realize how this had served to save them also from defenses, justifications, rationalizations, refutations.

"These young people now...so shrill...so public. Decency, a sense of the private life—do they remain at all?" These were the only further remarks, over luncheon of chilled white wine and fresh asparagus, that Charlotte allowed herself.

Yes, Eleanor thought, but did not speak, *and with that privacy, shame, subterfuge, distortion?* How could she, who found herself sometimes now walking to the car, from classes, to the library, briefcase swinging against her leg, forgetting the time, her errand, even where the car was parked, she, of all women, who had dedicated her whole life to the pursuit of the truth, the imparting of that truth to others, to the young—have lived with such denial?

*And yet...*the ceaseless conversation she could not have with her companion, in fact, with no other living being, rattled on now, instead, inside her head... *What other choices had we?*

The girl Eleanor—thin, shy, bespeckled, supposedly frail, studious—had not appealed to men. But what other girls might have felt as rejection, Eleanor enjoyed with relief. She was left to be free.

Her own versions of both strength and passion emerged with her greatest devotion—to her own mother, amateur botanist, conversationalist of wit, devoted homemaker and helpmeet to her writer husband. After her mother's early death—one that medicine today could have prevented—all Eleanor's intensity flowed instead to her college history professor, Miss Ingles: high of brow, pure of intellect, fervent beyond all telling—in front of the class, on the shady green paths of the cloistered campus, in her book-lined study, sherry glinting in the tiny glasses....

The only job without graduate school, which without money was impossible, was in public school. (After his wife's death, Eleanor's father could write no more; checks dwindled while medical bills drifted in unpaid.) The school—noisy, barn-like, understaffed, with a library that was a wound that would not heal—swallowed her up. Yet a few eager, promising students, and those evenings at the Literary Guild, Historical Society, and Symphony Committee kept her alive.

Alive enough, anyway, to realize in Charlotte Conroy a woman whose potential matched her own. The two walked, talked, listened to music, discussed—with charged voices and snapping eyes—plays, lectures, political speakers. When the shabby but genteel neighborhood where each had a solitary, capacious apartment—good woodwork, fireplaces—fell sudden prey to greedy developers eyeing the trendy young professional market, rents doubled. How sensible then to share—each her own room, her own life, yet, companionship. And so it was between them—the richness, confluence, deep as the river that Eleanor had always known to lie below ordinary events.

No one spoke to either of them of marriage—seeing not, of course, that they had a sort of marriage—that image being invisible. Each became serious about her work, the rise of her own career. Eleanor moved up from high school to junior college, grinding all the way at the night courses that brought her finally to her doctorate and the university, where she, like the long-lost but not forgotten Miss Ingles, might burn, and, so burning, ignite others.

Charlotte progressed steadily from simple bookkeeper to full accountant to office manager in several firms, finally now to executive
administrator of a small but prospering computer outfit.

The two women had begun their lives in a time when females of
such ambition paid for it with a narrow bed and an empty womb. As
times changed, which, despite Charlotte's view to the contrary, Eleanor knew indeed they do, women—who now had careers, babies,
husbands, lovers (sometimes both), even vacations alone—merely
assumed that these two who continued to share home and hearth
long after financial need could have been the reason did so only out
of some lack of nerve, some failure of the imagination.

Despite their silence, nothing could have been further from the
truth; what happened between them happened earlier than one
might suppose, long before either would have had to relinquish all
hopes of male attention. What they had in every other way simply
spilled over easily enough—given the circumstances and the times—
into that final, inevitable passion that women, especially those of ambition and the mind's delight, possess in abundance.

Eleanor could remember, as if looking over long, hazy hills to a
horizon dreamt of as much as seen, that amazing night—the sherry,
the music, the talk, the warmth.... When the time came there had
been no words. *"Sweet,"* she had always thought, tenderly—and
now, with anger, *"crippling."*

The bed in her own room that first night had lain empty, the
spread neat and tight; every night thereafter, with no comment, empty it remained. Though neither really had been the first to reach
out—so full and mutual that coming together had been—it was then
and always Eleanor who came to Charlotte, to the bed of her be-
loved, for their nightly resting close to the comfort of each other's
breathing in sleep and each other's waking to the sun.

But now, for Eleanor, this was no longer enough.

Across the way, the growing light and warmth, the gritty slush
spilling into clear, nourishing rivulets, brought their flamboyant
neighbors even more into view. Lawn chairs were dragged to the
patio; music could be heard that seemed—Eleanor at first feared au-
ditory hallucinations brought on by her insominia—to consist solely

of phrases like "Gay and Proud" and "You've got to ride the lesbian train."

"Lesbian train?" All she could envision was car after car rattling down a winding, ceaseless track, all the windows overflowing with women leaning out as they flew past, beckoning and blowing kisses. *I must be hearing things!*

Eleanor would shake her head in hopes of clearing it, straighten her spine, hoist her briefcase, and move briskly to the car. Those words, which had meant for her whole generation only degradation and defilement, did not slip easily now into her vocabulary as terms of affirmation, even celebration. She felt the very insides of the folds of her brain undergoing alterations. So, she imagined, had entire systems of ideas shifted, nations fallen. Ideas, the exhilaration of them, and the danger, were part of life's study. That is how she knew about Darwin, Freud, France in 1789—with an academician's distance. Now in the same way on a smaller scale, inside herself, revolution began to smolder.

Eleanor neither sought—nor avoided—the inevitable meeting. One morning, as she passed the opposite front yard, one of the young women moved swiftly into the sun, calling out to her: "Hello! Hello!" The girl's hair was long and a little wild; her breasts, firm, high and youthful, bounced freely under a T-shirt silk-screened, astonishingly, with an image of a naked woman astride a unicorn. Her face was open and clear and—amazing to Eleanor, used always to such guardedness and caution—friendly. "Could I ask you about something—that is, if you have a minute...."

"Yes. Certainly. A minute." Or, she thought, a lifetime. Eleanor stopped, gravely, and waited.

"Hi, I'm Willow. I guess we've never met, but my friends and I see you out here all the time...."

"Yes...." Taking the eagerly proffered hand, Eleanor realized with further astonishment that this young creature seemed to have impaled her earlobes with tiny silver battleaxes. "I'm Eleanor Barnett, your..." she faltered but a beat, "...neighbor. What again is your name?"

"Willow." The child grinned ear to ear. "My real name is Sue. I chose it last year. We had a ritual...."

"I see," said Eleanor, calmly, as if she did.

"Well, anyway, Ms. Barnett, I hope you don't mind, but...our other neighbors," Willow gestured vaguely back over the clipped hedges that separated units, "told us you were a history professor over at the U. I go to the community college...all I can afford...I work part-time at The Edible Mushroom. You know, the health food deli over on South Street...and I'm trying to help get us a women's studies program, writing a proposal, and I need help...you know."

Yes, Eleanor realized easily, I do.

"...and I thought...well, maybe..." Only just then did Willow's eyes drop a bit. "...you'd help us." She looked up again; on her face, in her eyes, was all the hope in the world. "There are no women faculty we can count on...they're all married with kids and only work part-time. We thought you'd be...different."

A week later as they nursed their coffee after dinner, the candles guttered low, throwing large, almost menacing shadows on the wall beyond. "At first," said Eleanor to Charlotte, "I didn't know what to do. Thirty-five years in the field...she's right, we haven't taught this...I haven't taught this...women in history...half the human race! You know, the worst part..." She stopped only for the space of a breath, to try to read the face of her companion in the flickering half-light, to gauge the silence that was now, irrevocably, only one-way. "...was feeling somehow that I'd failed. There was a sense of grief for an instant so deep that I couldn't touch the bottom of it...and why? For a girl I'd never met before?"

"And now?" Charlotte's voice reached her from a distance measured by a shadow.

"Well, I've made a beginning on what we need..." The pronoun came quite unselfconsciously. "...and it wasn't all so difficult. I have the skills, after all, years of them. There are possibilities—so many I'd never guessed at."

The energy in her voice, her body, which had been building all week, a fierce joy, yet shot through by fear, took her up from the table, away from where their two cups sat, two napkins lay, where the pool of light had just touched the perimeter of the circle that held them, to the wide window where a rose and lilac twilight deepened around the stark skeletons of trees whose fuzzy growth could not yet be seen but by full day.

"So I gave her everything I'd found—notes, lists of books.... I'm meeting with them all, this group she belongs to—a study group they call it, but certainly not the sort of study we used to do—next week. She, Willow...." The name still seemed impossibly odd to Eleanor, like all words in a language one is newly beginning to speak. "...wanted to offer some kind of fee. I told her, of course not. They're only kids; I have no need. And besides, I do feel that in some important way I'll be fully repaid...."

"Their apartment..." Eleanor was aware that her words were toppling out, one after the other, as Willow's did, nothing like her usual measured way, yet that silence of her companion created a hungry space that seemed to pull them from her into itself. She could not stop. "...it's such a curious place. The three of them live there. Two, Willow and Gina, share a room." This was the best Eleanor could do to describe their obvious union. "Jesse has her own, but the place is quite full of posters and   pictures...books...newspapers...journals, all about..."

She paused, then pushed the words out, "...women...like us. I never dreamt all of this existed. It's like unearthing an alien civilization, yet..." She gazed off, as a silver rind of moon glinted through branches. "...one that you know you've been part of...somehow. Perhaps in a dream...." Her words tapered off; there seemed to be no energy or breath left, only the fear gripping, constricting her heart. Her eyes suddenly stung. Turning away from the window, the night-gathering sky, to the room that was now cloaked in near-darkness where only the two low guttering flames gleamed, where Charlotte's face had been swallowed, Eleanor felt that she was looking into an emptiness, as if twenty years were no longer there.

Could death be worse?

The time that passed was long, long as the leaving of breath for the last time, long as the moment of waiting before the midwife, exclaiming, sees the head begin to crown.

When it had finally passed, as all moments of this sort inevitably do, Charlotte was beside her, arm warm about her shoulders solid, real as earth and rain.

"Tell me," she said. "Tell me more. Tell me all about it."

Sunspots

It's Labor Day in Connecticut, steamy as a chestnut on Fifth Avenue in winter. My mother's making Christmas ornaments and wants me to help. This involves sitting at the dinette table, usually cluttered with piles of newspapers—"I just cain't," she laments through the faint traces of her Appalachian accent, "throw anything away"— poking slivers of steel through the very eyes of iridescent sequins, then sinking the pins deep into the hearts of styrofoam balls. Each year for the garden club boutique she produces five hundred of these wondrous objects, five hundred less than the number of plastic bags that live inside her bread drawer.

"Ma," I say, "can't we do something else?"

My mood, low enough as I've been hanging around since Thursday, has not been improved by the appearance of my sibling, Sharon. As usual, she's got her fiancé, Dexter, in tow. This visit's purely duty for them, not to mention a pit stop on the way up to New Hampshire to go spelunking. In fact, they're outfitting themselves with supplies right now, preparing for their honeymoon, during which Dexter will be continuing his research on bat guano in Central America, a field in which he's one of the world's experts. This preparation is no easy task since they're not only all-natural, but gourmet.

At thirty, Sharon's three years my junior. She's a literary agent for a New York firm. I teach English as a Second Language in a cold church basement funded by a grant that probably ran out last Tuesday. My latest lover's left me. In a good year, I average three; in a lean one there's nobody to lose.

Sharon and Dexter just drove off in their Audi to purchase little backpack envelopes of freeze-dried stroganoff. Ma senses my restlessness. Anxious to please, lest I take off on her, too, she offers, "We could go out back."

As we make our way outside, she lights up another filter-free Camel. Ma's smoked for sixty years, ever since she and her brothers used to sneak out back the shed and smoke catalpa pods. You couldn't get a high from them, she's told me, but it was wicked all the same. The air in this large suburban split-level ranch in which the windows are never opened, reeks of nicotine; every room's cluttered with the excretia of my mother's life as it's evolved over the years.

Starting out as typist in Columbus, Ohio—as far as she could get from West Virginia—Ma met my father, the son of a revenuer from the North Carolina backwoods. He'd gone from the pickle factory during the depression to accountant trainee in a mattress-making company to sales director forty years later. She came to be able to afford excess: the plastic bags, sequins, the styrofoam balls, green felt Xmas trees, yarn octopi with pigtail legs, old handbags limp with fatigue, tangled clumps of costume jewelry. Now, she could no more let any of it go than drown one of us.

"I haven't spoken to Elsie Zipko in three years," Ma gestures to the right, across the fence, with her cigarette, "not since Pierre died." She's dripping ash onto her floral cotton housecoat; three large burns already decorate its surface. Pierre was Elsie's poodle; Elsie left him home all day to work in a bank as a data processor. While she was gone, he made a noise like a squeeze toy ten hours a day non-stop. When cancer was discovered it was too late. We'd assumed his pain came only from loneliness; perhaps after all it did.

"And Phyllis," that's the neighbor to the left, "I haven't talked to her in four years. Last time was the day of the hurricane. We got together during the eye."

Now Ma's watering her amaryllis. There are twelve of them, lined up on the picnic table's benches which border the cracking flagstone patio—one for every Christmas my parents've had the house. The instructions say with careful watering and feeding a new set of blooms will appear a second year. None of my mother's have. Each stands now mute; no trumpet-shaped blooms, tall fronds drooping from each withered bulb. Still, she waters, tends, hopes.

"Where's Daddy?" I ask. I'm stinking with sweat, polo shirt sticking to my nipples, throat raspy with humidity and cigarette smoke. I'd like to tell Ma about my latest romantic failure, but I know from past experiences all I'll get are reproaches and lectures on things like shaving my underarms. Then, later, she'll tell me how she stayed up late, listening to Sally Jesse Raphael, the shrink who talks on the radio, all about 'love problems,' and crying for me.

"He's at the short-wave." Ma shuffles over to the faucet on the side of the house, fills her watering can.

I'm not surprised. My father converses fluently in four languages—learned initially in night school, improved on later in the service— with people all over the world on the short wave radio rig he installed a while back. I say people; really, they're men. Few women have leisure and money for radio amateur status; usually they're C.B.'ers with cute "handles" like "Doll-Baby" or "Powder Puff."

Daddy talks to men all over the place: Albuquerque, Rio, Cleveland, West Berlin. His favorite, Georges, comes from Marseilles. Georges is a civil servant who lives with his aging parents and his pet squirrel. He used to call Daddy every morning, up until this year when sunspots intervened, rendering transmission impossible. Georges still writes though, on whisper-thin transatlantic paper, and sends him books like *Captain Fracas,* a kind of French wild-west sheriff.

Right now I can hear, faintly, through the open basement-level window, the hum of the radio, the occasional crackle of energy along the high-tension wires that link these men, land to land, each spilling out to another what secrets they dare. As far as I can tell, the talk is always about how big of a rig they have, how much power it can handle. Men everywhere are really the same, always talking about their equipment. Daddy seems out of sync somehow; he's looking for foreign language speakers—other displaced persons.

Once Daddy talked to me—the week his father died. He spoke with his eyes turned resolutely away from my face, told me all about how the kids up north where his family finally moved used to make him the butt of persecution, laughing at his backwoods accent. I guess that's why I keep hanging around—hoping to catch some more of the story.

The other thing Daddy has are telephones, a little odd, really, since he hasn't got any friends to talk to, unless you count Mario, the barber, or Morris across the street. The phones he got mostly at tag sales, some by mail from *Popular Mechanics*. They've all got special features like digital calendars or the capacity to store frequently-used numbers for push-button re-call. Daddy's got four numbers stored: me, Sharon, Mario, and Morris.

One Christmas, hoping to capitalize on this newest fad, I got him a digital watch, and even a digital ballpoint pen; it told the date in teeny numerals along the barrel. I thought the pen would go nicely with the clock Daddy got from "the girls" in his office when he retired; the clock displays the lighted time across the ceiling while you lie in bed at night, the numerals changing second by second.

He never liked those things, though, as well as the phones. One of them's cordless. When my mother carried it out one day while watering the amaryllis, it rang. Overjoyed—no one calls her either, except the garden club chairwoman asking for styrofoam balls—she told the person at the other end who had the number wrong how nice it was he'd called her in the garden.

Daddy's got another phone now, a touch-tone, hooked up to a place that tells you the stock market reports when you push the buttons on the telephone's face, generating electronic pulses that sound like the ones in *Close Encounters*. The voice that tells you what your stocks are doing, or not doing, is that of a computer. It is female—assuming, of course, that gender, for computers, is a valid concept.

Sometimes, like when another lover has left, I'd like to call her up. It would be a voice, after all. I can't reach Georges and I don't know how to reach the wrong number from the garden.

After another cigarette, my mother shuffles into the house again—insisting on my presence—to watch her one P. M. show. It's on every day and seems to feature a nun who's frequently pregnant. Then, I have to make a sandwich for myself and for Daddy, or we won't get lunch.

We usually have deviled ham on whole wheat Home Pride. This

is a concession to Sharon and Dexter who only eat whole, live foods. (I wonder if freeze-dried stroganoff was once whole?) With deviled ham, we always have a smattering of pickle relish, the green kind.

During a commercial, my mother supervises the amount of spread I'm allowed to put on each slice of bread. "No, no, Debbie, that's too much. No, don't use that knife." Her brow knitted with anxiety, she whips one knife out of my hand, rummages in a drawer of utensils worthy of a medieval enforcer's collection, and hands me another which appears identical. I take it without rebuttal; having no Audi to escape in, I've long since learned how to survive on site.

Next I take the sandwiches on plates on a tray downstairs to my father. Since the upper regions of the house are hers—monopolized by the plastic bags, the octopi, the rejected jewelry, not to mention the India print bedspreads she's got all over the "good furniture" in the living room—he's had to carve out such territory as he could. The lower reaches work out fine; for one thing, they're cooler; for another—as she gets older and stiffer—it's hard for her to negotiate the stairs.

He's got it made down there, really. There's a large room we call the recreation room, complete with an ancient leather-padded bar behind which he keeps various lethal liqueurs—the artichoke for example, could take the rust right off your lawn furniture—some of which hide in a secret cubbyhole behind a trick panel. Here, also, Daddy positions his radio and several of his phones.

A huge chess set procured at a tag sale dominates the rest of the room. It's the size of a bridge table with pieces about the height of catsup bottles. He's never forgiven me for only learning how the pieces move, no strategy. Therefore, I can't play. It's been a problem I've had most of my life. Still, I remember my grandfather visiting, before his death, sitting up night after night over that board with Daddy, never winning, just setting up those knights and bishops one more time. Not me, boy. Dexter won't play either, even though he knows how. He always asks instead for bridge, at which he's an ace, never Trivial Pursuit. He knows I can beat him; he's desperately weak on early TV.

"Dexter giggles," Daddy says, the only reason he'll ever give for hating the guy. Me, I've got lots more; Dexter's fond of telling me how he makes fifty-thousand a year for teaching two courses while I make a mere fifteen. "Yeah, but," I always throw back, "I don't have to hang out at faculty meetings." Dexter never answers, just slinks off to the guest room where they keep their gorp in ziplock plastic bags. I do think plastic is a dead substance; I wonder if they know.

"Dexter giggles; he's not a man's man," Daddy repeats himself. Presumably, though, Georges is, and also Morris, who once, in his cups, a frequent occurence, backed his car down his own driveway, across the street, and up my parents' sloping lawn to leave tread marks on the slim trunk of a young maple my mother had been growing from its own wings these past six years.

Mario the barber is not a man's man either. Desperately fond of my father—that dog-like devotion makes sense to me; it's what's driven every one of my lovers away—he likes to call him in the evenings to speak Italian, sends him clippings on Tuscan architecture and the opera, gives him special bottles of wine after every haircut, plus stamps he's soaked off letters from his sister still over in Naples. My father despises these offerings, makes fun of them, considers letting his hair grow out. Nevertheless, every Thursday he returns for a trim and even offered to call Mario's sister on the short wave through a phone patch to Naples.

Creatures of habit and need—my parents. Standing in the garden, I wonder for a fleeting instant if the amaryllis ought to be moved into the sun?

Sharon and Dexter return from their shopping trip to Eddie Bauer where a marathon Labor Day sale was taking place. Daddy and I call it Eddie Bow-Wow; in the absence of real conversation we indulge in puns, word-plays, double entendres—never sexual, of course— anything the others can't catch onto, especially Ma. It gives me a sense of solidarity I get nowhere else, except, perhaps, on the first days of terms when my students—terrified Cambodians and Haitians—gather with me to begin to learn how to survive in an alien land. Besides, it beats the hell out of getting checkmated.

"Look what we've got!" Sharon's pulling packages out of the

Audi, talking non-stop. Thin, sharp-featured, relentlessly perky, she manages to pour forth an uninterrupted conversational stream throughout entire visits. This seems to function as a kind of *Star Wars* energy shield. I guess she feels she needs it. After all, trips home are excruciating for her.

Her success and my depressions make it seem I'm my parents' favorite. She won't make puns or sequined balls, thinks artichoke liqueur gives you cancer and amaryllis only need watering once a week. She seems to believe that chattering away about the books her authors write can prevent Dexter and Daddy from locking horns like stags on *Wild Kingdom*, or me from snuffling on about romance down the tubes. "Your standards are too high," she tells me brightly each time I flounder again.

Now, looking at Dexter as he rummages through the Eddie Bauer bags to show us his many-pocketed vest, his fanny pack, his cans of sterno, I'm glad. I feel sorry for her embarrassment, remember how close we once were, playing Ginny dolls and dyeing our mashed potatoes blue. I'd try to talk to her more now if she didn't keep recommending I get a better haircut.

She's going on now about one of her authors, the doctor whose book, *How to Live as Long as Possible*, explains every imaginable way one might eat, exercise, sleep, excrete, think and have sex to achieve extraordinary longevity. Whether a particular individual wants to or even ought to live that long is not discussed. Sharon and Dexter are suitably impressed by the good doctor, plan to follow his regimes to the letter. Sharon's only worry is that the guy has the personality of a used Brillo pad, can't be considered for talk shows, and therefore the book won't be a best-seller. She's never had one; the *Great Religious Leaders of the World* in twelve volumes sold in supermarkets just didn't make it, nor did the cards on home repair tucked adorably into a plastic toolbox file. (My mother got one free; she keeps earrings without mates in it and opened and unopened bags of sequins.)

"Here comes Morris," my mother says. We're all standing in the driveway, the Eddie Bauer bags perched on the hood of the Audi. Myself, I travel by bus.

"Be nice to him. Ever since his mother died, he's very unhappy."

I can still see the tread marks he made on my parents' maple and I know.

"After she died, 'Meals on Wheels' forgot to cancel her order. He gets two meals every time, and tries to bring them over here. Daddy likes them, but I don't."

"They use white bread." Sharon sniffs. "And canned vegetables. That's an appalling diet for senior citizens. Dr. Brewer says.... "

"Morris was a staff sergeant in the U.S. Army," Daddy interrupts, threateningly, as if daring Dexter to giggle. "He was in the offensive up Omaha beach." Daddy, who was a communications officer in the Allied invasion of Italy, never talked war stories until Dexter came into the picture. Sharon and I, mere females, couldn't be trusted to grasp it all. Somehow, Dexter's testosterone qualifies him. Daddy's favorite—which Dexter always listens to silently from behind his wire-rims, before he slips off for a date-apricot-fig chew—is about how he had to stand in front of a four-star general and explain why his jeep had gotten stolen by Fascisti. This was somewhere outside Bologna in 1944.

"I told him the truth," Daddy reminds us for the thousandth time. "Always tell the truth. It saves on complications. I told him, "I left the keys in it.'"

"Let's hear about Omaha Beach, Sergeant," Daddy hails Morris heartily as our neighbor shuffles up the drive, honing in like radar on the source of human noise we represent. I wonder idly where the cordless phone is; could we hear it ringing, for example, if it were stuffed under a sofa cushion, or smothered by plastic bags?

"Omaha Beach. Yes, sir," Morris starts out in a peppy tone, which sinks rapidly. "That was when I got the letter telling me Dad was failing." He searches each one of us, face by face.

Behind us, through the open garage door, from the depths of the recreation room, I hear the crackle and whine of the radio. Perhaps Georges is calling. With the sunspots due to leave pretty soon now, he and Daddy should have another eleven years, free and clear, until the cycle comes round again.

"That was very hard on me," Morris beseeches each one of us

with his gaze, mutely in turn. "I flew right home, but when I got there they'd put him in the ground."

Tight-lipped, my mother moves closer to him. Within her—I know from every crisis I've ever had, the few I've ever let her know about, anyway—war wages between the horror of emotional mess, personal dishonor, and the yearning her own pain has for company. "That was very hard for you, Morris," she murmurs, her accent slurring the words. She grubs in the pocket of her housecoat for another Camel.

"I told him," Daddy says louder, "I left the keys in it. Always tell the truth."

I'm shifting now, from foot to foot, wishing I were home in Boston. My old bedroom here—where I sleep now—has the clock that flashes the time all night onto the ceiling. I just can't take it. I miss my tiny apartment, neat and spare as a military barracks. I miss my two cats, Watson and Holmes, and their antics. I miss my students, their gratitude, their surprising senses of humor, the walks we take after their lessons are done, practicing with street signs and using American money. There's no one here to play with, unless I want chess. I know how to open the secret wine compartment. Even Pierre is gone.

"We're going for a walk, Ma," Sharon announces. Dexter's moved closer to her side. His plump knees bulge out from the khaki canvas many-pocketed shorts. He takes her hand. "Honey, let's do three miles. We've got to get in better shape for Mount Katahdin."

"Mother's gone now, too, you know," Morris tell us, ignoring everything else. His eyes, close-up, look rheumy, pale, naked blue. "I go out alone," he says, "I talk to myself alone."

Morris, I look at him, I understand.

Underwater Women

"...*Roxanne and I may be part of a vast majority of underwater women, making love in the back seat of cars after PTA meetings, in the morning after the babies have been nursed and put down to nap.*"

—Jane Rule—*Contract with the World*

Tuesday, April 6, LUCY. Here by the window in our quiet suburban neighborhood, treetops caught full of dusk, bronze ball of a sun sinking over the ranch next door, I'm waiting, as women do, for my lover. Dorothy Sayers' mystery is on my lap, Pickle is purring in the crook of my arm, and Annie and Brad are upstairs blessedly asleep. With the whole house, now that I am sole mistress of it, as I like—ordered, still, and tucked down tight—I wait. My heart is not still. This is not a state of contentment. But then, even though now at thirty I've finally learned, as every good woman does, to cultivate a placid outer façade, I've never waited well. Yet, Lord, how I've waited.

First, I suppose, to be born. The third, probably unplanned, child of modest working parents, I was two weeks late. Sometimes at night, now, waking, fighting for breath, sweated, tangled, in darkness and sheets, I wonder: Do I recreate that sensation—womblocked, no place to go? There was always more waiting—to be old enough, big enough to do something, be somebody.

Older brothers had bikes and guns; I had plushy pink elephants to sleep with, reams of companions with fixed smiles stamped in colors on paper awaiting the liberation of my scissors. Most of all, I

had books, full of princesses and unicorns. As my parents waited—
to be richer, happier, live one day in a bigger house, a better part of
town—I, too, kept on waiting—for school, for dancing lessons, for
breasts, blood, nylons, a garter-belt, clear skin, a kiss, a fuck, a husband, a name, a life, a face....

When Jeffrey came along—solid young man, plain and straight as
the pine boards he worked—I married him; I nurtured him from carpenter to contractor. He made money. We moved to this place
where two generations ago we would have been denied property.

Finally I had the life my parents wanted. (brothers were far gone
to jobs and wives on distant coasts). They smiled and sighed and
died. Inside, of course, dying was what I had done all along. Now,
in what is supposed to be the prime of my life (anyhow, all the
books that were always my best friends, say so), here I sit and let it
all reel past. The dreams of my mother and father, that I always
wore like the clothes of a relative not quite my size, pass on. What
do I have now to show for all this living? Thighs, belly, veined like
the Mother Lode herself. Nothing I've had so far feels like it's really
mine. For my own real life tonight in this deepening dark, I wait....

Pickle rouses herself, yawns, boldly flicks a narrow pink tongue.
The soft night settles over us like a bowl. And Cat, wild woman, sister of my heart, knocks her muffled knock at my back Dutch door.
It's a desperate, secret life we lead. I rise, blood pounding at tem-
ples, chest.

Pickle bolts. My book slips to the floor. Unlatching, I welcome
Cat into the dark entry—for all we know, her husband's lawyers
have hired as paid informants all of my most respectable neighbors—into my arms, my loins, my sacred chamber....

Wednesday, April 7: CAT. Holy fucking shit! What the bejesus do I
think I'm doing? Thirty-four, Barnard grad, mother of a teenage kid.
Cited by a recent newspaper feature as the "helpmeet and power-
behind the throne" to my husband Hank—prominent Liberal politi-
co, soon to be tapped for the State Senate. Standing on another
woman's doorstep at 6 a.m., decked out in a Jantzen jogging suit,
squinting at the rising sun, about to run for my (her? our?) life

through the manicured streets of this bedroom burb.

Voted Class Cut-Up at Miss Porter's, I never dreamt in what a sleazy mess I'd find myself. I look around. Fucking bastards. This street's full of them: tight, trimmed hedges, Volvos, Mercedes, Lincolns (dark colors only, please), heavy drapes barely parted revealing the merest wisp of an observer behind. Right now the coast's clear. Off I go. Two miles. Jesus. Every step shakes my bones. I'm too old for this. Passion all night, then off like a gazelle? Maybe when you're seventeen....

Yet what else can we do? Soon I round the corner of Tumbling Brook Lane to the stiff austere Colonial mausoleum where—until I threw him my kick to the balls—Hank and I lived with Robert, our son, acting out the American Dream (performance nightly, Saturday matinees.)

Up the long driveway I chuff, enter through the back porch where, thanks to a handy hardware gadget, the light has snapped off at midnight on the dot, thus proving to all snoopers that I was home alone in my celibate bed. I collapse over the threshold, peel off my stinky top and pants and stumble into the shower. What a wacko way to live! Yet, as the hot water sluices over my hard limbs, firm breasts, secret puff of hair so recently caressed by Lucy, my lover, the one with the liquid eyes, the fierce mouth, I understand why....

Saturday, April 10: LUCY. Catherine, Cat, Caterina, Catherine the Great...I scrawl your name all over my paper napkins, my shopping list, as we used to do in school to our brown paper book covers. Catherine, Conqueror of my Heart, Lover of my Body, friend...I cherish this time, this safe Saturday afternoon when no one can suspect us of other than a neighborly visit as I sit here at my dinette table, cup of tea in hand, knees tucked up, catered to, nurtured, at last, at last, as I've done, good wife and mother, for others all these years....

As you fix us lunch, I relish your movements—crisp, competent, precise. The way your hands wield the knife—chopping onion fearlessly, slicing deli bread, tomatoes. Grating cheese. Fitting it all together—sandwiches to grill like a short-order cook. Flipping them on the skillet with a turn of your wrist. You're a woman, like me, who's cooked for years, packed endless nutritious lunches, chosen just the right recipes for business-associate dinners, yet you've never lost the soul of it. What you serve us—Annie, Brad, and me—tingles with a spice we don't own in any jar.

And bewildered still with the abrupt exit and infrequent visits of their father, how they adore you; blocking tackles in the back yard, dressing and re-dressing endless scruffy dolls, you've befriended them all the way, just as you've done with me. I never dreamt or imagined any of this, yet—in my broadloom-carpeted living room, by the mahogany occasional table—when you reached out your hand, (although in my girlish education I had not studied such a language) I answered at once, fluently, with full understanding....

CAT. Thin spring sun can't beat the wind. You bundle up the kids, go off to play ball. I sit, Pickle rumbling on my lap, savor a cigarette while the lunch dishes soak, remembering, a year ago, how we met. At the YWCA. In yoga class. Afterwards, in the locker room, I used to watch your creamy body out of the corner of my eye. All my life I've committed perverted acts like these. Only recently have I realized they are not perverted acts.

I wanted you. I wooed you. Swinging wildly between terror and bravado, I'd swagger across the Y lobby under the evil eye of the desk girl—hired precisely to keep out the likes of me—to call out to you—for coffee, a gallery opening, a tennis date....

The blood of my youth—girls' schools, girls' teams, women's college—coursed in my veins as I steered you toward my car. My limbs came alive again after years of joyless matrimonial sex. (Hank never sank below the weekly Kinsey average.) Once I'd had the cuddles of an infant, the sticky hugs of a toddler; then a prickly adolescent emerged and pushed me away.

Ambitious Hank became too tired for anything but fuck and snore. You, Lucy, angel-lover, bring back again those desperate summer Sundays in the Berkshires—days off from the camp where I worked as a tennis counselor to go out to Bear Mountain State Park where—proving manhood—guys scaled trees while their dates giggled below with the lemonade and the ants. And there I'd be, deep

in the woods' heart on a scratchy blanket making forbidden love—
with Judy, with Corky, with Marianne.

I hear those mess hall whispers to this day—*queer, queer*—the
ones that drove me to the altar. Hank married me for my backhand,
my legs, my flambéed duck. I'd launch his career, he felt. He'd
launch my normality, I fervently prayed. Now, I take those words,
sing them to myself, an anthem of power—*queer, queer—lesbian.*

What blows me away now is not that I reached for you, but that
it wasn't hard. You'd known only the flat loves found between pages
in a book, flattening marriage, yet you leapt into this life like a sal-
mon to the uphill swim. Well, my love, we've tasted the fruit. Now
the price comes due. Easy enough to rid ourselves of the men who
sucked our hearts hollow. Not so easy to rid their hearts of rancor.

Jeffrey—contractor, wood-solid—survives just fine. He's dating
already, you said. Forgot Annie's birthday, Brad's big game. I, in my
Red Sox cap, did my damndest to fill many shoes—mommy, daddy,
lover.

What's the real pinch, though, is money. You have none; he has
it all, and lately won't make more. He doesn't want you now; he
doesn't want your babies, but no way in hell is he paying those bills.

Me, I'm baying under another moon; Hank, out of Tumbling
Brook Lane (to the utter shame of his political cronies), lodged in a
plush, furnished apartment, wants it warm from the jugular. He's using against me the pillow confessions of a honeymoon, fleshed out
in the "unnatural acts" his filthy detectives (the real perverts) have
documented for him. He can, if he wants, take it all.

Well, time to polish off the dishes, join you and the shrieking
kids out by the forsythia hedge tossing a ball. (Never thought my
tomboy youth would serve me like this.) We've planned my public
departure at five—you waving from the driveway's foot.

Later, under cover of darkness, we meet in a distant movie, hold
hands like teenagers. Why, oh, god, goddess, whoever you are, do
you make it so cruel? So sweet? So costly? House, stocks, good
name—I care for none of it. Take it, Hank, you bastard, and run for
your tarnished glory in a corrupt legislature. But leave me my son. (I
remember Robert, fuzz-headed, tugging at the breast—how it hurt. It
still does.)

Later, after the movie, we figure a brief interlude at Friendly's can't hurt. A quick scan about the place reveals no one in a trench coat. We talk in earnest about the future. No idea yet how it'll fall, both of us scanning the want ads daily, knowing we've got to find work. Only a matter of weeks now till the Jaws of Justice creak closed. Family Relations have already sniffed their way up and down my staircases, herb garden, spare bedroom—I remember, heart beating, snatching up a lacy pair of Lucy's bikini's from the bathroom floor, stuffing them into my blazer pocket, just seconds before the snoopers, clipboards at the ready, glided by. Afterwards, I collapsed against the insides of the front door and laughed like a banshee.

The lawyers have met—mine one year out of school, silver women's symbol hidden deep between her breasts under her button-down shirt. I'll pay her meager bill out of nickels and dimes the next five years of my life. I don't care. It's worth it.

Up the dark driveway, my love, I walk you to your back door. The porch light's off; I sneak inside, catch you to me. All we can do now is pray and wait. As I kiss your face I taste the salt of our tears.

Wednesday, October 15: LUCY. Finally, soaking my feet in a red plastic dishpan—"No, Annie, you can't sail your boat in here. Go fill the bathtub!"—I grab a moment's peace. We're working now. What jobs could we get, women as we are? I'm a hostess out at The Nutmeg Inn on the river, just far enough out of town to eat up my tips in gas. I smile and smile—luckily, I've got just the right training—and swish about in my pseudo-Colonial garb, complete with ruffled white cap, ushering bilious salesmen and their polyester wives to decorated tables. If, after this, I ever see another popover, I'll scream! Cat's at a nursing home doing the books, math major finally paying off.

A gleam of hope: maybe next month a landscape designer's going to take her on for the spring. You know he'd pay a man a living wage, but her unmistakable way with herbs and blooming plants, those hands, the rippling muscles of her lean, sweated back, have him convinced, after a little fill-in work in September, she can increase his profits. So we survive, the four of us (and Pickle) in my house, which, with all of our combined resources, we don't quite pay for each month. Each week, Robert dutifully calls, reports to Cat—coldly, severely—his activities. Their once-a-month visits, away from this house, leave her silent and tight for hours. Annie and Brad, without quite realizing the facts, swarm over her afterwards with hugs as vigorous as the massages that bring frozen limbs back to life.

We fend off bill collectors with clever strategies, unearth old budget cookbooks with honeymoon inscriptions, deal with middle-of-the-night phone calls that have either palpable silences or crude slurs at the other end, find our love-making tempered now, traded often enough for the embraces of the sort of people in bomb shelters and box cars must have shared.

Still, in each other's care toward ripeness we turn. I am older now. Behind me I have put my girlish fancies, the musty pages of life in Magic Kingdoms. The curls above my brow spiral with strands of white. Veins in my legs show up blue. I answer my children's questions with a choking throat. Yet, as my hand meets Cat's—over a sink, pulling weeds in the garden, at night at the edge of a child's quilt—I know I am no longer waiting.

Dinner Party

Caitlin, my amazing friend, PhD physicist, poet, musician, the one I met in a seminar "Myth, Ritual, and The Great Goddess," the one who carries a hunting knife, blindingly sharp, in her leather bookbag on the subway late at night, is married. Suddenly. To a young corporate accountant she met at a gallery opening. The wedding, a civil ceremony, was simple and local. Her parents in Galway are too old to make the trip, his parents too conservative to approve of her.

I want her happiness. She's so often confided, "I'm lonely. The men in the lab treat me as a girl or a neuter."

I asked her once about women. Without meeting my eye, she slowly shook her head, "Once there was someone...it didn't work out." I changed the subject.

Now I'm invited to dinner. She's left her funky attic apartment in Jamaica Plain near the pond with her weavings on the walls, her pots on the sills, futon on the floor, for his glass-and-chrome highrise out on the high-tech strip, blondwood, square corners.

We sit in the living room, drinking Chardonnay. William has expressed his extreme joy at meeting me—"having heard so much...." His eyes devour me. He's so liberal my stomach hurts.

If he tells me what I do in the privacy of my own bedroom is nobody's business, I'll smash my brie in his face.

Caitlin is silent, not unlike her, but this new kind of married quiet is different, bled of the power her silences once contained.

He wants me to know he's sensitive. A-OK. He takes the dishes to the sink. He's baked the cake. He tells me about giving Caitlin's cat Morgaine catnip. "Ha! You should've seen her! She kept shuddering all over like she was having multiple orgasms!" His eyes haven't left me all evening. "I'm trying," he says further, tapping my glass when some question of male privilege comes up in conversation, "like eighty percent of the men in America."

I beg Caitlin to sing. She demurs, but finally picks up her guitar, gives us an Irish ballad, not one of her own. While she sings, he weeps openly, the sides of his hands brushing tears from his cheeks like wings.

She leaves the room to put on coffee.

He moves next to me to show me a book, his lanky arm stretches the back of the couch, fingers brushing my shoulder unnecessarily. I freeze. I'm not surprised, yet also I don't quite believe, my mind stretching for explanation, justification. I grab another book, change my position just enough to escape his touch. He hitches in again— those fingers, their slight weight burns against my arm. His knee nudges mine.

"Caitlin...." I jump up, scattering books as well as the orgasmic Morgaine. "I'll help you. Then could you read us one of your poems?" I take the tray of cups from her hands, chatter on nervously about publication possibilities, how much I want to hear her work again. As with the guitar, she's reluctant, but I persist. It seems crucially importantfor me to find out somehow that she's still there.

My friend takes a manila folder from a drawer, reads a re-telling of an Celtic folk tale in which a young woman, a sorceress, goes through a mirror to confront a wizard who offers her the loss of her powers for the promise of lifelong earthly companionship and love. I know before the last line what the choice will be.

Afraid that William might weep again, I babble my excuses and dive into the closet for my coat. At the door I embrace my friend. Her shoulder blades rise and fall, the delicate bones of a bird beneath my hands. As I leave her embrace, he's waiting. I try to give him a perfunctory hug; he crushes me instead to his chest, kisses me on the lips.

"You needed a hug!" he chortles. "I could tell." (Has Caitlin told him of my recent separation from my lover? Could he deduce it just from my face?) "I like you. You're a nice person. You deserve the best."

I mumble my goodbyes, plunge out into the street, dodging potential rapists all the way across the vast asphalt parking lot to my car. I drive the long, dark way back to the shambling triple deckers of Somerville where I live. As I round the corner onto my street, a police cruiser, blue lights flashing, careens by me, ejaculating its siren all over the night.

In its looming headlights I see William's face.

Endangered Species

Martha, in her plain, sunny kitchen, shuttles back and forth from the scrubbed butcher-block countertop to the littered desk, then to the wall-phone, waiting busily for her daughter Hanna, who is always late, to arrive.

Martha has never understood Hanna's chronic disrespect for time. For Martha time always seems inadequate to the urgency of the tasks it must contain—as an oasis to irrigate a desert.

Hanna was due at one; it is now one-forty. Martha knows she can easily squeeze in a few calls before her daughter drifts in. "Hello, Joyce? Martha...I'm calling to remind you about the rally Thursday. Yes. Can you call the others on your list? Thank you."

Hanging up, she reaches for the plastic bags of raisins and sunflower seeds, mentally calculating whether she'll have enough for two pans of Crunchy Granola Bars; one for her affinity group training tonight, one for the fundraiser Saturday.

They were boycotting the A & P for carrying non-union produce. Would there be time to run to the food co-op for more seeds? She looks up to the large calendar tacked up by the bulletin board above her desk piled inches deep in petitions. Martha fishes her fat red marker from the ceramic cup decorated with a leaping dolphin. She charts a few plans into the empty boxes on the calender which represent the days of the week ahead. Thus reassured, she turns back to the sunflower seeds.

As Hanna's old Karmann Ghia finally rattles to a halt outside, Martha starts, runs a hand, despite herself, through her short, no-nonsense hair, tugs at her denim skirt—fleetingly, desperately. She wishes she'd worn something floaty and brightly-colored even though nothing she owns remotely fits this description.

"Mother!" Hanna, as always, overwhelms—with her voice, her scent (musk oil? patchouli?), the clouds of her hair—dark, wild curls, her various drifting brilliant layers of ornament and dress, hugs. Martha submits.

Tea is put on, camomile. They sit. "No, thanks," Hanna pushes away the mug, "I brought this instead." She produces from her capacious untidy bag a bottle of Greek wine. To Martha, sipping as they face each other across the breakfast nook table, the liquid Hanna has poured tastes like turpentine.

"When I was in Crete we drank this endlessly! I was thrilled to find some just the other day in Harvard Square. So, Mother, how are you? How are all your Causes?" As she talks, Hanna sifts through stacks of thick envelopes; the desk and the nook table are the only clutter piles Martha permits. "Mother, you have the most illustrious correspondents! Senators, movie stars...." Hanna's hearty tone contains no malice, only her constant eagerness for a good laugh.

"Hanna...." How Martha hates the prim, cold tone in her own voice the presence of her only offspring always produces. Hanna's frivolity frightens her; it seems such a dangerous approach to life in such an imperiled world. Every so often, in a rare self-reflective moment, she wonders, how ever did such a creature come to me? She feels more nurturing by far of the tiny brown nut face in the photograph "Save the Children" has sent, identifying "Maria" as the grateful recipient of her fifteen dollars a month. Even the whooping cranes and the whales Martha worries about, which Hanna loves to mock, are far more in need of her care than her own child.

She remembers once ripping open yet another of the fat creamy envelopes that jam her mailbox, daily bringing into the heart of suburban Wayland the details of torture in the Central America, illiteracy on Mesa Flats, black lung in Harlan County—to see a picture of a bludgeoned, bloody baby seal, the mother hovering nearby, mute and bewildered with grief, and how she herself began to cry and cry and couldn't stop.

Such moods, thank Providence, were rare.

Martha takes another sip; the wine has not improved. "Hanna..."

she starts again, "...what I'm...we all...are trying to do is important work. You are an educated young woman...." A sore point—Hanna had left Radcliffe for The Art Institute, her classes for an astonishing number of beds. "...You are certainly aware. Surely you must put aside some time to read the papers; the latest unemployment statistics among minority youth have just been released—quite shocking—and Helen Caldicott spoke last week at Brandeis about the escalating Arms Race...."

Usually, Martha finds in her zeal for a just and peaceful universe—despite the horrors one must face—a deep and satisfying release. Now she begins to sound, even to herself, wound to a snapping point. Hanna's presence never fails to create this effect.

"Mother!" Hanna jingles her silver bracelets bought on a hitchhiking tour of Mexico. "I'm not putting you down! I just wish sometimes you'd forget all this save-the-world crap and think about yourself! When's the last time you took some space for you?"

Hanna's vocabulary, to her mother's ear, has steadily corrupted itself ever since her parents agreed to fund her therapy. Rejecting Wayland Psychological Associates, Hanna chose a women's counseling collective in Cambridge in order to "get in touch with her feelings," a phrase that always sets Martha's teeth on edge.

"I mean, really, Mother, Abigail Doherty works on all the causes you do and when I saw her last week in Harvard Square, she said she was cutting back and taking a trip to Alaska. You could let things slide a bit, too, you know. I know lots of activists who nurture themselves, too. The missile silos will still be there."

Choosing to ignore the travesty of what Hanna considers a joke, Martha answers primly, "I'm in no need of a vacation, thank you, dear. I do very little these days, actually, now that the referendum is over. All we're working on now is the nuclear issue—that being the most crucial, of course. My affinity group meets tonight. We've received training should we be arrested during the action. You know, I believe..." Suddenly she feels moved to reach out blindly, wildly toward this creature born of her yet so foreign, knowing that Hanna could soon leap forever past any need at all for her care. "...my group must be something like that women's support group you go to...."

"Yes, it really must be. I never thought of it that way." Hanna smiles eagerly, reaches for her mother's hand.

At her daughter's touch, from which she frequently flinches, Martha allows herself a rare flood of feeling for this hearty, overwhelmingly healthy creature who had emerged grinning on the exact date she was due, walked at ten months, talked at twelve months, spent blissful summers at sleep-over camp from age eight on, kayaked the Colorado at thirteen, lost her virginity—"No blood," Hanna had casually bragged—at fifteen.

"Mother...." Hanna goes on, leaping into the warm mood, "Mom...I have something special to tell you."

In the flush of rare emotion, pleased that Hanna has shared so much, Martha allows herself to slump back a little. The sips of wine, though small, have reached her head. "Wonderful. I love news of your life." Usually this is a lie—yet what more shocking news could reach her now? The married Harvard professor had been the worst—except perhaps the summer spent in a cave in Crete after the tuition refund from the Lycee. Pregnancy or V.D., Martha does not fear. Hanna is never irresponsible or careless—only bold and self-indulgent.

"It's my new lover."

"Oh? Not another Geoffrey, I hope?" The professor left his wife soon after beginning to see Hanna. Hanna refused marriage; Geoffrey entered analysis; the affair collapsed.

"No, Mother, no!" Hanna is laughing. "Far, far from it! No, I just wanted to share..." Martha suppresses a wince. "...that I am in love now, for the first time, maybe ever. I felt you'd be pleased. I know you and Daddy have never stood in my way, but I'm aware that you think I take sex and relationships too casually."

Martha is silent. This last is an understatement, yet Martha has signed petitions for sexual freedom, picketed for reproductive rights.

"Her name is Shell."

The silence lengthens. Martha is capable of hearing endlessly, without flinching, about how many babies in East Africa have had no food each year, how many political prisoners in various totalitarian regimes are forced to talk under electric shock, which dyes and chemicals cause which kinds of cancer, which parts of the natural world—the lakes, the tundra, the sea—are dying now. She sees in her dreams at night exactly how the very earth itself would come apart should certain Pentagon generals tap certain red buttons, yet now she finds herself unable to take in what her ears receive. Finally she says, "I'm not sure, Hanna, what it is that you're saying...."

Through all this Hanna has been beaming. "That I'm in love, Mother. That my lover is a woman. That we're very, very happy. That I've finally found a joy I didn't know was possible!"

"Then...are you..." Martha's mind scrambles wildly through her memories of every demonstration, pamphlet, speech, for something that would help. "...are you saying...that you're *gay?* You've never brought this up before. You've always, well, seen so many men...."

"Well, Mom...." Hanna's stretching now, wide purple sleeves drifting off her arms which gleam, mottled and pale like the insides of the skins of baby seal. "...You *know* how I hate labels, but if I must have one, then, yes, why not? Not gay. That always makes me think of men in push-up bras and eyeshadow. Lesbian...yes...lesbian. Sounds lovely, doesn't it? When should I bring Shell for dinner?"

"But...but...." Martha has no idea how to feel, to behave, to respond. She has been taught, has taught Hanna in turn, to feel no disgust for any human choice, to respect all life that involves love as sacred. Hanna has always been full of a passion for all creatures— goldfish, mice, playmates of different colors, yes, even married Harvard professors—with sincerity and ingenuousness. Martha does not doubt for a moment the validity of her daughter's choice of this...this Shell, whoever she is.

Rather, Martha can't help shying away from what lies smoldering in Hanna's eyes, the glow of her complexion, the cat-like repose of her satisfied body. Edward, Martha's husband, Chief Paleontologist at the Museum of Natural History, has been a compatible mate. After the conception—their only moment of blaze—of Hanna, each had retired to a twin bed, coupling briefly, wistfully, at distant intervals, neither having the heart to tell the other they'd rather not. Instead, for Martha, passion finds expression through a stack of completed petitions thrust into a Senator's hand, or when, on a long, parching march, the pain of one's blisters becomes entirely submerged by the full-throated rise of angry, unified, hopeful voices.

Her immediate second rush of feelings is fear. This sojourn we call life, and what it may lure us into, lies fraught with danger, a fact not fully realized by Hanna, blessed from birth by happy family Christmases, birthday cakes and candles, Montessouri schools, the green illusion of suburbia.

Martha, early, learned this from her father, a frail, upright, gentle Unitarian/Universalist minister, who died, a bit before his time, of (she had always believed) a genuinely broken heart. In the same year that Martin Luther King was shot, Gene McCarthy defeated, her father's church was vandalized by a young addict he had sponsored. The boy accepted the immunity from prosecution Martha's father offered him, then promptly O.D.'d. No one spoke of it. Instead, the family, hostessed by Martha's efficient, dedicated mother, continued to put on dinners for visiting ministers who spoke of apartheid, Appalachia, voter registration. Martha yearned, as do all adolescents, to run away—not to New York or L.A., rather to Mississippi. Her senior thesis at Earlham focused on the origins of the Nazi Holocaust. On her post-graduation trip to Europe, she left her traveling companions in a Munich beer garden and made a pilgrimage to Dachau.

Now, here, suburban Wayland seems as far from that awesome spot of earth sifted deep in human ashes, as Shangri-La. Despite the apparent safety of lilac bushes, Volvos in driveways, trim, clipped hedges, whole families in White Stag suits out jogging in the summer twilight, Martha feels gripped with old terror for her baby, her own. Involvement of the heart, she knows—as her father before her knew—stands as the ultimate peril. Jake, the young addict, had been, in secret, her first lover. After his death, the rare blossom they'd picked together could no longer on this earth be found.

"Hanna..." She forced herself to push on. "...I certainly respect whatever you choose. Not that what I think or feel has ever influenced you...."

"Not true, Mother! We're really a lot alike."

"Now, let me finish. I'm glad you're happy, and I hope this girl—woman—is good for you, but we don't live in as enlightened a world as we might." Anxiety was rising in Martha's throat; she felt compelled to caution her daughter. What she warned of was not truly what she feared, so deeply had time and the will to survive left some things buried. "I know that Anita Bryant was a laughing stock, but nowadays there are other people like her but...more serious, and more sinister. People have lost jobs, apartments...."

"Mother! No one's going to fire me for being queer!" Hanna earned a good living at The Art Institute as a nude model. "All the male teachers are queer themselves! As for my apartment, two dykes live downstairs, and...."

"Hanna! Such language! Surely homosexuals.... I mean gays ...lesbians...whatever...." Martha's mind reels now full speed—away from seals lying in blood, picket lines and billy clubs, burning crosses—toward new images, calming itself by force of habit. "...have been degraded by such terms, and, as you say, this is a happy choice for you...nothing to be ashamed of...."

"Mother!" Hanna is really laughing now, pouring herself more wine. "It means something good! We reclaim it like some black kids call themselves nigger. Dyke means strong, powerful woman."

Martha has already ceased to listen. Instead, she is focused utterly on the mental image of her calendar and how to make space for new and pressing priorities. This way her rapid heart feels slowed, as if by a lullaby, this way she does not remember certain secret picnics in daisy-wild fields after Sunday church, certain nights in which her option for life hung in the balance. All she remembers now are Monday mornings and daylight, her ultimate choices, and the calendar, every square full.

By the time Shell comes to dinner, Martha has already subscribed to *Gay Community News*, joined the National Gay Task Force, and, due to her formidable past experience, been elected Ways-and-Means Chairwoman of the Greater Boston Chapter of the Parents and Friends of Gays. She has flustered the local Wayland librarians by her unselfconscious combing of the stacks for every possible relevant text. She has begun therapy with a slightly nervous social worker at Wayland Psychological Associates who seems to ask a lot of questions about her mother—or is it her father? Martha can never remember.

In deference to his lifelong residence in the Jurassic, Edward has not been told; which meetings his wife attends do not, anyway, stick in his mind. Martha remembers, during their courtship, asking him why the dinosaurs became extinct. As he answered, she saw—for the first and only time—a misting of tears gather in his eyes. It was why she married him. Now memories of that mist, of him, her father, of Jake, of Hanna, her child, find protection under her own strong wing.

On the humid mid-June Saturday when lesbians and gays and Parents and Friends of Lesbians and Gays—Martha herself has helped to sew the felt banner—march through the streets of Boston to demand their rights, Martha feels entirely safe, full of new vigor, anchored to her purpose. It's been a long time since she marched; the last time *War is Not Healthy for Children and Other Living Things* was emblazoned on her placard. Sweat pours off her brow, her throat rasps itself raw from shouting, "Two-four-six-eight, gay is just as good as straight."

As she follows the bobbing mass of heads, the green and purple balloons, the huge streaming banners—all flowing before her to a disco beat, as far as the eye can see—she feels inside her a rise of rippling waves of warmth that let her know she is alive.

Above the street in the bedroom of an attic apartment in Cambridge, oblivious to the date or the event downtown, Hanna and Shell twine—easily, simply—in the aftermath of love. Each seeks the other's eye; each traces with a finger-tip silver pathways of moisture from brow to cheek to shoulder to breast, and then, curled and secure as babies, they sleep.

Nicotine

Thursday eve. Tonight C. came in from class, announcing, "I'm going cold turkey!" She'd been telling me this for days now: "After finals—that's it!" I'd only nod, murmur vaguely, "uh-huh." Something I'd learned very early in life—seems to me it started with an old car we had that always got a dead battery before outings—"never get your hopes up."

"I'll sleep all day tomorrow. That'll deal with the cravings." Reeking of cinnamon gum, she kissed me.

I didn't believe for a minute she'd succeed—too many memories of our year together. Never lucky in love, when she came along, I was available. I broke my rule of no smokers. (One thousand nights of an empty bed bends one's will.)

Rooms hazy with settling smoke, over-flowing ashtrays (always, always emptied by me), learning how to spot all the calculated little deceptions of the addict—"Just stepping out for some air, a little walk" …yeah, sure, to the corner gas station vending machine.

So many nights turning over in bed to find an empty space—to realize she was out in the kitchen hunched over a paperback science fiction book, TV droning ("Lift Every Voice," "Bonanza") chainsmoking. The next day—most of it spent heavily drugged with sleep—accomplishment, the moving on with one's life, has been made impossible.

"How come," my sophisticated friend, Liz, the hotsy-totsy lawyer who owns her own condominium with a swimming pool, asked me, "you keep choosing lovers less capable than you?" Well, the one before C. used to think she could visit her friend in the Peace Corps by taking a Greyhound from Morocco to Kenya; I feel I deserve some credit for improvement.

"Gee, how old is C…twenty-eight? She sure has a lot of…things," says Ruth, my sweet, straight, cozily married friend, whose kids, at ages four and seven, undoubtedly don't even suck their thumbs.

Is this any way to live? Every day I come home from The Project, my battered canvas briefcase stuffed full of students' stories and poems, to find the kitchen full of the sound of "Bewitched" or "Hogan's Heroes," choked with the acrid odor of smoke. We have no kisses that do not impart to me the sweet stench of death….

Friday, 5 P. M. Today was a wonderful day! Somehow, today, I believe in the possibilities of love and loving, in the strength of our relationship, C.'s and mine. I'm on vacation break; so is she. Her night courses—they are financed, as is her share of the rent, by her aging parents in a distant city who are kept, by a system of Byzantine elaborateness, from knowing she is a dyke, or that I am more than her "roommate"—are intended to make her ready to take a "good" job in an "up-and-coming" field.

We wake together—rare for us, since usually I must be off to the Project, and she, because of her nights with the "cigs," as she calls them, is always out cold. We cuddle, hug, laugh, and talk in bed. I want to make love; she can't. Morning's too early for orgasm; she isn't really awake yet, although she's willing to stroke and suck me without satisfaction to the point of exhaustion.

I sense the craving rising in her—all that lies between her and a puff is my flesh. Yet I love the unaccustomed intimacy: we tell stories, tickle each other. I finally rise and sing, "She needs me. She needs me, therefore," as the water sluices over my body in the shower, I add, "will never leave me."

The rest of the day we play together , yet each time I suggest sex, she backs off—her stomach hurts, hunger pangs on top of the craving for a cigarette; she had always smoked instead of eating.

Long about afternoon, anxiety in earnest begins to roll in, something like a tide—inexorable, huge, submerging every delicate-colored shell on the beach. Still full of missionary zeal, I draw her out.

I am an excellent counselor; all my students and colleagues say so. I teach writing to city folk who never got much of a chance before, and I find they come to me before or after sessions with their pregnancies, troubles in love, lack of funds to finance their particular dreams for school or creativity.... I soothe and bandage and allow myself to feel worthwhile.

And thus I coax C., to bring out, one by one, the tawdry, shabby fears that had lain on the closet floor of her mind all those months while nicotine barred the door. "I'm a failure. I'll never get a job. Every door is closed to me. People just won't give me a chance to do what I want to do. This society denies people a real chance. I'd rather go to Israel and live on kibbutz!"

I hold her and stroke her and kiss her. Ah, heaven! no stench! only the cinnamon tingle of the gum. She confesses that while out earlier at the library, she had scrounged a butt from an ashtray and smoked it.

"Promise me you won't do that again."

Her eyes are large, soulful, limpid with unaccustomed tears. "I won't. I love you. I promise."

I feel like a goddess, all-nurturing, all wise. This is what love is all about. She will be able to quit. She will get a job. We will buy a house with a garden, and summer on the Cape, winter in the Bahamas. Tomorrow I plan to coax her up by ten, and we'll sit together and go over my manual on writing resumes. Then I'll help her go through the want ads. Life is sweet.

Saturday morning 4 A. M. Ashes. All ashes. How could I have been such a fool? After dinner, as we sat sipping tiny glasses of apricot brandy, I began eagerly to discuss my plan of want ads and resumes. C.'s hands, already trembling as she held the stem of her glass, tightened. She made a gesture, which, I realize now, was the "reaching-for-a-cig" movement which she has now to redirect—to what? Gripping the throat of her lover?

She sat, silent, nodding, as I talked, going on and on, about job-search skills and techinques, about re-directing one's energies, selling oneself, "hustling" through the personal contacts and inside information gained by calling up.... (I forget! I forget! how, as she approaches any potential phone call, the "cigs" follow one another with astonishing rapidity, the ashtray, as she talks, begins to choke with butts. I've even heard her, when she's had to call me at work, take miniscule pauses between words to suck in the nicotine.)

Finally, she speaks, fingers kneading the delicate glass stem, turning it around and around and around, about not being in the right field after all, about switching over to another—more obscure, more unlikely, it seems to me—that would, of course, require a PhD, but eventually, would be easier for her to break into....

Suddenly, I feel as if a huge force, held at bay by a reasonably sturdy but not invincible barrier, has broken through, and is, that very instant, engulfing me. My only salvation is speech: hard, clipped words, rapidly delivered, as if lecturing my class on the absolute necessity of specific detail in fiction, on their utterly inadequate efforts to do so. "School is just a game you play! It's a safe one—the only thing you know how to do. Taking money from your parents! Lying! Moving to the couch in the den when they come! Adults work! Adults earn their own living! Where do you think my students would be if they had your attitude for one day? How do think I would've gotten through school, my father sick like that and out of a job, if I hadn't sweated my butt off?"

Tears flood her eyes. She jumps up. Her hands flail for the lighter and pack. Nothing there. Nothing there. In nakedness and betrayal, we confront each other. I feel monumentally ripped off. As she grabs her coat and runs down the back stairs to her car, I know, just as I know that a stone will sink to the depths of a deep well, that I had driven her to nicotine. Hatred—of her—of me—rises through my body. I begin to do the dishes, breaking two of her favorites.

Yet—apparently not—her will power has held. When she comes in—still tearful and shaking at eleven—and holds me, she says she has had only one, scrounged from an ashtray on the counter of the coffee shop where she's sat out the evening with two elderly men in stained raincoats. I did not ask how exquisite it had tasted, how sweet the relief of the smoke stinging her tear-filled eyes. We apologize, make more promises to each other, make agreements about the limits of my strength, patience, and endurance, the necessity of her talking to other friends, of–my suggestion only, not responded to by her—seeking out a new therapist. (She has gone twice to mine, fled with righteous anger when pushed to consider the theory of addiction as applicable to her own life.)

We—finally—make love. "How much more you kiss me now!" she marvels, as her hands travel hungrily and ceaselessly over my body. Her mouth, as I settle, thighs open, into the posture of ecstacy and abandonment, has never been better. We sleep.

I am awake now. I sit at her chair in the kitchen, the TV a silent, blinded eye; old ashtrays, filthy but unused, litter the countertop and window sill. The room smells mercifully of our chicken dinner, not smoke. The smoke, I had begun to feel, was part of the molecular structure of the universe I lived in, so thoroughly integrated was it with every texture and surface of my surroundings.

I fear the day to come. Grotesque impulses overwhelm me— to rifle her purse for possible butts stored in bits of cellophane, to remove matches or lighter in order to decrease her chances of cheating. My fantasies—as garish as any produced by clouds of opium— involve her rising immediately to begin again to chain-smoke, to spend the day with her real lovers—the re-runs and the cigs, never the want ads. I fear breathing, week in, week out, the acrid, stinking air, tasting it on her sullied breath. I fear coming and going from my classes, teachers' meetings, student conferences, trips to the library and finding her always immobile at the table wrapped in the hazy arms (dream-lullaby-fantasy-sleep) of her first and last infatuation.

Perhaps I should just leave. Be alone again. Perhaps I already am.

Jesse

I

How I survive is I use my shield a lot, the shield I figured out when I was pretty little I had all around me. It starts with a feeling I get about my body like there's something—not a wall, not anything that hard or heavy—but something more like a wrapping of air or electricity all around me, something no one else could see. It's full of power.

When I have to walk down Franklin Avenue past the tough guys hanging out in front of the Town House Café on the way to the Cumberland Farms to buy milk for Mom and Bertie, I pull the shield all around me. That way I don't feel the ugly words they throw at me, the ones that sting like sharp little stones. The shield also makes me invisible, like in school, in the back of those crowded classes full of sweaty, squirming bodies.

Before I had the shield I could only get away by day-dreaming; I'd think up pictures in my mind of those green-and-yellow days back at day camp with Dee Dee, my favorite counselor, or the good times with Mom. I'd imagine myself breaking free and running— kind of like a horse in some movie on TV—over the rolling hills, like the ones Mom would tell us about sometimes, back home down south. The horse would go fast; it was always alone.

I'm at the Junior High now, not with Bertie and the little kids anymore, so I just hang out at the Cumberland Farms or the ceme- tery with all the other kids who don't have any place to go, smoking cigs or grass if we can get it, rapping, bragging to each other about all the amazing stuff we're gonna do, like rip off a Cadillac and bust outta this freakin' town and head for Miami to work undercover or for Hollywood to score big drug deals. Talk, a lot of talk, like all the old women back in our building waiting for the mailman to bring the checks.

I don't really like the other girls in the group. Too much eye-make-up, purple and green like bruises, sweaters too tight, hair brassy or dead black from cheap dyes. They put out for guys all the time. I know—in the backs of old shit-kicker cars or, in the summer, even behind the gravestones. I won't, and no one ever tries anything on me. It's like they feel the shield. Somehow we all know something about me, about how I'm different. The guys just treat me like I'm one of them. I know I'm not a guy, of course, but it's hard to figure out how to be a girl and not be like the others who'll do anything just to get chosen. So I just go along, hanging out, not saying too much, smoking and swearing and hunkering down out of the wind as long as possible without heading home, or for what passes these days for home.

A lot's changed. That's why I need the shield, need every scrap of my own kind of power to muster up to survive. Mom yells a lot now. Last week she threw a pot at me. If I talk back she gives me the side of her hand upside my face, if she can get close enough which usually I won't let her do.

Bertie's just not as good as me at taking care of herself. She's four years younger than me and real skinny and kind of whiny-voiced so she gets it a lot more. Every time Bertie gets hit I just die inside. I've tried talking to Mom, tried taking Bertie out with me to hang out, but Bertie started bad-mouthing me for hanging with such a rough crowd and started calling me names as if I were really one of those creeps, so I quit trying. It's almost like she wants Mom to come after her—provokes it sometimes. At least then, I figure, she feels like Mom's paying attention to her.

Last Tuesday was one of those warm clear September evenings that make you hurt inside, in your gut, but in a nice way like when they read poetry in school or you touch yourself secret in the dark. I was walking down Hillside. Something strange happened I haven't got all figured out yet. The grammar school there was all lit up, a yellow glow coming from out the windows, streams of people heading up the stairs—grown-ups. 'Night school,' somebody told me. Typing, and English for people who just got here and only know

Vietnamese or Spanish or Portuguese.

This night I was going to just amble on past the school and see what was goin' down at the cemetery, or over to the liquor store where sometimes we could score some grass, when out of the corner of my eye I saw some girls—women, really, I guess—older than me, older than high school, most of them, but not like Mom or her friends. They were all in a group, laughing, moving into a side door, the one that led to the gym.

I had my knowing in me then, that night. That's the feeling kinda like the shield, that tells me I'm different but tells me who I am. Seems like it's always been there, like the world was some huge jigsaw puzzle with lots of crazy pieces but all of them fitting together somehow. The knowing tells me where to put that piece that's me.

This night the knowing pulled me in the door, into where those women were in the gym starting up to play basketball. I remember the feeling—it was steady and warm like the hand of someone you love helping you walk along. I could hear them fooling around.

"Hey, Karla! We're really gonna bust your ass tonight!"

"Oh yeah? You'n what army?"

They were talking like that and tossing around a battered old basketball, filling that dingy gym with voices, laughter, bodies moving. I wasn't used to women like this, not broken like Mom or weak like Bertie. Being with them right off felt OK. One called me over, the one I found out was called Karla—she's short with short brown hair, no nonsense and big-framed glasses, strong with legs like an athlete.

"Hi," she said. "I'm Karla." She stuck out a hand to shake. Firm. "What's your name?"

"Jesse," I told her, "Jesse." That was the name I'd been practicing, the one that sounded the closest to Jessica. That was my grandmother's sister, back home, the only really brave woman I'd ever heard about. I don't much want to be me these days, at least the me that school and the kids on the corner and Mom, when she's hitting me, make out I have to be. This way I can start over.

"Wanna play? Every Tuesday and Friday seven sharp."

"Sure," I said, and she tossed me the ball.

Now I'm trying to figure them all out. Today's Saturday; last night

I went again and now I'm counting the hours till Tuesday. Might even head over, tomorrow, to the outdoor court at the park where some of them said we could practice for a couple of hours if it doesn't get too cold.

They're all ages—one or two as young as me, some even gray-haired they're so much older. Two of them are black and I like the way they carry themselves, proud-like. Mom's had lots of black friends, "colored," she'd say, but sometimes she'll talk like they aren't as good as her. These two—their names are Nesta and Carol—wouldn't take shit like that, I can tell. Two of the women come together in a beat-up old car with three little kids between them. I can't take my eyes off of those kids sitting on the side lines with a big bag of toys and games and books—nothing fancy, just stuff probably from the Goodwill, but anyway, all for them. They don't get hit, don't get yelled at. All the women fuss over them and help out when they need something—the bathroom or the drinking fountain. These women all look something like Karla, good muscles, no make-up, short hair, backs straight, eyes clear. Watching them I feel like something big's gonna happen to me—like maybe here I can be me—like I don't have to have the shield as much. One thing I've realized about the shield is how it can melt away in places to let something good in—like when I come to the gym to play and talk to the women, or like long ago when Dee Dee held me at camp when I cried. The only trouble is when I go a long long time without ever letting anybody in, it gets really hard to do.

Living with Mom and Bertie I have to keep them out even though I love them—feel stuck loving them. I can't let them in because they know how to hurt me—not so much with the hits but with words, names they call me. Also because if I do let them in, I might get trapped living the same lives as theirs.

The fighting we've got now in the apartment isn't much different from how it always was before. We were down on Franklin Avenue then, and Saturday nights were always noisy—breaking glass, men shouting, women screaming then crying—so it didn't seem like my family was doing anything different. I guess they weren't. The differentness was in me. Holding Mom's head, stroking it, I remember that. I can't even say how young I was, or how I knew to use touching like that. I know what went through my head was not how someday I'd find a man who didn't hit and yell—someone gentle and kind who'd give me all his love wrapped up like a fancy birthday present, but how I just wasn't going to go that route period. Something deep inside told me this wasn't any way for a woman to be living, that there was more, a different way that I used to get glimpses of sometimes in dreams but couldn't really ever hold onto.

After Dad left—the exact day he split I couldn't say—just that he was hardly ever there except to come in yelling and slinging his fists around, and then, all at once, there wasn't even that, just a calm, sweet time I especially remember—another thing I still see in dreams. I was about seven.

Everything in those dreams—I have them waking or asleep, especially when I'm stoned—is warm with the bright, yellow sunshine of early summer, things growing, me just out of school going to the day camp out of the city we took buses to for free. Mom singing, hanging out the wash in the breeze and the light when I'd get home every day holding my grubby little art papers to give to her.

My sister was about five then, too young for camp, but happy, I guess, to be at home with all that quiet and singing and Mom not getting hit so everything seemed special.

I remember too, right before bed in the long, sweet twilights— we had a big bush that grew all over with flowers down by the porch out back—Mom would tell us stories about the hills down south when she was little and used to live there. We'd lay in our room listening to her, watching the dark creep up the sky. My favorite was the one about Aunt Jessica, a true one about Mom's mother's sister. I used to love to say the name over and over in my mouth, "Je-si-kah," like rolling hard candies over my teeth. Anyway, Jessica married young to a man who owned a business in the little town, Gardners Gulch, just over the bridge from the crick out where Mom's folks had their cabin.

I don't remember what their store really was like, but I always imagined a really neat place where they sold stuff—nails and screwdrivers and junk like that which I loved and also bolts and bolts of beautiful cloth, all satin and silk. Her husband died soon after and left her the business. She never got married again, because of a broken heart Mom always said. I didn't think so, but kept quiet. Anyway, she lived for years and years and years—till her face got to look like a shriveled-up old apple, Mom said. She lived long after Mayleen—Mom's other aunt whose husband stayed alive—died of cancer and really suffered and Mom had run away up north with Dad. Aunt Jessica ran the store herself and even had some tough guys come in—college guys on a joy ride, out-of-towners, drunk, wanting what was in the till, maybe more, too. She ordered them to leave, swung out her old shotgun, Betsey, and they did!

She made money and had a house on the best—the only, really—street in town with a horsehair sofa that hurt my mother's bottom, when she got to go there for lemonade and cookies. I'd beg for that story over and over.

At night, the three of us—Mom, Bertie, and me, around the supper table or in the bedroom telling stories—felt like a family. Not like the ones in all the books in school, sure enough, with a big, smiling wonderful Dad, but a family nevertheless. Mom would sing a lot and sometimes make us corn bread with thickenin', a white gravy with bacon grease they used to eat down home when she was little.

Bertie was always playing; she liked to build things out of an old kit of little wooden logs Dad had bought her once when he had some cash. We had a few stray cats we'd feed out back too and Bertie really loved them. She used to be so sweet before everything went rotten.

I used to pretend Aunt Jessica was there too, at supper in the seat where Dad used to sit. And once I even passed her the butter, mumbling to her half-aloud. Mom gave me a dirty look and told me if I kept on with that kid-stuff, pretending and all, the teachers would throw me out of school and lock me up in The Institute—a big walled place not too far away where all the crazies lived. I decided there and then I had to grow up, keep the dreams and make-believe secret inside my head. Probably that's when the shield came although I don't know for sure.

What else was special about that time was camp. First of all, I liked being with all those other girls. It felt really safe sitting on the grass in the middle of all of them packed around me singing camp songs about friendship and loyalty and fig trees, feeling our voices rise and blend.

And then, there was the one that was special, that I still dream about—Dee Dee, the head counselor. She used to wear a white camp shirt unbuttoned just enough to show her throat, brown from the sun, smooth skin all the way down over her breasts. She wore a whistle on a chain that would settle between them, pulling the shirt tight over her nipples. I loved her. Her eyes were so gentle, her voice, too. And when the other kids ganged up on me one day, laughing and calling me names, she took me in her arms and held me, my cheek against that whistle. I can feel it still, cold and cutting into my face and how soft and sweet-smelling she was.

When the oldest girls and the counselors played against each other in softball, I sat, hot, in the dust and cheered till my throat was raw. Dee Dee was the best; hair plastered with sweat, she swung like a demon and hit a run clean out of the park. I can still see her, running like an antelope between those bases.

After that summer, though, things started getting rough again. It crept up on us like summer leaving does, especially in the city. One minute the trees alongside the cemetery fence on the way to the playground bush out all thick and green and the air hangs heavy and sweet all mixed up with the smoky sting of pollution, and the next, you can feel a cruel wind whipping through and see the leaves all dropping off and brown.

We always got a fine Indian summer here after that, but somehow I just couldn't enjoy it. I knew what was coming next.

Dad never did show up again after his job in the plant got axed. Seems like after Vietnam they didn't need those helicopter parts so much. He didn't send money either, and after the first feeling good with just the three of us, the stories and the candy, I guess Mom just wanted him back. Right then, figuring that out and figuring out, too, that my sister, young as she was, felt the same way, I knew for sure just how different I was turning out to be. I knew for sure that love was nothing I was going to sell my soul for, nothing I was going to trade for hits.

Anyway, Mom never really liked being alone; the only way she knew how to be was to have a husband. Kids didn't count. Even though I'd done all that holding and stroking, and even though I knew we could talk together just like two equal people, and sometimes we did—she never counted that. Being with other people, with women—like how I felt at camp singing—just wasn't there either. It had to be a man.

And then there was money. We didn't have any and she didn't know how to get any. My father had made her quit her job. She used to be a typist in a nice office after they moved north. I only know this from her telling me those times sitting in the kitchen when her coffee was hot and ready and the radio down low and Bertie playing down the block, when I was a real person to her for just a little while. But Dad said "his woman" wouldn't have to work, and we would always have everything—a big, white house in the country with a porch swing for Bertie and a pony for me; that was when the aircraft was paying good and the work was steady. That part—him telling us that, I do remember, but I never believed him; when he talked that way he always had beer on his breath, and later, when Bertie and I were in bed, the voices would rise and the shouting begin, and then the hitting.

So Mom didn't know how to work or get money. We must've been on welfare for a while. I remember a lot of talking with the neighbors—other women starting to sag like her, in the building down on Owens Street we had to move to which was much older and smellier than the one on Franklin and had darker rooms and fewer—about checks and the "first-of-the-month" and extra payments and how to wangle them. A lot of energy went into that kind of talk, I remember, bodies heavy and slow, eyes dull, but voices just going on and on, words and words and words spilling over and over—and Mom and me never talking to each other anymore.

Later, one morning all of a sudden, she got up from the living-room sofa where she used to sleep on part of it that folded out—Bertie and I had the one little bedroom—in the chilly kind of half-light just before real dawn and told me I was a big girl now, "in charge," and then she left....

After that we had door keys, Bertie and I, on chains around our necks, and we'd come home alone after school—walking real fast past the cemetery together, then running the rest of the way, down the long blocks past the stores and the movie house where only

men went and where Mom had said there were no shows for kids—
to the place where we lived, tall and shabby, all the apartments with
something in them broken. At first we'd just sit there waiting for
Mom to come home, but when she did, it was never happy. She'd
be bone-weary and angry, wanting to know why I hadn't put the
grits on. That's when she started hitting us.

II

It's June now. It's been a time like nothing I've ever known. The
whole group at the gym took me right in like a long-lost cousin. The
one that's the youngest, Sue, she goes to my school. It's funny how
we never talk there, just give each other a kind of hidden smile
when we pass in the hall. It's like we've got to protect a special secret and keep it for when it's safe. We meet on the corner of Zion
on the basketball nights and walk over to the gym together.

I work at the Pizza Hut now to earn extra money, but I never go
to work on those nights. They're sacred. Sometimes we all go out after the game to a different pizza place, Luigi's; it's darker and sells
beer, and everybody who's got an I.D. drinks a few, but they'll let
Sue and me sit there and get cokes. I feel so good then, like I've got
a real family.

I'm a good player now. Karla works with me, and sometimes
some of the others do, too. They're not in school. They're like regular grown-ups with jobs and apartments and even cars. Karla meets
Sue and me early to drill us; we shoot baskets and she helps us with
our form. She works for a bank as a computer programmer.

She's always asking me about my plans for after high school.
This is the only bad part; I just clam up then, 'cause I don't have any
plans or hopes. My grades are OK. When it's rainy or bad out, I
head over to the Park Street Library and read or do my homework.
I'm not failing in anything; I just know there'll never be any money
for college or any of that shit these women seem to take for granted.
They all accept me, and out here on the court, or in Luigi's, it
doesn't feel like we're different. But really we are.

"Jesse," Karla would say—she never doubted it was my real
name—"you gotta make something of yourself." I wouldn't answer.

Jessica, my aunt, was one reason for the name; the other one was that I felt like an outlaw—not by breaking laws which I only do with dope—but because of the differentness, the being outside of the world of regular folks. "Education, a good job—that's the ticket out of a bad scene," Karla would keep on saying. She knows all about Mom and Bertie and all the trouble. I had to tell her once when she found me early outside the gym with a shiner from Mom's hand. We let the others think it'd happened in the school gym, a ball gone wild. Karla said she understood. She said that Jo, one of the other women who played with us, one of the gray-haired ones, did counseling and stuff at a place where women who got hit—battered women, she calls them—go to get help.

"You can crash at my place anytime," she said. "I live by myself right now."

"Did you used to be married?" I never dared to ask her any personal questions. On the team it seemed like we had a kind of unwritten rule that we just talked about our playing and stuff and things like movies. What she said made me wonder, though, because I knew that Sally, one of the women with the little kids, had just gotten divorced. The others did talk some about that, how the ex-husband was hassling her, trying to get the kids.

Karla started laughing when I asked about a husband. I couldn't figure out why. She plunked her hand on my shoulder, really nice, like a big sister. "Oh, Jesse, oh, Jesse," she said, "I hope this isn't a bad idea, you getting in so thick with all of us."

I've been thinking about that ever since. I never had a chance to ask her what she meant because the others showed up then and we started playing. It seems like finally I'm getting the big idea, who these women really are, why they're the way they are, how I fit in. Seems like it came to me like part of the knowing, just the way it came to me that I couldn't live like Mom or those girls I used to hang with who wore the purple eye shadow.

Sure and easy and just right—that's how it feels to imagine women being just for each other. The way I'm learning to play ball. The way I'm learning to be in the world for the first time. It's like a door nobody ever told me about opening up in a brick wall, showing me a green, green world beyond, with a sweet little crick flowing and flowers blooming and birds. Women together—strong and free. Women loving each other. Women who don't take shit from men.

Of course I've heard of it before, words like "lezzie" and "queer," people thinking women like that must want to be men. I know that's not true. It's more like wanting be real women but still get some of the stuff men get, respect and all. I know I can't ever let anything about this slip at school. This must be why Sue and me keep a distance there; somehow I knew all along what these women were wasn't something you could talk about, that it was so good it had to be kept a secret. Hell, I don't care. I've been dodging questions about guys and dates and making out for years now. This must be why nobody ever hit on me before when we used to hang out and the other girls were fair game.

What this all means to me in terms of love and sex and stuff, I guess I really don't know. I never wanted that with guys because it leads to getting hit and then getting left, with a few dozen babies in between. I know how those babies get here; it makes me sort of sick. I know with women it must be lots different, softer, kind of like Dee Dee holding me, only more.

I can figure out now with the basketball crowd who's with who. A lot of things I didn't understand fall into place now. Joanne and Sally, the ones with the kids, they're a pair for sure. And Nesta and Carol. Everybody pretty much has somebody except Karla. She seems to be a loner. Like me.

I let Sue in on how I knew what was up and now she wants to talk about it all the time—how her old man beat her to a pulp when he caught her and her old girlfriend last year in the bedroom and how the priest told her she'd burn in hell, how the counselor at school was very nice with a stuck-on smile and said it was "natural at her age," but that she'd grow out of it and want to have a husband and kids like everybody else. I figure I'm lucky. Mom's so out of it she'll never figure it out. No one at school guesses. Sue's kinda decided she and I ought to go together since her old girlfriend got sent away to Catholic school, the sleep-over kind, and we're in the same class and the two youngest on the team.

But what's happening is, I think I love Karla. I just try to avoid Sue now, at school and after the games, so she won't think I want to get mushy with her. She sulks and acts hurt but she's still my friend, I think. She'll come round. But Karla is the last thing I think of at night before falling to sleep. Sometimes I touch myself and pretend it's her. After I do that, I can drift off to sleep OK, dreaming of my mother in the far-off sunny time of Aunt Jessica and ol' Betsey ordering those creeps out of her store. I woke up laughing at that one once.

Karla never says anything, just keeps giving me buddy-type hugs. Nothing else ever happens. She goes out after practice to Luigi's, first with that one, then the other. I can't stay out that late or Mom'll beat the shit out of me. I started studying a lot; it keeps my mind steady. I try to daydream about other stuff—women in the movies or my school gym teacher. The days are getting shorter now, colder, the nights deeper. Maybe my feelings are changing, too. Love, the kind I've been going through anyway, feels like a fever. Finally you get over it, stop feeling weak.

After a while, I want to hang out more with Sue again. I don't think about Karla as much at night. I feel older now, smarter, going on to high school next year. Going to work full-time this summer at the Pizza Hut or maybe Bradlee's. I'm not really any safer.... Mom's still angry a lot and ready to lash out—but I'm stronger. The shield comes over me real easy when I need it, slips off soft and silky when I don't.

Meantime, we've got basketball practice every night now; Karla got the gym to open up the space, made us into a real team that gets to play other women's teams from other towns around. I've been getting invitations, too, to parties and stuff at the women's apartments. Now they know I know about the gay business and that I'm one of them, everybody talks a lot more personal. The young ones like Sue and me don't get left out. I like that. Mostly Karla makes that happen, and Jo, the one who does the work for battered women at the shelter, and Deborah, another older woman who works for an insurance company and told us her two kids live with their father and he won't let them see her. There always seems to be something to do—potlucks, touch football on Saturday afternoons down by the college, birthday parties and stuff. Lots of times some of the crowd goes over to the Oak Street Café, a real women's bar. Sue and me can't come in because we're minors, unless Jo or Karla, who both know Lucille, the owner, bring us and promise we won't drink. We don't care. We catch a beer before or after.

The bar is incredible. Women in there touch and kiss and dance slow. Some look and dress exactly like men. I don't really like that, but it's pretty fascinating to look at. I love to just watch everybody, really. It's a real scene. Once a guy came in, all decked out in an evening gown and a wig. Jesus! If Mom or Bertie ever knew! But the music in there's way too loud for talking, and talk's the best part when I see my friends.

Except for the couples going off sometimes smooching, talk's what our whole group really wants to do; we settle in with a joint or a big jug of Lambrusco or something, music on low, and get on down to it, not like Mom and her neighbors, or my old gang, but real. Words, like our basketball, bounced and tossed, up and down and back and forth between us with that same kind of heat. We talk about everything—being gay, our parents, whether they know about us or not, lovers, quarrels, break-ups, "ex's."

Since I've never had anybody, all these stories about love sound rich and mysterious, tangled and complex. Loving another woman, the way my new friends tell it, sounds dangerous sometimes. I know some people really got their hearts broke, like Deborah who left her husband for a minister's wife, then got dumped by her. She hasn't had anybody since. Karla loved a teacher at her college and got dumped, too. Dangerous, though I figure I can handle. What I saw Mom go through with men was worse; it was lethal.

Some of the women, Karla especially, and Jo, are into women's lib. It's a new thing, in all the papers with angry-faced women waving placards and raising fists. I always figure the papers pick the stupidest and ugliest pictures to print so you can't tell what the hell is going on—like the clipping Karla had from the Gay Pride parade in New York City, with a guy on roller skates in a wedding dress. Shit! All due respect to that guy, whoever he is, that kind of picture hasn't got anything, really, to do with our lives.

I'm learning a lot I never knew from all this talk—about battered women (what my Mom was) and rape, how the victims get blamed and the cops don't care, about banks not giving women credit, and discrimination on jobs. Sometimes I get really depressed, but after, in bed, just slipping off, I remember, not the angry faces and words when we talk about the shit women get, but how it feels when we hug each other good night, or just sit, stoned, giggling, piling in on each other like puppies or kittens. Yeah, the world's full of problems all right, and a lot of it women getting beat on, but we have each other and some of the women are working hard for change. Jo's speaking to clubs and classes now about battering and how women can get help; Karla's part of a group to start a credit union just for women to be able to get loans; even Deborah started volunteering at a daycare center that's open Saturdays so she can be with kids.

I don't know yet just what I can do, but it's finally started seeming like the future could hold a promise for me—something to work for, study for, so I could get a scholarship and get a degree. It isn't that I think college grads are better or smarter, or that a piece of paper means anything about how I really am, just that, like Karla keeps telling me, it could be a ticket out of the hole I live in, that Mom is probably always going to be stuck in. I just can't go that route; I'd rather die. Also, no man is ever going to pay my way; I'm going to have to do it on my own. Maybe I'll even be able to help Mom and Bertie someday, but, for sure, I'll be able to help some other woman like my friends do.

The longer I hang around the women's crowd, the more people I get to know, even ones who never come to basketball. Karla and Jo are trying to start a women's center, a place where women can come and get counseling and all kinds of information on stuff like lawyers and women doctors, job openings, and day care. Jo says we could use it for other things, too, like coffeehouses and maybe even dances—where women performers could sing and read poetry. It would be a place to meet women without smoke and noise and booze like the bar. They found a church that's willing to put up the space for pretty cheap rent plus utilities.

I've tried a few of the meetings; one really angry woman named Chip kept talking about a lot of shit I don't understand. She won't ever let me speak, keeps interrupting. Karla brought someone named Bonnie, a good friend of Chip's, who has kids, too. She's really anxious to get something going about violence against women. After what I've seen, I agree. Her style puts me off though, like Chip's—talking too fast and sharp, not listening. I guess I'm learning I don't have to love everybody; there's room for all. I just don't like it that some of them treat me like I don't belong; that's never happened before, not with the basketball women. Karla seems really sweet on Bonnie. I can't figure out why since they aren't at all alike but, as Sue says, that's what lust will do.

I know I'm not as close to Karla now. It hurt a lot at first and I cried one night, but now I talk to lots of the other women more; I make a point of it, and it feels OK, like I'm more grown-up, don't need a big sister. I can handle stuff on my own terms.

Meanwhile, things at home just get worse and worse. I'm there as little as possible, staying over anywhere I can with my friends. Mom lost the awful job she'd had at the plant sticking one little part into another all day for shit pay, back on welfare again.

Bertie's become just like the friends of mine she used to scorn, with the makeup and the loose ways. I guess her life's so empty of any love and affection, she gives her body to guys just to be held. Every time I try to talk to her, she mocks me or slams the door, and once when Mom was out, she called me "queer," and split. Nothing else about that has ever been said. I cried about that half the night, after Nesta's birthday party, Nesta and Carol and Jo holding and stroking me. Now I've decided to give it up. Jo tried to make me understand that we can't rescue everybody. One of the women at the shelter, she's spent weeks trying to help, went back to her battering husband; she'd rather get beat than be alone.

Last weekend, while I was taking the short cut over through Owens Street to Sue's where I thought I could crash, I saw Bertie standing out on the corner with two other girls all dolled up like what Mom used to call chippies. They had wigs on and short tight minis made out of leather. It was so gross I thought I'd puke. Bertie stared straight at me bold as brass but didn't speak. I didn't either. A car cruised by real slow then, a big shiny rich one with a purring motor. A man put his head out the window and the three girls clustered round. I hurried on over to Sue's, wouldn't talk, got real stoned and slept half the next day. I found out yesterday from going right up to an old buddy of Bertie's outside the junior high, that Bertie's got in with some older dude who likes to drub up the young girls who're looking for trouble, tell them they're his only forever love and turn them out on his behalf.

I feel numb now because of knowing all this. Mom doesn't notice, doesn't care, and Bertie's never home either, so I haven't got any family anymore at all—except the women. I try not to think about anything except studying and basketball; it helps.

It was February, gray and mean and slushy, the time when you think maybe winter's forever—outside and in your soul, too. This is when Sara came to me. "We always get what we need," she told me later. I guess she was right. It was at a party at Joanne and Sally's; everybody was there. I was sitting quietly in the corner on a couple of big, stuffed pillows Joanne had made which they use for furniture. She and Sally live on next-to-nothing, AFDC Sally gets and Joanne's part-time wages as a mechanic at Sears Automotive. Jo and Karla had told her to threaten to sue if they wouldn't give her the job; she puts batteries in cars three days a week.

Candles were burning all over—that was the only light—and something soft and low and honeyed was on the stereo, some jazz singer Nesta and Carol like. I'd had just a half a glass of wine, no grass, feelin' mellow and easy inside my own skin, being with my friends after such a hard time for so long.

Sara walked in. Her eyes turned right toward me. I felt—words can't describe it. I realized then, and all the time since, how we've been cheated, we women, in this world—not just by having no laws to protect us and no good ways to make ourselves independent with money and jobs and all, but no words either to talk about how it really is for us and how we feel about each other. None of the old words I'd heard my Mom or my old friends or the women on TV use would do; all their talk sounded like it came from outer space.

Joanne clapped her hands, made everybody shut up. She put her hand on Sara's shoulder. "This is our friend from Oregon, Sara. She's passing through so make her feel welcome." Everybody clapped and smiled. Sara, who was dressed differently from us—a long, purplish Indian print skirt, boots, a thin gauzy shirt—set down her big, bulging pack which looked serious and sturdy. I wanted to rush up and pull her over to me, start talking, say anything, just to attract attention. Something held me—more of my knowing which I was getting surer and surer with. Something said, "Wait. Be still. Your heart's desire can never be struggled for. It always drops when it's ready into your hands."

And just like I always know when one of my long shots're going to make it dead center from the edge of the court, I knew I was right. When she came to me—soon enough after speaking to Joanne and Sally and going in to the kids, who, of course, in p.j.'s, were not sleeping but bouncing and screaming on their little mattresses on the floor, and after she had had something to eat and said "hi" to a few others—she came all the way with nothing left over, and without hanging onto anything past or extra or even in the future.

I don't remember what we said at first, not much probably. Her hair was short and dark around her face like a cap. Her eyes were gray and did not waver from my face. A crystal on a colored thread around her neck caught the light and danced. She likes stuff like that and meditation and astrology. I'd always thought it was silly before. Now I wanted to know all about it.

She was twenty-one, from Maryland, living now in Oregon, home for a while to visit her folks and friends back east. "You can't imagine how green it is and the rain smells sweet—the women are strong and beautiful." She'd met Joanne and Sally at a lesbian mother's gathering out there last summer. They'd taken the kids and the clunky car and just barely made it in on their last gallon of gas and peanut butter sandwiches.

Sara'd been living then with a woman, thirty-five, and her little boy. "That's over now—I've learned this year about letting go." "Me, too." I told her about Bertie. She listened. About halfway through our talking, I realized we were holding hands. I don't know who had reached out first. It didn't matter. Later, I realized my shield hadn't left me, just melted right around Sara and let her in.

All the candles had burned to pools of wax. The kids had been zonkers for hours. All the guests had gone and Joanne and Sally were tiptoeing around trying not to send us knowing glances as they picked up crumpled paper cups and dirty plates. Finally, they went off to their room. I could hear the soft sounds of their love-making, comforting as rain on a roof in the summertime, as Sara and I let our words trail off, our bodies curl together, the low murmurs and cries we began soon to make to join those of our friends. Much later—lying in Sara's arms, in moonlight, on the big, soft pillows, the itchy wool of her poncho covering us—I wished I'd grown up like those kids fast asleep in the next room, wrapped as surely as we were in the sweetness and power of women's love.

III

After I got the letter from Sara telling me she'd found somebody new out in Oregon and that they were really in love and planning to build a log house together, I felt numb for a long, long time. It was like the shield turned to lead. Nothing could get in or out. By then, I was in second-year high, working full-time—vacations and summers, and part-time after school, saving money, making the grades to get into college. Yeah, I was still different from Karla and Jo and Deborah—they had families who paid for them to go to fancy colleges, get training for regular jobs. But just because I never had anybody to help me didn't have to mean I'd have to settle for nothing all my life. I just feel bitter and angry about it a lot. I guess in the long run, though, I refuse to let anything stop me. I don't want to end up with nothing I can ever call my own.

But when I knew I couldn't ever have Sara's love anymore, I let my whole life slide, spent a lot of time drinking in the Oak with Sue and her pals, playing pool, smoking dope when we could scrounge it, missing work some, not saving money any more. Losing Sara hurt so much inside, I just didn't dare feel it. Nothing except what happened to Bertie had ever hurt so much.

I'd fall asleep stoned, dreaming of Dee Dee and Mom and bright summer days and love scenes with Sara in the redwoods—a lot of stuff that won't ever be again, or ever be, period. I stopped going to basketball a while back. Just couldn't face everybody asking me when I was going out to Oregon, did I get a letter, you know, stuff like that.

Sue's fallen in love by now with a woman, Gina, from softball from the summer. Gina's out of school, got her own place. They're pretty tight and I don't see Sue much. Karla's totally gone into Bonnie's crowd and the new women's center. I just can't hack some of those women's center political types and their head games, much as I believe in some of the causes. Jo moved away to Arizona 'cause she started getting some arthritis bad. Wrote one postcard; she's working with a shelter there. Deborah's just as depressed as me. Her ex-husband sent one of their kids away to a prep school in Chicago, the other one to college in Texas. She might never see them again. Sometimes I really have to laugh at myself about how I used to believe so much in this bunch of women—in the real family we were going to be for each other, and the perfect love Sara and I would have, everything all rosy and sweet. It feels like life is just full of shit now, sometimes. I'm never home at the apartment with Mom except to sleep.

As soon as I can, I'm going to get me a room somewhere and be on my own. The counselor at school told me how to do it—to still be a minor but have a legal thing that your blood relatives can't have any rights anymore over your life.

Mom's dating a new guy, Larry. He seems real decent. She hasn't hit me in weeks. He's talking a lot about them buying land down south where he used to come from too. Maybe growing stuff and trying to make a new life. Maybe it'll work. I keep thinking about what Sara used to say about how we always get what we need. I guess I think that's probably true, but what it ends up meaning, sometimes, is something really hard to swallow.

What you need isn't always what you've dreamed you would finally get to have. All's I know now anyway is, I've got to get out on my own. Mom will go her way and I'll go mine and maybe we'll meet again without the hate some day, but not for a long time.

I wish I could say what it was got me through, pulled me back to myself, to my own power. Since I've done better at school and taken books Karla or Jo would lend me and gone to the library a lot, I've learned about stuff—how in all the books people see a blinding light or feel a visitation from a god or something to turn them around. It hasn't been like that for me, getting myself back on track, nowhere close.

Instead, it's just been the slow relentless turn of the earth, I think. Day after night after day, light over the tombstones out at the cemetery where I always walk changing from pale to brighter to dark again, trees leafing out and budding, flaming up in the fall, dying back, sprouting out again, even if you don't care, even if you just want to lay down and sleep and never wake up. Staying away from the basketball crowd was good for awhile because I found out I'm no good at drinking or smoking alone. Instead, I just read and study, 'cause it numbs my hurt heart, and lots of nights I keep on walking, up and down all those city hills, those winding little streets with their falling-down tenements, past wash frozen on the lines in winter, straggly tomatoes by the wire fences in summer.

A whole year slips by fast enough sometimes, if you're just marking your breath minute by minute, keeping it even. I got into advanced algebra in school by some fluke, then calculus. I'm crackerjack at it. It's like playing basketball, a game that's not only a game, instead, it's skill and precision and joy. Getting the equation just right feels like it does when the ball slips, whoosh, through the hoop. A couple of teachers noticed me. The new counselor got on my case about scholarships and college, all the while helping me to get my rights free from Mom. I like them all. They remind me of the old crowd even though one's a guy.

I don't want to trust anybody, but sometimes it's like I haven't got a choice—anymore than the sun does about coming up and going down. I think I'd like to be a teacher, probably in math, when I get out of school, and help kids like myself—or maybe work in science somewhere and maybe discover something that would help people. I want my life to matter, that's all, and it's up to nobody but me to make that happen.

Finally, one day a couple weeks ago, I got a card from Oregon addressed in purple ink with goddess designs stamped on it from one of those little rubber stamps they sell in the new feminist bookstore in town. I've been hanging out there some, never talking to anybody, just leafing through all the new books. My heart almost stopped when I held the card in my hand. I couldn't wait to get alone so I could rip it open. Of course it was from her—my lost Sara. For a split second I dared to believe she'd be calling me back, back to her arms, her mouth, her breasts, to that safe special place where I could curl up and never have to go through anything hard again. Of course I was wrong. But what she said made me feel warm inside: "Dear Jesse—I think of you often and I will always love you and hold you in my heart." She wanted to give me her new address. She's still with her lover—it's working out real good. They built their log house, but now they're going to rent it and go to San Francisco for two years, where Sara's going to acupuncture school and her lover's going to try to sell her paintings and stuff.

That night I cried the whole night through. The next day I went out and went to the bookstore and looked up the flyer I'd seen that advertised women's basketball at a new school that got built over by Prospect. I've been going to practice now three times a week. Sue even showed up once with her lover, Gina. They were real friendly and invited me over for supper one night to Gina's place. They told me news. Deborah was in a psych hospital for a month; she's out now and doing really good, seeing a shrink or something, I guess. Jo's got a great job out in Phoenix; she's coming for a visit at Christmas. Karla broke up with Bonnie; she's taking it real hard but promised she'd come by to play basketball as soon as she felt up to it. Nesta and Carol are still together, bought a house. Joanne lost one of her kids who decided to go live with his father; she and Sally started a wallpaper-and-paint business. I liked hearing the news, good and bad; it made me realize I missed everybody and that all of us seemed to weather our fair share of ups and downs. Sue and Gina and I talked about starting a league again and playing other teams. We meet now before practice and walk over together.

It feels good now to get back into it, dribbling, passing, holding your breath praying for the ball to sink down into the hoop. I met a new woman last night, sturdy, clear-eyed, a freshman at the community college. "What's your name?" she said.

"Well, they call me Jesse, and I grew up being Carrie, but it's Caroline, really."

"Nice. Who for?"

"My mother." I feel fine saying it now. My mother, who gave me life but whose life will never be mine. "She's Carrie, too, but she was born Caroline. You can call me that."

"Sure thing. I'm Bobbie. Hey, look over there—a kid, I guess. She's been hanging around here a lot. Should I tell her she's too young for the team?"

"Hell, no." I strode over. The kid had freckles, braces. She looked scared, but I could tell from the way she grinned and didn't back off she had potential. "Hi, kid. Wanna play?" I passed her the ball.

III. Islands

Islands

On the night of the largest march on Washington for lesbian and gay rights ever held, a woman sits up late in the living room of her home nursing a glass of brandy, watching television. As usual her husband is asleep upstairs, as are her two children. This is her regular routine, yet tonight she has switched from the old movie channel where her favorites are frequently re-run, to make sure she catches the late news.

She watches intently hoping to see, as indeed she does, a brief snatch of an impassioned speech delivered by a woman about her own age— who is the chairperson of the National Alliance for Lesbian and Gay Rights.

The same woman appears from time to time on certain talk shows and in the more liberal newspapers. Her face can also be seen on the back of more than one book jacket.

Now on the television, as she speaks, she brings her hand up to her hair, sweeping it back on one side.

When the spot is over, the first woman leans back on the couch, flips the station back to the movie channel by remote control, and pours out a little more brandy.

Back in her hotel, exhausted, having finally waved away the crowd of reporters, hangers-on, and would-be groupies, the woman who has spoken to the crowd kicks off her shoes, lets her slacks drop to the floor, drapes her shirt over the back of a chair, and crawls, numb all over, into the wide bed, alone.

It seemed from the first that the island didn't want them. That first day driving up from Boston with the U-Haul, the rain slammed down so hard they could barely find the entrance to the causeway that would take them out to the far spit of land that was now to be their home. Once on the high arching bridge, Megan, who could never ride in a car she wasn't driving, cursed as the whole structure seemed to bounce up beneath the wheels of the Rabbit. "Jesus, Mary, and Joseph, I'm going to puke."

"Keep calm, hon. It'll be all right. Remember, the real estate agent told us this usually happens in a high wind." Carole had the knack of establishing serenity where there was none—a dubious skill.

By the time they were unloaded into Headlands House—a U-Haul will only hold so much and the house had come completely equipped right down to Hudson's Bay blankets and bone china tea cups—the wind had blown the rain out to sea.

Carole stood on the headland the house was named for and saw before her what she had come to claim. The harbor, nestled into the curve of a tiny cove, could have been—and was—a postcard. Angles and planes of all sorts—the vertical of the horizon, the curving swell of small bluffs and sea cliffs, mounds of tiny islands, piercing spires of pines, wedge-shaped juts of sails—all seemed to merge into a composition of almost unbearable harmony.

Colors, too, were married to each other—grays, gray-greens, pearl-whites, soft mauve. Breathing here was a privilege rather than a forced necessity as in the city. She was just reaching up her arms, feeling her vertebrae stretch apart and reassemble, when curses and crashes behind her, not unfamiliar, pulled her back.

Megan must have lost the cords to the VCR, the only thing their landlady, a businesswoman who lived most of the year in Manhattan, was not providing that Megan felt she couldn't live without.

When they'd been trying to pare down their possessions to what the U-Haul could hold, Carole had had to agree to allow the color TV and the VCR to come with them. Megan had argued that she should, at least have something; Carole was getting everything else— the time free from work, (she had resigned from the teaching job she had held for the thirteen years since she'd left college) money to live on, (a lump sum equivalent to what she'd had to pay monthly into the union-mandated retirement fund) and the ambition and inspiration to write.

What was Megan getting by coming up here but the opportunity to work at yet another nursing job she hated (Carole had not yet learned to be suspicious about a pattern that stayed intact, no matter how much exteriors changed) unless it could be for all this?

Carole threw one last wistful glance around the harbor, the sea, the vault of the sky beyond, before the desperation in her lover's voice pulled her back into the house's dim interior. For Megan, she knew, the beauty of this place meant nothing.

That night, under the Hudson's Bay blankets, Carol reached for Megan who had already turned on her side and begun to snore. Sadness pierced her. She remembered other nights, however few, in which Megan had been eager, puppyish in her affection, yet generous. Carole did not realize until this moment how much she had hoped, once she was up here, not only for the freedom to write, which seemed forbidden to her in the city with all of the demands of papers to correct, constantly ringing phone, neighbors' noisy kids, but for things to be different between herself and her lover.

"Sex always falls off after the second year! Haven't you heard that?"

"Yeah, it's called lesbian bed death!"

Angie and Jan, friends Megan had made through work, were frank about how 'extra-marital' affairs were the way they'd stayed together for eight years. They liked to crow and cackle after a few too many drinks whenever Megan grumpily alluded to the problem.

What was so bewildering was that, increasingly, Megan would humiliate her in public by mentioning the issue, then at night when Carole turned to her, feign sleep or plead another of her favorite old movies on the tube in the den. She'd crawl under an afghan, a huge bowl of greasy popcorn beside her, to fall asleep alone later on the couch. The station signal would buzz till dawn. Sometimes it was hard for Carole to believe that most of their three years had passed in this way.

After the VCR cords had been found, right where Megan had packed them, Carole persuaded her to walk down to the town which lay in three or four small clumps of buildings—some houses, a few shops, a couple of inns—at the foot of the steep drive that ended at their house.

Megan seemed to perk up then, raising her head, sniffing at the air, practically frolicking like the small puppy she could resemble.

Her dark, short, curly hair and round wire-rim glasses always gave her the air of a school girl.

Carole, by contrast, was slimmer, taller, with soft brown hair worn mid-length and swept to one side. She was steady, serious, looking always the schoolmarm.

Playfulness from Megan wasn't frequent, but always endearing; Carole would find herself forgetting the huffiness, the cutting remarks that had become the norm. "So, lots of ideas here for poems, you think?" Megan had her hands crammed into her slicker pocket. She shoved glasses up her nose.

"Well, it would seem so." Carole couldn't help gesturing again, just to feel her arm cut through the bracing air, just to imitate the wheel of one of the many gulls that keened and dipped above the harbor. Suddenly she felt glad, despite Megan's choice of sleep over love last night. That moment of failure of nerve on the bridge was forgotten. (Another pattern she had not yet come to be entirely suspicious of—this one of hers of forgetting.) All promise seemed before them. The only slightly out-of-kilter detail in this landscape of fantasy-come-true was the faces of the townspeople: cold, expressionless.

Back in the city, before sleep, dreaming, plotting this moment in her mind's eye, the people had always been ruddy-cheeked with beaming smiles—the crusty old lobsterman who'd spin yarns, the genial, buxom housewife who'd offer them fresh-baked cookies.

Here, now, they saw almost no one. The few they did see, including a liver-colored dog who skulked by, were sallow, thin, and did not meet their eyes. One or two did stare boldly, but only from behind the glass in front windows that were quickly pulled over with shabby lace drapes as if the gazer had been but a phantom.

Uneasiness, for Carole, about this lack of welcome from the town did not really surface until the third day. She'd been busy filling drawers with warm sweaters and flannel nighties, trying to learn how the woodstove worked, fixing up her writing studio in the attic room that their landlady had had renovated with modern skylights and a picture window that overlooked the harbor. On that day Megan had had to start her new job in the hospital in the nearest biggish town, which, of course, wasn't big at all, a forty-minute commute.

Carole's aloneness, then, felt sharp, like walking barefoot on bits of glass from an accident. Maybe fear of such feelings was why she'd stayed so long in a relationship that clearly wasn't working.

"Nonsense!" she told herself, her words echoing in the cold room. "Time alone is what I came for. I'm going to seize it!" She pulled a chair to the butcher block table that served as a desk under the picture window in the studio. After scrawling a number of trite lines about the view, she balled up her efforts and bolted down the steep stairs out into the ragged September garden.

The weather had held since the storm of their arrival. Standing amidst the frozen mums, she tried again with herself. "Nonsense, a writer's task is to be in the world gathering material. I'll walk to the store for what we need, and then this afternoon I'll make notes on my impressions. Tomorrow I can start work in earnest."

Walking back up the drive to the house after her brief stop into the small all-purpose store that offered everything from fishing tackle to cans of tuna, Carole tried to sort out her encounter. The sales clerk, a woman with greenish teeth, a few in the front actually missing, had looked old, but was more likely in her twenties. She had spoken only in grunts or monosyllables, refusing to respond to Carole's chatter. Her eyes, though, had followed Carole everywhere about the dusty store as she collected what was needed—a few grocery items, and lots of fuses.

They'd learned that everything in the house ran off of one fuse; they'd blown it already each time they tried to use a hair dryer or an iron while the TV was on. Since Megan kept the TV always going, the problem was a real one. "We can't get anything here!" Megan had wailed. "Find somebody to come put in an aerial. I'll pay. I'll pay," she shrieked, when Carole looked hesitant.

This issue of the use of money was a sore one. Megan's salary was to be miniscule. Still, it was more than the monthly stipend Carole was allowing herself out of her lump-sum fund which would give her a year for her writing if she was very careful. Then, if they wanted to stay, she'd have to find work herself.

Holding the bag of her purchases in the crook of her arm as she climbed the hill, Carole attempted to count and recount her change in the palm of her other hand. She was an English teacher. Math had always been her weak point. Still, if the fuses cost 69 cents each, as the price tag had indicated, she should have a lot more left than she did. Could that toothless girl have short-changed her?

God knows, education up here seemed pitifully lacking, Carole told herself. Maine had a much poorer system than Massachusetts—plus in these isolated islands everyone had to take buses to centralized schools miles away. When the snows drifted high they couldn't make it at all. They had to drop out young to go to work, and so it cycled around.

All her life, Carole had been coached to have empathy for the "less fortunate." Her mother had championed several charities of the less-controversial kind and had carefully explained to the young Carole what the benefits she went to on evenings when her daughter wished her to stay home were all about. Now Carole saw that her mother's activities had been an advantage in her career (helping her to make the leap from teaching into administration), that altruistic acts could mask self serving ones. Yet Carole's childhood heart had been deeply impressed with the goodness of helping others, excusing their weaknesses.

Her parents' philosophy had stood her in good stead in her relationship with Megan who was always in need of excuse and rescue; now it seemed, dealing with the people of this town was going to require more of the same. Carole realized, as she tried to calm her mounting rage over the short changing, that her jaw was clenched. "Let it go," she urged herself, "let it go."

She looked at her watch. Megan would be off shift in fifteen more minutes, in an hour she would be home. If Carole washed the breakfast dishes, put away her purchases, peeled some potatoes for supper, then the two of them could walk before they ate, along the coast. Carole had found a stretch of shore a few miles down from the town that especially appealed to her; she'd promised herself they would explore it as soon as they could. I'll write tonight, she vowed, when Megan leaves me for either sleep or a movie.

The first car stopping happened late that night.

After the walk, Carole had lined the purplish sea urchin shells which she had collected all along her desk. Megan had been persuaded to let Carole build a fire, and they sat like children at a picnic on a rough blanket and ate their supper in front of it. They had had wine with their dinner and finally made love. Of course Megan wouldn't make love before the fire as Carole wanted. Upstairs in the dark under the heavy blankets was less satisfactory.

But Megan had offered, "That was nice," as they finished, stroking Carole's hair in a gesture more tender than any of her more explicit touches. Carole had been soaking in the rare warmth of it, when she realized Megan was now dead weight beside her. Megan's sleep was frequently instantaneous, heavy, seemingly dreamless.

Carole usually dropped off less readily but tonight she was stark staring awake. It was too cold to get up and go to her desk. Myriad ideas wheeled in her skull like the gulls over the pier and would not settle.

That was when she had become aware of the car, of the motor running as it sat by the stop sign at the corner on which their house stood. Cars went by sparsely during the day, a few more at both morning and evening "rush hours," and not at all at night.

Now, in the tremendous silence that existed in this place, any unusual sound took on uneasy proportions. When the car did not move on after ten minutes, Carole finally got up. She pulled her thick robe around her, found her moleskin slipper boots, shoved her toes in, and walked with the heels squashed under to the window.

The car was a battered heap, like most cars up here. Their own shiny red Rabbit seemed almost obscene by contrast. The occupants of the heap—as much as the lone street light could reveal—appeared to be adolescents. The faint rise of voices came up to her with what sounded like a harsh laugh, a few curses. Finally, after ten more minutes, the wheels screeched on the gravel and the vehicle moved on. Carole returned to bed—but not to sleep.

"Jesus fucking H Christ! You won't believe this!" Megan was huffing in from the car, bearing a grocery bag, a six-pack, and the inevitable little polyethylene tote from the video store she'd luckily found in the town where the hospital was.

"Did you learn *anything* in parochial school besides swear words?" Carole was raking the yard. The straggly heads of mums and the last few burnt-out heads of marigolds lined the floral border by the house. The lawn was full of dead brown leaves. She'd done two whole stanzas today. The raking was her reward.

"Precious little! You'd curse like a trooper too if you'd had Sister

Benedicta. Listen to this." Megan flung her bags down onto the red-wood picnic table, shoved up her glasses. Her white uniform pants stuck out below her expensive but stained trenchcoat; her white shoes were scuffed. "I stopped into Bailey's, that ratty little store next to the liquor store to get that oregano you said you wanted...." Even in the midst of her tirade, Megan paused at this, as if asking for a pat on the head.

"Yes. Go on."

"And that bitch in there, the one with the green teeth..."

"Yes."

"...well, she had the friggin' nerve to tell me the oregano was a dollar sixty-nine, when it's plainly marked sixty-nine cents. When I called her on it, showed the price tag and the same one on three other bottles, you know what she said?"

"What?" Carole was feeling a cold chill around her heart. So far she hadn't gone back to Bailey's. She'd driven with Megan Saturday evenings into the bigger town to the supermarket, then they'd gone to the movies there despite the wretched selection, shows that had hit Boston a whole year earlier.

"She said, and I quote," Megan was already ripping one of the beers out of the six-pack, popping the top, "'Price just went up,'" mimicking the island's singsong inflection. "And she told me the milk was a dollar forty-nine. I saw what the woman behind me paid her. That old biddy who lives down the corner of Seawall Avenue, the one we saw out in the yard with her dog the other day?" Carole nodded. "She was only getting milk, and she gave the bitch a one dollar bill, and got a couple cents change! We are being over-charged!" Megan chugged half the beer, slammed the can down on the table, eyes flashing, the sunset glinting on her lenses.

Carole straightened. Her back was killing her. She leaned on the rake, swept the fall of her hair on one side back and away from her eyes. "I didn't want to tell you this before, but she's done it to me too."

"What!" Megan squeaked. "Why didn't you tell me?"

"Well, hon," Carole sank heavily to the picnic table bench. "I guess, well...." For a poet, her words seemed to be coming awfully slowly. Why could she never think of exactly the right ones to calm Megan's fury? For three whole years now, she'd been convinced that if only she could crack the code, find the magic syllables, she could tame something wild in her lover's eyes so that they could rest sweetly together.... "I was the one who wanted to come here when we drove up from Boston that day, when we found the ad in the newspaper...for the house...for your job. This place seemed magical to me. I knew I could get the money from the union fund. I guess I've felt I had no right to ask you to come up here with me. I've been afraid you were unhappy."

"Oh, honey," Megan slumped beside her, her coat flapping like untidy wings. She embraced Carole and tried to wipe her tears. Carole leaned against her shoulder, knowing why she had tried so hard for so long to love this troublesome woman—knowing what, after all, made Megan a good nurse.

At times like these, the brief warmth from Megan seemed all the more desirable because Carole knew how hard it was for her lover—sandwiched as she had been as a child between many sisters and oftener than not left out—to give at all. When Carole heard Megan's stories of her childhood she could almost picture a young version of her lover—runny-nosed, scruffy-kneed—running desperately after the others, stopping to pull up her socks, teased and then forgotten. Thinking of that lost child, she hugged Megan tighter.

"Listen Carole, it's okay. I don't like it here much, but I don't like Boston either. And hospitals are all the same. The same crew of harpies and shrews, the same decaying bodies, the same shitty pay. What difference does it make?"

Carole pulled back a little, wiped with one finger the tears coursing down Megan's cheeks, too. "What does make a difference to you, babe?"

Megan released her lover from her embrace to blow her nose with a vigorous snort. "Beats me."

Later, Megan refused to sit by another fire. She hunkered in the den to watch *Dark Victory*, which she'd brought home from the video store.

Pleading revisions to her stanzas, Carole sat alone in front of leaping flames, the notebook untouched by her side, and remembered their first meeting three years ago at Daughters of Bilitis in Cambridge. This D. O. B. was the only remaining chapter of the oldest lesbian social group ever to exist in the U.S. A sense of that proud history used to move Carole when she served as recording secretary and often as a "rap leader" for the weekly discussion groups. At one point, she had even tried to start a political action group to do lobbying at the state capitol for gay rights; the plan failed when the women realized that many of them could lose their jobs were they to come out so publicly.

The group fizzled; Carole felt deep remorse for her own cowardice, yet finally contented herself by picking topics for the raps that dealt with issues of discrimination and the importance of social action. She had no lovers, but allowed herself to luxuriate in the pleasure of the company of her own kind after all of the days of the school year that had to be endured in the closet.

Megan had been brought to her first and only meeting by Angie, shortly after they'd met. Angie had sought out Megan at work, sensing a kindred spirit with that infallible "dyke radar" some lesbians develop. After weeks of cajoling, Megan, whose only previous relationship had been with a lay teacher at the Catholic college she'd attended before nursing school, finally gave in and went to a meeting.

Carole, still smarting from a dangerous crush on a student teacher who had had the same eyes she now saw in Megan, the same bizarre sense of humor, had fallen hard for her without really checking out the terrain. They'd gotten over their mutual initial shyness while on a D.O.B. sponsored whale watch. Carole could still recall Megan's excitement as their first whale breached, sending a delicate spume of spray above the choppy seas.

"Oh, wow! Carole—look! It's just like Moby Dick!" In a bright green slicker, droplets of spray glistening along her eyelashes, her nose sunburnt, Megan had literally jumped up and down and clapped her hands, then grabbed Carole's arm. Carole grabbed back. Within days they were enmeshed. It hadn't seemed possible to retreat then, and it didn't now.

Carole's family absently accepted her life choices. Her mother, a classical historian at a large midwestern university, kept Carole's father, a drunk who was discreet enough so that no one really knew why his life-work—an opus about revolutionary France—was never published, why he could never hold a teaching job for long. Her parents had met in graduate school. Her father had worked for a few years, slipping from a prestigious university post to a junior college

to private tutoring. On the other hand, her mother's career has ris-
en—publication, tenure, national recognition, eventual entry into the
university administration. She kept a clear island in the center of it
all for her husband whom she cosseted, whose endless manuscript
revisions she still typed herself.

Carole had existed on the periphery. There were no other children; her younger brother, over whom much fuss had been made,
had died of spinal meningitis when he was five. What she did now
seemed of little real importance to her parents. They were pleased
enough, in an absent way, to see her when she visited, never asking
personal questions. They were probably just as glad she didn't bring
home a demanding man or messy children.

Megan, on the other hand, had grown up in a tangle of children.
Her mother, an upper-middle-class Catholic matron whose valiant attempts at the rhythm method never succeeded, kept pushing out babies year after year. Seeing them all off—adorable stairsteps in their
neat somber uniforms, plaid pleated skirts, or creased slacks and
monogrammed blazers, to Roxbury Latin for the boys, St. Catherine's
for the girls—became her life's vocation. Appearances were what
mattered, not how her children felt.

Megan had gone on to Regis College, and then, because she
wasn't married and couldn't bear the thought of the novitiate, to the
only thing that was left—nursing school. Her family had no idea, at
least not consciously, why she wasn't married and producing candi-
dates for their old alma maters like all of her siblings. She went
home only on obligatory holidays and lied when she did.

Crumpling an empty page of her notebook and pitching it into
the fire's heart, Carole told herself, I guess Megan and I are really
each other's only family. That's why it's so hard. We expect each
other to be everything for ourselves and we can't imagine letting go.

She was climbing the cold stairs to join the snoring lump under
the blankets when the car stopped again. This time she retraced her
steps, walked into the dark dining room where she could get a better view of their visitors. After a few minutes another car pulled up
and stopped beside the first. Carole could hear more voices this
time, see the winking of cigarettes being lit. Almost twenty minutes
passed before they moved on.

"Nice the way you girls got this place fixed up." Bud Evans, the television repair man had consented, for the most exorbitant price, to come out to install the aerial so that Megan could get cable. He allowed his eyes to roam every corner and crevice of the rooms that were open to his view. "That New York lady who lives here always had dust covers on stuff, and lots of those nice pretty plates and all packed away." He gestured to the hutch where Carole had displayed the china and some lovely New England pewter. "Two city girls like you must be pretty lonely up in these parts. None of that nightlife I'll bet you're used to—nice-looking girl like you, anyway. That other's a bit dowdy, but you're OK."

Shocked by his bluntness, by the way his eyes took all of her in—moleskin slippers, old sweats for writing in, a scarf around her unwashed hair—Carole just blurted, "I didn't go in for nightlife in the city, Mr. Evans. I'm a writer."

"Call me Bud. Yeah, a writer, that's what they say."

"Who says?"

"Well, small town people like to talk. Listen, little lady, I've got to get into that upstairs right front bedroom to get out on the roof for the aerial. Which you girls use that room?" His eyes were piercing. What he wanted to know was obvious.

"Uh—it's mine," Carole said quickly. That room looked totally unlived in, as the other bedroom, warmer since it was right by the heating vent in the hall, was full of their tossed-off clothes, the laundry basket, paperbacks, notebooks, lotions, hairbrushes, slippers, robes on the back of the door. It had never ocurred to her that anyone else would be seeing the inside of the house. "Just let me go on up…to tidy away a few things. Help yourself to a cup of coffee. The pot's on," she gestured toward the stove.

"Don't mind if I do," he said, but he didn't turn as she mounted the stairs. His eyes bore into her back.

Hating herself, Carole dashed into the other bedroom. Grabbing a few items—a robe, a hairbrush, a bottle of lotion—she dashed into the unused room and put them about. Carefully, she went back to close tight the other door.

When Bud ascended, he looked boldly around again. "Quick work. You'd never know anyone ever lived here."

The job took four hours. Carole remembered a neighbor of her parents doing the same work for them in thirty minutes. During the time Bud was in the house, Carole hovered, making sure he didn't enter any of the other rooms. She was even afraid to go to the bathroom while he was there, but emptied her bladder in a searing rush after his truck finally pulled away.

"See ya 'round." He had winked as he left. Suddenly she felt terribly cold, even though the little wood stove was roaring. She made tea, poured a finger of Megan's brandy into it even though she rarely drank, sat in the rocker and waited by the dying coals for her lover to return.

Life seemed to settle into an almost familiar and therefore comforting routine for the remaining week of September. Carole had not spoken to Megan about the cars stopping. She tried to will herself into sleep each night without knowing or caring if they returned, although she was sure they had come by at least twice more. She'd taken to switching on lights, just after dusk, in both bedrooms, turning out the ones in the spare room right before climbing into their own bed.

Her writing was doing well enough. She had finished three poems, a sequence about a walk along the tide line, about what the ocean threw up, unexpected gifts, worthless trash. She felt pleased, planned to type fresh copies and mail them out to a small journal she hoped would take them.

The weekly shopping was still done at the supermarket. When she desperately needed something, Carole would swallow her pride and march into Bailey's. Having given up all attempts to engage the green-toothed girl in conversation, she'd just pay whatever was asked for what she bought, pocket her change without counting it.

She tried falling back on her social theories—what low incomes these people had and how few opportunities to better themselves— to justify the cheating that was going on. It's a small donation to help them out, she told herself. I can afford it. Years of practice had developed Carole's ability to rationalize.

She found herself remembering the times the gay rights group at D.O.B. had failed and the self hatred she'd felt. She had been a coward then. Now, slinking out of the store each time, she felt a coward again.

Megan bitched a lot about her job. "They keep asking me questions about why I came up here, about if I have a boyfriend back in Boston. They want to know all about you. At least, in the city, half the nurses were gay and the other half didn't care." She loved the new cable stations though, and developed elaborate rituals of taping movies at all hours—using the advance timer—to add to her collection, which she painstakingly labelled and filed on the landlady's empty shelves according to major stars—Gable, Davis, Bogart.

There was no more love-making, but Carole told herself that Megan was tired from working. There were lots fewer technological amenities at this hospital and a very short staff. Megan had to do things she had never done in the city—lift people, do bed baths, change linens.

And then, on Saturday, two things happened. Years later, Carole was to mark all of her life different from that day forward. Megan was in an unaccustomed good mood because a superior had praised her at work for managing a belligerent patient; after rising late, she gave Carole a bear hug and suggested they go out to the beach that had become Carole's favorite—to beachcomb, to sit on the high rocks in what promised to be the last bit of warmth the season could possibly offer. After a makeshift picnic which included a bottle of cheap wine Megan had insisted on picking up, the two returned. Megan was eager to set the timer for *Key Largo* which was coming up at 2 P. M. They were horrified to find a broken window in the dining room. As Carole knelt to discover the cause of the breakage— a beer bottle lying on the oriental rug with a vile brown stain leaking from its mouth—Megan, who had run upstairs, not able to wait for the bathroom, let out a piercing shriek.

"My God, Megan, what is it?" Carole rushed, heart pounding against her ribs, to the foot of the stairs.

Megan, standing just inside the bedroom door, just kept on shrieking, like a stuck record. When Carole reached her side she saw what had terrified Megan so. On the bed, which had been empty before save for the neatly spread quilt, lay one of her bras and two pairs of bikini underpants. The dresser drawer in which they had been stored was no longer tightly closed, but stuck out an inch or so.

"I am not leaving. They are not going to force me out." Over and over, Carole chanted to herself. Sick to death of feeling the victim, she willed courage to flood into her veins as she rocked violently back and forth in the bentwood rocker by the woodstove.

Megan was pacing the dining room with a glass of brandy in hand. Every light in the whole house was blazing against the deep moonless night, a symbol of Carole's defiance. She said to Megan, "There's a gay rights group in Portland. I remember contacting them back when I was going to do political stuff with D. O. B. I've got that newsletter from them I picked up in that bookstore last summer when we took the trip up. I saved it in my papers. I'm going to dig it out and call them tomorrow."

"It won't do any good. What do we do now? Wait for them to come and rape us?"

"No." Carole kept staring into the fire. "We just have to lock the door from now on. Breaking and entering is an offense. We have our rights. Leaving the door unlocked just because all the locals do it is a sure-fire invitation. Newcomers and outsiders always get harassed in small towns, at first. Anyway, they're just testing us." Carole felt the high flair of her anger begin to subside, the familiar excuses come flooding back in.

"You know it's Bud who came in after the underwear. I saw him leering at me when he drove past the other day."

"He's a pervert. He's got a problem. We don't need to deal with him again."

"And the cars? The beer bottle?"

"Kids. Drunks. Out for a joy ride."

That was what the sheriff had said when they'd rushed to his office right after the incidents. He'd looked at them over the rims of his pushed-down bifocals, not bothering to raise his substantial bulk from the chair in which he had been leaning back, reading a magazine, when they had entered his office. His breath had smelt of beer. His eyes had undressed them. The slowness with which he spoke, the way he finally whipped the glasses off, began to polish them with a filthy bandanna, the way he'd pulled the magazine, something with football players on the cover and nude women in the ads on the back, closer as a dismissal, told them he was going to do nothing.

"Listen, Megan...." Carole felt confused inside. Torn between her dying anger and her rising despair, she found herself turning to face her lover who had gone to the sideboard for a refill on her brandy, "Maybe if you'd try to get to know people here a little better, warm up more—I had nice talk with Mrs. Joyce up the hill. Her son was killed in Vietnam."

Carole had finally gotten up her nerve to speak to a few people after her failures in Bailey's. Impatient with poems about the seashore—although she'd sent her sequence off—she'd thought to elicit stories from the locals and try some local narratives. "...And Mr. Haskell, the one who builds model ships in that little hut down on the corner of Church and Seawall. He talked to me, too, told me how they really get a ship inside the bottle." Carole glossed over that converation which had been mostly monosyllables, although it had taken place. Mrs. Joyce was so lonely and full of grief long held in she'd speak to anyone, even a town pariah. Still....

"You're so cold and superior," Carole couldn't stop herself from barreling on, despite the wounded-puppy look that sprang to her lover's eyes. Carole felt so hurt by the toppling of all her lovely dreams—so let down with her own habitual failure of nerve—that all she could do was hurt in return. "No wonder they don't like us."

Megan rallied a bit, her gaze hardening. She strode over to Carole, hunkered down, her face inches from Carole's. "Listen Carole, this is not my fault. Got that? Who the fuck do you think I am? What do you think you're trying to pull? I never felt good about this, I never wanted to come here. You think I *like* emptying filthy bedpans full of diarrhea and giving enemas just so Ms. Shakespeare here can fritter her lovely little life away pretending to be somebody great?"

"Please, Megan," Carole had burst into tears, her first since the afternoon. "This is just what they want, for us to turn on each other so we'll have to leave. If all the gays who ever get persecuted just turn tail and run, then we don't get to exist at all! Don't you see?" It seemed as if Carole could feel the embers of her anger stir. The thought flickered across her consciousness that whatever it was that she feared so much could not be worse than this perpetual wavering, this continual not fighting for herself and what she loved.

Megan stayed put, silent, impassive, not pulling her hands away, not really grasping Carole's either.

"Let's go up to bed."

They mounted the stairs, undressed to one candle, crawled in under the Hudson's Bays, and clung to each other, not sleeping, till dawn streaked the sky the colors of a bruise.

The next day Carole took a long cold walk on her special beach during which she pushed herself to retrieve and solidify her flickerings of strength of the night before. The conviction to fight, she was surprised and gratified to realize, had not actually deserted her this time; her nerves seemed steady, something to count on. When she returned to the house, she sat down and wrote to the gay rights group, after failing to find any kind of listed number.

"Please help us," she wrote. "Please be in touch as soon as possible." Never before in her lesbian life had she felt so keenly the lack of community, something she had always taken for granted since she had come out in Boston—a place where women's dances, bars (not that she frequented them), bookstores, concerts, theatre productions and services like counseling collectives and law firms abounded. Because she was a public school teacher of fourteen-year-olds, she had had to be closeted—at least until 3:30 P.M. every day. After 3:30—though never flamboyant—she just didn't think about it.

Their apartment in a two-family house—shared with a young cohabiting heterosexual couple who belonged to a food co-op, Greenpeace and several Central American support groups—felt safe even though she had never come out to their neighbors in so many words.

Megan's work was anonymous enough with, as she had said, both gay staff and those who were indifferent. Their friends—although increasingly Megan would complain that she didn't like the people Carole brought around, preferring instead to sit in front of the TV—were mostly from D. O. B. The few straight friends they had were Carole's from college. They all knew and felt fine about it. Other than Angie and Jan, Megan had no friends of her own. Her family she saw only at Easter and Christmas; they were outraged, of course, but had long since given up hopes of changing her.

Here, now, with just the two of them and absolutely no recourse, Carole realized what it was to be truly afraid. Her former zeal for political action she saw as an almost laughable attempt to one up her mother; see *I* can do social change work too, but for real, not just tea-party play. Now she knew, in her bones where the fear really lived, just how vital that kind of organizing was—not to put a feather in anyone's cap, but simply to save lives.

One afternoon, soon after, as she was walking on her special strip of beach without at glance at what treasures were underfoot to be scooped up to sit on her windowsill or desk, the thought came to her that perhaps they *should* go back. They'd lose their seven-hundred and fifty dollar deposit on the house. She would have wasted the portion of her stipend already spent on rent, and the citizens of this village would know that women on their own, "queer women," were easily dealt with.

"No," she said to herself, then again, aloud, "NO," and kicked a piece of driftwood into the steadily encroaching waves. (Much later in her life, this moment in which she had said no, in stark contrast to the one in which they'd first rushed trembling through their violated house, seemed to mark the time from which she would really begin to live.)

A new offensive was mounted. All doors and windows were kept tightly locked. Carole took to going in and out the big oaken front door which had a double lock although the landlady had said she never used it. She would prop a kitchen chair under the back door handle each time before leaving. Once she did find it kicked over, although there were no signs of actual entry. Just a draft from the windows that leak, she told herself. A storm had been brewing that day and the gusts were strong. Or maybe I didn't prop it up sturdily enough, she told herself. All the lights blazed at night in every room. No lights were turned off in the two upstairs bedrooms until Carole, always the last one to go to sleep, turned out the bedside lamp. No more trips to Bailey's, no matter what. If they ran out of something, they'd just have to wait till Saturday. Megan took to bringing home a quart of milk from town every other day without prompting.

When the sheriff stopped by the back door one morning to ask how things were going, obviously trying to get himself invited in, Carole was cold and abrupt. "I'm working," she said, and sent him on his way.

The cars were stopping outside every night now—always two, one time even three, one a Jeep Cherokee. The yard became littered with tossed bottles, cigarette butts, and crumpled empty Frito bags. Carole would clean it all up carefully each afternoon before Megan returned. She'd will herself not to think, not to feel, as she threw the trash into plastic bags which she stuffed into the metal cans by the end of the drive. She and Megan discussed calling the state police while the cars were outside. They'd decided that could put them at greater risk. The troopers would arrive; the boys would deny everything yet perhaps come back later in the night, enraged, and go after them. No, better to stand firm and show the boys that they refused to be intimidated.

Every day she checked the mail for a letter from the gay rights organization, praying that, when it came, it would be in a discreet envelope. When she finally got something, it was cursory, naming several organizations she already knew of, all in Boston.

The cars began stopping, then, in the daytime about three in the afternoon—only briefly each time, but long enough to feel like a menace, enough to tell Carole that they weren't just pausing for the stop sign. It was always the battered heap with an ugly rust spot on the side and eaten-away wheel wells, another heap not much different, and the Jeep Cherokee which was new—sitting on souped-up wheels with a pair of fabric dice dangling from the rear-view mirror.

Inside, she could always see three or four boys ranging in age anywhere from their late teens to their early twenties. She tried to ignore it all each time—tried to keep her mind on her work which was progressing either slowly or not at all.

One Saturday early evening while a thrown-together stew was simmering on the stove, Carole ventured out for a head-clearing walk. Dark as it was, she could at least take in the sea air; the day had been unseasonably mild. As she passed the small, weathered wooden church in the village, she was surprised to see the place brilliantly lit. Figures she recognized, Mrs. Joyce, the old man who built the ship models, others she'd seen in Bailey's or out in their yards raking leaves, were hovering around the lit doorway, bundled into winter coats with covered dishes in their hands. Laughter and the rise and fall of voices punctuated the soft damp dark. One bundled figure slapped another on the back. Two women touched cheeks in greeting. Several scruffy children hurled pieces of driftwood at each other, shrieking, as they played a kind of tag around the building. It must be a church supper, just the kind of event Carole had once imagined she and Megan would be invited to with warm welcomes, fed New England brown bread and baked beans and regaled with stories of ships and the sea which she would put into her poems. It shocked her a bit now to see the people who had so relentlessly shunned her acting human—even warm. Then the last arrival hastened up the steps and inside; the heavy door, beyond which could be seen bright lights and a flash of color from the Christmas decorations, swung firmly shut. Carole hastened home to scorched stew, a fire burnt too low, and a grumpy Megan glued to the tube.

Megan had, in fact, retreated now into a frosty silence. She'd started smoking again, something she'd given up a year earlier in Boston after a severe cancer lecture from a young intern at the hospital. She'd sit in front of her VCR, hour upon hour, not speaking. In bed, her back was always turned. Megan was having no trouble sleeping since her pre-bed cigarettes were always accompanied now by brandy.

Lying there sleepless next to Megan, waiting for the late night run by the boys, after which the yard would be littered, Carole found herself drifting back to her childhood. The images that came most often to her were of herself waiting, waiting in her own room, nicely furnished, with a little white wooden bookshelf full of classics— *Black Beauty, The Little Princess, The Secret Garden, Jo's Boys*— listening to the rise and fall of her parents' voices down the hall, as they prepared for a faculty dinner or a concert or evening lecture.

The two of them always stopped on their way out, to say goodnight, bowing almost formally to their child in their evening clothes. The live-in housekeeper was ostensibly the babysitter, but she always sat in her own little bed-sitting room with the radio on, the door closed all but an inch. Carole tried to reach for what she must have been feeling then. As now, feelings seemed elusive. All she could remember was a stubborn will that held, like a seawall, against her emotions.

She'd tried, these sleepless nights, too, to understand how Megan was feeling, what her needs could be, so that Carole might meet them. Megan's job had gone from bad to worse. Although closemouthed about it, Megan alluded to the fact that the harassment and innuendoes had stepped up at work. Carole wondered if some of the boys weren't related to hospital personnel. There were only four basic extended families on the island. Everyone, eventually, was related to everyone else, and gossip was the life-blood.

She knew this from Mrs. Joyce, who was the only one who passed the time of day with her, throwing a few tidbits before drawing Carole into her pathetic sitting room to see more pictures of Bobby in his uniform, as well as, once again, the framed letter from his commanding officer, telling his mother how Bobby had died on a landmine in glory.

She'd try sometimes, before a fitful slumber would finally claim her in the pre-dawn hour, to touch Megan's shoulder, to feel warm flesh, the pulse of blood deep underneath. She'd try to conjure up images of their former happiness, the day on the whale watch, the mess of scrambled eggs they'd devoured sitting on Carole's living room floor the morning after they'd first slept together, even that last picnic on the beach a few weeks ago. At these moments Carole felt the most lonely.

How like islands all of us are, she thought, each to one another. How near by—even side by side—we lie, yet all the oceans in the world sweep between us. There is no bridge.

Finally, after trying to work after the cars pulled up at 3 P.M., Carole pulled on the high rubber clam boots she'd paid an extorted price for trying to look like a native, shrugged on her parka, and stormed out to the edge of the yard. She waved her arms, a gesture of bravado she did not feel. In reality cold terror lodged in the pit of her stomach. A window was rolled down. A young male face, pimply, greasy-haired, with the same sallow, closed, islander look, peered out, grinning broadly. Thank God, this one had teeth, though they were yellow—from nicotine, she presumed. He chucked a butt into the yard.

Stupidly, Carole seized on that. "Don't throw butts in my yard!"

"Sorry, lady." He kept grinning, made no move to gun the motor. Two boys actually got out of the other vehicle—the jeep was not there today—and leaned against the side, one with a hand in his lumberjacket pocket and a cigarette hanging from his lips; the other held a beer in his hand. They looked her over thoroughly, nudging each other and grinned.

"What do you boys want?" she said in her best school-teacher voice, choosing the word "boy" deliberately. "Don't tell me you aren't the ones who stop here every day—every night, too. I see you. I know all about it. You've been reported to the sheriff, you know." She plunged on knowing that was foolish but having no other response to their silence and their leers.

"Don't want nothin', lady." They laughed raucously. "Where's your girlfriend? Huh?" "Why don't you go back to the city?" The one with the meanest face spat out. "We don't want your kind here."

"What kind? I'm a person, just like you. And we're NOT leaving!" Carole spun on her heel, strode back to the house. She locked the door and leaned against it, breathing hard. The cars didn't roar off for another ten minutes, leaving behind more empty bottles and crumpled bags for the yard.

That Saturday, while they were out, another window was broken, this time with a rock. The embers of Carole's anger flared again. "Enough," she said and called Megan to put her coat on.

Carole and Megan drove in the Rabbit the thirty-five miles to the State Police headquarters just off the island on the other side of the causeway. It was a tiny office, not worthy of being called a barracks. A young officer, his face red with the rash of too close a shave, greeted them. He was neither warm nor friendly, yet more attentive than the repugnant sheriff. He took notes as they spoke.

"Has anyone actually threatened either of you? I mean, by bodily harm, made explicit threats? Has anyone put a hand on you?"

"Well...no," they had to confess.

"But we're scared...." Megan implored, with a pathetic look.

Stop whining, Megan. It'll only hurt our case, Carole was screaming inside, although she didn't dare speak out loud.

"Listen, girls..." the officer went on. Carole winced. He seemed unconscious of his word choice. "...about the...uh, undergarments...uh...when people are in a hurry, to go out to work, or whatever, sometimes they forget things. Don't you think maybe you just left those things out and forgot that you had?" His voice strained to be persuasive. He wants no part of this, Carole realized, with a familiar sinking thud.

"No, officer," her voice was crisp. "I'm positive. I don't forget things like that."

"Let's go over this again. It was *your* room the things were left out in; they were *your* things...."

"Ye-es," Carole stammered, her hand ever so slightly on Megan's sleeve to make sure her lover kept silent. She had told Bud that the other room was hers. What if they questioned him? It seemed so unlikely she decided not to try to switch her story. Besides, they could always say they had changed rooms. "Girls" always did that sort of silly thing.

"And Bud Evans was alone with you in the house for several hours while he fixed the TV antenna?"

"Well...yes...what of it?"

"You're an attractive girl, miss, and single. Up here alone." The implications of his words hovered in the air like the stench of something rotting. All Carole could think of was his word "alone." The presence of another female in the house was invisible to him.

She and Megan left right after that, fighting bitterly all the way home with Megan urging Carole to decide that they could both move back to Boston. "But my stipend won't last with the rent we have to pay there. I probably couldn't get anything but subbing until next fall. Besides we'd have to get a new place. We gave the sub-letters a year. You know that."

"I'll get a weekend private duty job, too." Megan spoke wildly. "I'll make up the difference." This seemed highly unlikely, as Megan hated to work, had all too easily malingered after a muscle pull on the job, letting Carole support her for nine months their second year together when she could have gone back after three weeks.

As they pulled into the driveway to find more garbage in the yard including the decaying body of a dead seagull, Carole had had enough. "All right, all right. You go. I'm staying," she screamed and stormed out of the car, slamming the door, and into the house. She flung herself onto the bed, sobbing till her whole body shook. These outbursts came to her rarely and only after a build-up of weeks of strain.

When she came down much later—hair combed severely back, swollen face washed—she found that Megan, who could not cook, had managed a makeshift supper, canned soup and cheese sand-wiches. She'd built a fire with too much newspaper, which was dy-ing down quickly in the woodstove.

"When will you be leaving?" Carole said levelly. "I need to know. I'll have to find some kind of work. I assume you'll let me keep the car since I made the downpayment and most of the insurance and monthly payments. I'll reimburse you later on for what you did pay. I won't be able to give back your half of the house deposit for awhile, either."

Megan said nothing, just got up to get the mustard. She did not mention leaving again. She fell asleep the next few nights on the couch in front of the TV without ever coming to bed. The two barely spoke or interacted at all as the next week began.

When Bud Evans came to the door the following Wednesday, Ca-role was not suprised. She'd started a series of narrative poems about the island natives—Mrs. Joyce, the girl in Bailey's, the old man who made ship models. The work felt clumsy; it was a form she was unpracticed in, yet it seemed important somehow that she salvage something of their stay here—that she give herself a reason for their refusal to leave.

"What do you want?" she said coldy. The tea kettle was whistling inside; she'd been taking a break. She reached over to snap off the gas, returned to the door, which she opened only narrowly, leaving him no room to imagine an invitation. The fact that he could easily overpower her, that the law was that vile sheriff who sat like a slug behind his desk, she tried not to admit to herself.

"Just to see how you're gettin' along." His smile was hideous.

"Just fine. Now, if you'll excuse me, I need to get back to work."

"Some of the boys told me you hollered at 'em the other day."

"What do you mean? They stop here all the time, late at night, throwing beer cans and garbage in our yard. We've had two broken windows...." Her face began to flush; she could hear the rising out-rage in her voice.

"We-ell," his drawl was slow and deliberate. His eyes had never stopped travelling her body. "Not much excitement up here, 'specially with winter comin' on. You kin hardly blame the boys. Lot of the girls leave here soon as they can. Easier for them to get work, offices in Bangor, or up to Bar Harbor in some of the resort hotels.

These boys see nice girls like you and your friend up here without no men—well, they get these ideas, you know. We do get the TV out here. They hear about things they think go on in the city. They put two an' two together...."

"I don't know what you're talking about. I really have to go now."

"Listen, how 'bout goin' on out with me Friday? A few beers down the road at Johnnie's? Or if you like, we could drive into Bangor. There's a real nice steak house there."

"No, thank you."

"Okay, okay. Catch you later." His smile was broad and knowing. He kept looking at her over his shoulder as he loped to his truck. Carole willed herself to stand straight, unflinching, in the doorway, until he was long gone down the road.

The end, when it came, was swift and merciless, in much the same way that Carole imagined Mrs. Joyce's Bobby must have met the landmine that had ripped into his tender belly as he set out innocently enough over that rice paddy.

In the morning mail came two items. The first was from the gay group in Portland which had sent out an emergency mailing informing all on their list of the tragedy that had happened only twenty-four hours before in Bangor. A young gay man had been thrown over a bridge to his death, despite his protests that he couldn't swim, by a group of toughs; the crime was supposed to have been fueled by hatred of gays. The flyer implored everyone to write their Congressmen, call their local officials, write to the newspapers, donate money. The other item was the rejection slip that accompanied the now dog-eared copies of Carole's poems, returned by the journal she'd sent them to. "We've seen this type of simple nature poem a thousand times—try something fresh, with a sense of specificity and life," was scrawled on the bottom of the printed form.

An hour later Megan whirled in, with both a liquor store bag and a plastic video tote in her arms. "Look at this!" She thrust at Carole a piece of paper crudely scrawled with red magic marker, "Lezzie, go home!" "Look what was on my windshield in the parking lot at work!" She seemed as angry at Carole as if Carole had planted the note. "What's *this?*" She scooped up the sheets from the gay center which lay on the kitchen table. Carole had planned to burn them in the stove before her arrival.

Carole had expected further hysterics from Megan after she had seen the write-up on the murder. When that didn't happen, when Megan simply put her brandy away, stacked her movies neatly on top of the TV, went silently upstairs to run bathwater as hard as she could, Carole felt cold dread seep all through her body.

She went through the motions of making a supper that Megan refused to come down for. Carole sat with her own dinner in front of the woodstove which she tried to stoke half-heartedly every time the flames burned low.

Finally, as the evening slid by, she wrapped up the untouched food, and continued to sit, waiting. She heard Megan's voice, low, upstairs on the extension phone, for what seemed like a long time. Once the fire was finally out, stone cold, no coals, and the cars outside come and gone for their nightly visit, Carole took an afghan and slept in her clothes on the couch in the den, or, rather, did not sleep, just stared out of the picture window until a faint dawn streaked the shrouded December sky.

Early, very early, she heard Megan make three more calls, didn't even turn and look as she heard her lover descend the stairs and go back up several times accompanied by bumps and thumps as if she were dragging heavy items down with her. When Carole got up to stand by the door with an afghan wrapped around her while Megan shrugged into her coat—the two bulging suitcases, a duffle, and a straw tote bag beside her—she had no words, no pleas, no arguments. Outside, she could hear, all the way from the harbor, the waves hit the seawall as a bad storm started to rise.

"I'm taking a taxi to the Trailways station. It'll be here in a minute. You can keep the car. Please ship me back my VCR and the rest of my stuff. I'll reimburse you for the costs. Here's the address. I'll be at my sister's." She thrust a piece of paper at Carole.

"But your job...."

"I just resigned, over the phone."

"But...your sister's? Which one?"

"Mary Catherine...in Rochester. There's a big university hospital there. I'll be there by midnight if I get the eight-thirty bus and change in Boston. Listen, Carole...I'm sorry, but...well, you know, except for Pam at school, which only lasted a couple of months, this was the first thing like this I ever tried, really. I mean, with women. How do I know I'm really like that?"

A horn blasted rudely outside.

"That's it. 'Bye. Listen, there's six dollars up on the dresser. Return my movies, will you?" And she was gone.

All Carole could think, as she climbed the stairs numbly to dress and to start packing, herself, was, But, Megan, you hate Mary Catherine!

Two days later, as she drove the causeway, Carole felt the bridge once again underneath her begin to lift. All around her stretched the vast expanse of ocean and sky, one bleeding into the other, no clear horizon, a flat, cold gray with no luminosity behind it. As the car rose, it seemed to her that she and it could just keep on moving, up and up and never come back.

Keys

Roads and then the ends of them seem all that there is or can be. I've been driving now almost non-stop just pulling off to sleep a few hours before dawn in rest areas, for more days than I can count.

I've come through the Ozarks, the highest place I've hit on all the long slide of the land down, down to this remote promontory, this fragile necklace of broken coral beads they call The Keys. Keys—I wonder to what? For me—another lock that refuses to open?

The journey has been one of increasing heat and suffocating air, from the mountains where all the concern is with God—even in the cafeterias, gospel hymns accompany your grits and eggs—down to this godless flatland where sky and ocean can barely be distinguished.

Route One. Here begins one of the longest roads in the U.S. If I turned around and kept driving, one day I'd see the tall pines and rocky coast of Maine. The road is a narrow ribbon. It takes all my concentration to avoid splaying right off of into depths I can't imagine, to disappear into a horizon which at noon lies suffused with haze, but at sunset looms with more color than the eye can bear.

Then the night comes down hard, the lack of light as suffocating as the air that seems far too wet for the lungs to absorb.

I lie in my little room in the guest house during the afternoon siesta. The kindly landlady calls it that, showing me how to use the heavy wooden shutters, hinged at the top, that come down, leaving only a gap for air and none for the cruel sun. I lie there until it's time for the cooler evening and the prowl. Everyone in Key West prowls: scams, drugs, sex, whatever will let the flesh later lie down and be still.

I try to remember why I'm running, what I've run from, and if there's anything left to run to. None of it seems to make sense. I had another life once in which I was somebody else; somebody with sinews, bones, nerve endings, blood pumping. This other self was capable of feeling—rage, pain. That's why I left her. That much I do remember.

As I follow the low tideline on the narrow, littered beach just past the relentless waves, I tell myself this story over and over like a child would, trying to fix the details in my mind:

Once there was a woman. She lived on a street in a city up north in an apartment in an old house, full of nooks and crannies and built-in shelves. Once she'd had photographs all over her wall that she had taken herself.

One day for no reason they made her angry; she began to rip them down one by one. The shelves she'd promised to fill with books remained empty.

Once, each day, she went to a job. It was in a high shiny building full of windows. She sat at a desk. Many people bustled about, talking, talking. She did something important with shuffling papers. The woman had some friends, even—once or twice—a lover.

As time went by she didn't want them around. Often she sat and let the phone ring over and over.

She had a mother and a few aunts and uncles and cousins somewhere far off in a place full of tall corn and weathered barns. She didn't call them or send Christmas cards. Why this was she couldn't remember.

At a friend's urging, she sought out a group, at a center, a place where people were supposed to be able to tell you why you woke up every morning angry, why you tore up things you used to love.

And, one day, she did remember—something.

Something that came out of a dark hallway at night, the only light far off and small like her body on the bed...something with tobacco breath and raspy edges...something with skin needing a razor...something with hands that hurt, hands that covered her so that breath could not come. She remembered.

I begin to run then, down the filthy sand, tripping over crushed beer cans, over tangled clumps of stinking seaweed, past a pack of scrawny kids playing war with sticks, past rusted campers where singing, jeering, ragged people pass beer cans before small fires.

I don't think, don't feel, till much, much later, deep in the fitful night when the drone of the landlady's small fan wakes me—the one she's pressed on me because I look so pale, she says, so ill, from the heat, not knowing that breathing well is something I have almost never done.

I can see my dream, vivid as the sunsets; myself cramming things into a suitcase, driving to the bank, taking out all I have, writing my boss a letter—"Emergency—it's an emergency." Walking out of the tall shiny building. Unplugging the phone in the apartment so that it will stop ringing. The ringing still echoing as I pull out of the driveway, head for the highway, drive on into the falling darkness.

Now the shops on Duval are shabby, garish. People saunter. I see tattoos, kids, hair orange or blue, wild spikes jutting up from their scalps, weathered, wizened street men who've spent lifetimes on small boats now claiming small alleyways, old women who mutter as they push shopping carts full of tattered rags and bags. I join them.

When I see the shell—pearlescent, creamy, fluted, whorled—I stop, riveted. I can't move. I try to will not thinking, not feeling. That's how I want to be, that's why I've been running.

It doesn't work.

The shell. The room at the center where Claudia held the group. A circle of faces, luminous as the moon. The shell on her desk to the side of the ring of colorful pillows. I used to stare at the shell again and again, fixing something in my mind like an anchor that would keep me from sinking deep into an ocean of pain. Her voice. I can still hear it.

"Selene—it means the moon. My mother named me that," I tell them. I can hear my own voice so far away, as if from down a tunnel. "She told me she'd read about it in a book. She liked to read books.

"Your mother?" Claudia would repeat my words softly.

"Yes. She always read books, from the bookmobile. It came on Tuesdays. She always got up out of bed for that on Tuesdays. Don't call me Selene—my name is Sally."

I find myself in the shop, clenching the shell so hard that bright red points form on my hand. I realize, what anchors me now is the pain. I feel real. I want to see blood.

"Miss—miss, would you like this shell? Six ninety-five—a special today."

I drop it. I move down the street fast, melting anonymous into the jostling crowd, the crowd with beer on its breath, cocaine on its mind, the crowd of people cheating death. I embrace them.

Next day I give the sweet landlady her money. She tries to convince me to stay. "You don't look well, dear. Can I call somebody for you? Your family?"

"No—there's no one, no family." No one. For years in school, when we got to that part about our father's name on all the forms, I made up a name from one of the Tuesday books—Roderick Hawthorne. He had a curling moustache and shiny boots and rode a horse. He's in the army, I'd say. He works overseas for the government. Yes, for something important, something secret. He sends me secret messages. Someday he'll be back, a hero. Someday he'll be back and take me away from her, the unwashed stinking clothes, the clutter of little plastic containers stuck all over with doctors' labels spilling all over the pile of books.

I decide to drive then, away from this small city on the edge, away from the Margaret Truman launderette, the lime green fire hydrants, the cemetery where the clattering skeletons lie each upon each in their narrow white boxes stacked above ground to save space—there will always be bodies, more and more; we must save space—to remain safe in case of rising waters.

I take the ribbon road again, this time in the opposite direction. Here in the Keys there is only one way in, one way out. I don't like that feeling—yet I know it well.

The bridges up ahead seem to heave and sway in the heat haze.

Big Pine Key. The name on the map sounds cool and sweet, a place to hide, a shelter. What I find instead is more of the same, what I saw coming down, what I tried my best to outrun until I came to the very end of where I could go. On both sides of the road one continuous shopping mall grows like a malignancy—dive shops, bait shops, fish joints, motels with plaster pink flamingos, each with a sign more garish than the last; promises, promises, each and every one with signs promising what they surely can't in truth deliver, but which you must believe you can't live without.

Just past the Winn Dixie Supermarket, largest on the Keys, a place I've learned has the coldest air conditioning in the world, a place where in two seconds your skin is blue and your teeth are rattling in your head—it's as good as any drug; no one can think or feel who is this cold—is a small blue sign: Refuge of the Key Deer.

I stop and read: *A relative of the virginia white tail deer, the key deer stand only 2 1/2 feet tall and weigh less than 75 lbs. Fawns weigh 2—4 lbs. At birth and their tiny hoofprint is the size of a thumbnail. It is a crime to hunt or hurt these deer in any way.*

I follow the sign to the parking lot and let myself slip into the landscape that springs up so close to the asphalt and the exhaust it's hard to believe. Palmetto scrub hunkers close to the ground, tall pines stretch on spindly bare trunks up to where next to the sky their feathery boughs fan out. Overhead, ospreys with wingspans as big as a man's outstretched arms wheel and dip, leaving shadows like inkblots over the forest floor.

The trailside abounds with exotic species, pigeon plum, poisonwood, silver palms and the gumbo limbo, big trees with bright orange peeling bark, "the tourist tree" because it looks like sunburn. A little brochure I take from a box on a post tells me all this. My heart, I think, feels like the gumbo limbo—raw, layer after layer shredding away.

I walk further and further back, veer off the gravelled trail into the forest until I reach the hammock.

A hardwood island in the midst of the scrubs and pines. Just a few more feet above sea level and everything changes.

Other kinds of growth become possible; species can live here—
sheltered, encouraged—that only a few feet away would die. Feathery bromeliads catch the sun in the treetops, a few of them flaming
purple or red at the tips. I want to reach up to touch. I wonder, if
the sharp edges cut me, would I bleed? I find that I am looking for
hoofprints the size of a thumbnail.

"And your father?" I hear Claudia's voice. The faces of the wom-
en in the circle blur into nothing. All I see is the creamy inside of the
shell, the muted pinks and browns. I remember swallowing hard,
nausea sour in the pit of my stomach. "He left. I was three or four—I
don't remember. My mother wouldn't tell me." But I do remember—
the hurting hands, the scratchy skin, the foul breath.... "I don't want
to talk about it."

There's a rustle in the undergrowth. Suddenly ahead of me starts
up a spirit of light and air. Huge ears, tender, scooped out like delicate blossoms or a shell, eyes so big and deep I could drown in their
centers, long spindly legs, fragile as glass, then the white fluff of dismissal, a tail disappearing into the scrub.

Back on the highway, I have to pull over. The Chamber of Com-
merce sign by the refuge has stated: *Approaching refuge of the key
deer. Endangered species. There are 250 key deer. Twelve were killed
by careless motorists in the last year.* I can hear the little leg bones
snap. I can see the blood spilled onto the white fluffy tail. The eyes I
know well, as they stare, open but lifeless. I have lived with those
eyes. After a long time I drive on.

The little motel on a rutted road out of sight of the highway—
funky rayon bedspreads, a vile kind of mustard yellow, a ceramic
lamp in the shape of a leaping marlin, the eye of the big TV domi-
nating the small whitewashed room—seems to take me in. Here under the shade of Royal Palms bigger than any I've seen so far, I feel I
will be able to sleep.

Another landlady, kindly as well, chattering on nonstop about
her son who helps her and how he's supposed to fly back late tonight in the seaplane he uses for his cargo business. She explains to

me that there are 70 palm trees here on this spit. I imagine her walking amongst them, counting. She's been here 30 years. Many of her guests are regulars. I was lucky to find a cancellation, an empty room. They like to come back each year and take her out to dinner up on Hawks Cay or one of the other fancier places. She has to go now to set her hair. Some of these very people are coming tonight to fetch her.

I go to the dock, wandering in the day's last light, wishing I had a place to stay in for 30 years, people to come back for me, to ask me out again and again.

"You run from us," the circle of women is chanting, all in unison while Claudia nods. My mother used to nod, too, but differently, nodding as she dozed, in the afternoon when the soaps were on, for which she'd put down her book. "You run from me," she'd say. "Stay, stay. I need you."

"You need us," the group would say over and over. I don't, I don't. I'm leaving, I told my mother, I told them. I'll tell them, I tell them all.

The landlady is stepping out now into the pool of light by the door of her apartment. She's natty in a flowered dress and a big hat. A middle-aged couple are by her side, resplendent in summer whites. Her son is there, shaven and pressed. They wave and wave. I turn away.

I don't need you. I don't need. I don't need.

I wander by the water's edge for what seems a long time, a time out of time. Sunset here falls swiftly once the sun's blazing orb hits the horizon, yet I float in this pre-twilight endless as in a dream. I am not sure where I am, who I am. I don't feel—yet not feeling is different from before. It is more like the split-second before really taking a breath. Anything seems possible.

Slowly a huge white bird with a wing span as long as my body floats over the shimmering water awash with colors of deepening nightfall—burnished gold, garnet, starshine. The wings of this bird embrace the fragrant air, drift in its silent descent so close I almost

imagine myself enfolded in their embrace—a feeling that I imagine
as so full of peace and utter relief that I could not bear it.

The bird's long graceful neck, slender beak, delicate legs and
feet, wheel past me, gently, so gently like the breath of a loved one
beside you in the night—something I don't remember either, unless
it was in a land where this bird lives, where maybe once before this
world of garbage and dead bloody deer on the road I had a place.

This night I sleep, deeply, no dreams. In the morning, so early
that the sunrise still flushes the edge of the mangrove swamps, I
walk the clean strip of sand, picking up tiny, tiny shells in my palms
and letting them go again in water clear as the night sky in winter. I
do not this morning know my name or where I have come from. I
do not remember the driving, the running. What is different is that I
do know I am here. The sand burns under my soles as the sun
climbs the sky.

"I think you'll love this boat trip, dear," the landlady urges me,
thrusting a tourist brochure into my hand. It's from the state park, a
trip out to a small key just offshore. *Lignumvitae*...the long cumber-
some Latin syllables soothe me somehow. I agree to go. She even
calls for me to make the reservation.

Like looking down the wrong end of a telescope, I remember
that back in the place where I had the apartment and the office in
the shiny building that I would have refused to let her do it, would
have done it all myself. Now, I cradle my cache of small shells, the
ones I've been holding all day in my hand. I am thinking about dusk
again and waiting for the bird to float in and hold me.

She even packs me a lunch. My mouth opens to say no. Hot
tears scald my lids. "Thank you." I take it.

I remember Claudia and the light touch of her hand on my arm.
"I'm glad you're here in the group."

I ran the next week.

The parking lot by the boat landing is small and full now of vans
and cars. A motley crew of tourists lines up for the boat. At this
point I balk. All that humanity. I can smell the suntan oil. The light

glints off the lenses of their shades, camera lenses bug out from their bellies, the eyes of monsters. They're jabbering amongst themselves. I am the only one who came alone.

A barge-like boat pulls up, drab green with a flat roof and seats in rows across its deck. Two rangers in olive uniforms leap off and one begins to secure the boat by rope to a piling by the dock. I am surprised to see that one is a woman, older than myself, mid-forties maybe, tanned a rich brown, hair in a practical style, sun-streaked, wind tousled. Her shoes are sturdy, her hands capable as she manages the complicated knots, unlatches the gate for the tourists to board the boat. The steadiness of her voice calling out names pulls me. She calls out mine. She's got it on a clipboard, my reservation. My place is reserved. I belong.

She smiles at me. Sun wrinkles gather at the corners of her seawater eyes. I smile back. My face feels unused, stiff. I take my place beside a family whose bodies are bristling with equipment: cameras, field glasses, canteens. They reek of Coppertone and Cutters, but they smile at me, too. "Ever been here before?"

"No," I say. "No."

The boat trip takes only twenty minutes. In that time we're beyond the sense of shore and civilization. Our competent guide, whose name we learn is Mara, gives us a history of the place: a rich family owned but hardly used it, eventually it became a park, preserved, safe for all time. We arrive at the island and once again Mara ropes us to the dock. Before we start off on the nature trail she is to lead us down, we enter the caretaker's cottage, vintage 1930. It's cool and dimly lit with wide old-fashioned floorboards, a scrubbed plain kitchen with pottery jugs and crocks on simple shelves.

As the others are lining up, juggling cameras and notebooks, sun visors and more Coppertone, I linger behind, caught by a small bedroom just off the rangers' office. The bedroom's as plain as the kitchen, yet it feels special. The bedstead is white-painted iron, delicate in design; a white wicker chair nestles under the window; a plain dresser with a mirror above holds a small bottle of wild flowers; on a stand beside the bed, a ceramic pitcher with a tiny painted pink rose design sits in a washing bowl. Eyelet curtains screen the sun, yet billow like birds' wings in the breeze from the water. The white chenille spread with a small blue figured design worked in is pulled neat and tight. Plump pillows are tucked under its edge. Blue and white rag throw-rugs sit on the wide washed floorboards. I don't want to leave.

I have to run to catch up with the group. Mara's voice seems to draw me, though. She's pointing up across the shadow-flickered path where gold and green splash themselves as far as the eye can see down a twisting lane of leaves and vines and scrub to where the path curves out of sight. It's a web, a spider's web. Caught up in its own glistening strands sits the Golden Orb, she tells us. The spider does not repel me as I had feared. Instead, she fascinates. A hand's span across, bright yellow banded with black. The web is as strong as steel, strands used, Mara says, for periscopes in the submarines in World War II. I touch the resilient thread; it bounces beneath my finger, delicate yet unbreakable.

We continue to walk past gumbo limbo, poisonwood, a wall made completely out of shell and coral. No one knows where it came from, who built it or why it's here, Mara says. I touch the rough surfaces, make out whole whorled shells embedded in brain-like formations. I can understand the whimsy of this, what it must be like to have the luxury of building something simply because it feels good, not because a purpose must be served, someone must be impressed enough to write you up for history. As we file out onto a small spit much later, far down the trail where mangroves squat reclaiming land from the sea, Mara tells us, we see here what the Caloosa Indians, the native people, would have seen—exactly the same. This is virgin primeval forest.

I pull off a smooth-lobed glossy mangrove leaf. I touch it to my tongue as Mara has shown us. Salt. Salt crystals encrust its surface, how it lives so intimately with the sea. I know the taste. It's the same as my tears.

"Oh, group..." Mara is calling out softly, "...we've really got something special over here. Gather round." Obedient children, we do. She shows us, close to the bottom of a huge tree, stuck fast to the massive trunk, lies the delicate fluted shell of a living land snail;

one of the rare *lignumvitae* species, she explains. "Each key or set of keys has its own species, each with unique markings." This one is pink and lilac, soft as a baby's breath, the shell whorled into a point. The whole thing's smaller than the span of my palm.

"Usually these snails this time of year would be high, high up in the branches. You'd never see them. This one must've gotten a late start. It's got quite a climb to make. They die from lack of water if they don't get off on their journeys early enough. These snails are so rare because of illegal collectors. Some people in the past would strip a hammock of all its shells, then set the whole thing on fire to destroy the species, make their own catch more valuable." I take in what she's saying. Hot tears sting my lids. I reach out a finger to almost touch the fragile shell.

The trail winds on. The tall trees filter the sunlight. It's cool here and soothing beyond words. Mara keeps talking, pointing, gesturing. I have ceased to listen for the facts, the information a bespectacled kid with several lenses and leather cases strapped around her is scribbling in her school notebook.

I listen instead for the cadence, the rise and fall of such a voice, for the rhythms of someone who knows land like this intimately, who walks these paths every day. She's worked here ten years, she tells us, through hurricanes and monsoon season and times the boat was mired in weeds and wouldn't budge—someone who has a place of such harmony in which to be, who harms nothing, who comes to no harm. We reach a turn in the path. She stops us. "We're going to come around the corner," she's almost whispering with reverence, "to see the *lignumvitae* tree in bloom. We believe this particular tree is sixteen-hundred years old."

The tree—which I had expected to be enormous, a tropical sequoia or giant redwood—instead is small, gnarled, intricately poised on the far side of a still pool in which the brilliant blue of its tiny blossoms lie reflected, a mirror image of itself for roots.

"There's a lot of legend associated with the tree," Mara says, "Ancient scholars believed it existed in the Garden of Eden and that to consume it was to achieve perpetual health, immortality and protection from anxiety and weakness. The wood is so hard that it can't be burned. The ancients claimed it had been purified by fire." I stand gazing at the tree for a long time, wishing I could touch it. I realize I am not holding my breath.

As I walk slowly back down the path—the others are long gone ahead—I am aware that I can feel each foot as it thuds softly beneath me on the path. I can hear every bird, see every leaf and flower. Mara is waiting as the path emerges into the clearing by the caretaker's house. The others are crowding onto the dock, talking cheerily about what they've seen and where they've been, offering to snap photos of each other's groups, passing around gum and canteens.

"Are you okay? I just wanted to wait to make sure you got back here." It's Mara, come for me. I don't know how to feel. My elbows and knees suddenly seem huge and out of control. I swallow and breathe and resist the impulse to run, run back into that forest with the greens and the golds and the great mother spider and the tree that will keep you safe and give you eternal life.

Instead I stay put. Surprising myself, I turn toward Mara. "I'm here," I say. I look in her eyes. I imagine looking into Claudia's eyes, the eyes of all the women in the circle in the group. I imagine beginning to talk about what I must.

I imagine getting back into my car and taking the highway straight up out and over all those arching bridges, following that narrow ribbon until it merges with other wider ribbons, until it begins to enter familiar terrain—the roads and arteries around the city where my apartment still lies, closed and dusty.

I imagine entering the city where I can look for work that fills me, so that my eyes can look like Mara's, the city where I can begin to make myself a home that will feel like a white chenille bedspread tucked tight over plump pillows. A home like a china jug with painted pink roses, a dresser with bottles of wildflowers and pieces of driftwood and smooth pebbles in earth colors snatched from the waves, with one perfect fluted creamy pink-and-ivory shell resting in the center. A place with lots of whitewashed wooden shelves which I will fill with books, with walls I will fill once again with photographs of how I see the world.

A place in which I, like the tree snail, can begin the climb.

Bodies

The first day the suggestion box appears in the fitness center, I've got plenty to say. Of course I've always got plenty to say, but those square little pieces of paper and those little pencils, like my mother used to use for ladies' bridge club for keeping score, are just too great a temptation.

"How about the hot water?" I scrawl. "Sure would be nice to get some. In the shower, I mean." Or, "What about starting the 4:30 light aerobics on time for a change? It gets pretty sickening standing around reading *Runners' World* or *Nutrition Weekly!*" I go wild. I write so much they have to put out more of the little pencils.

It's not surprising. Me and the fitness center—there's always been a quarrel or two. In fact, just the very idea always made me a bit antsy. "Exercise makes you feel worse," I say to my lover, as I stumble in after aerobics, heading for our bathroom shower because all we've had again in the center is ice. "It's a known fact that people who exercise regularly have a shorter life span." A woman of few words but a rich inner life, my lover just smiles her slow, deep smile, and puts on the blackberry tea.

"And another thing," I like to bluster, stuffing my L.L. Bean tote to go to the center, "Aerobics can do substantial damage to one's joints and tendons." My lover just kisses me, and sits down on the living room rug to do her yoga stretches, which are a lovely thing to watch, with her dancer's limbs so straight and long.

My tote was originally a ski boot bag, but I decided that as dangerous as fitness is, skiing is worse. I also find that the best way to entice myself to the center is to fill the tote with a luscious little assortment of body creams, oils, sponges and the like to take along just in case the water heats up, or I want to protect my skin, after the sauna, from looking like a seriously crinkled camel.

Bodies, that's the real trouble; that's why I hate the fitness center so much. I scribble on another little square of paper, "Why don't you let some women in here with bellies or thighs, somebody who maybe has a little fat pouch under her chin? Huh? Why don'tcha?"

Bodies, it's always been my only really serious complaint about anything. We have them. We love in them. They die on us.

Yesterday, I received the letter from Marya's support group. I stuffed it in my tote so my lover wouldn't see it. If she did, she'd try to get me to talk about it, about my feelings. I really hate her for that, the way she'll move up behind me in bed in the night, our bodies like spoons—she's the soup spoon, I'm the tea—and wrap her long arms tight around my middle and breathe warm and sweet into my ear, and say, "Thank you for talking to me," when all I had been doing was blubbering and moaning all my problems out to her, snuffling like a puppy that's lost its milkbone. "Thank you for talking to me."

That's why I chose her—let her choose me. That's why I broke two years of celibacy and a routine of deprivation as sophisticated as a monk's, after eight years of weird affairs with married women, straight women, women with other lovers, women who hated sex, women who hated talking—to risk it all. I hate her, you know. I think we need a suggestion box around this apartment. "No talking," would be my first one.

Bodies. The fitness center, for example, is full of them, just like I said, young ones, thin, supple, fit bodies with aerobic target zones in the mid-teens, bodies that can manipulate rowing machines and Stairmasters and Nautilus contraptions that look like the Inquisition is trying to get you to recant.

And this is the lady gym! I joined it after I dropped out of the dyke gym, which I had innocently stumbled into for a six-week trial run last year. I kept waiting for one of their bulging-biceped, furry-calved women, all of whom wore horizontally-rolled bandannas around their foreheads, to offer to kick sand in my face up at Herring Cove Beach. The contempt of the instructor as she tried to put me through my paces brought back seventh grade gym so vividly I fled.

Still, visions of what I would look like at seventy, curved like an archer's bow from osteoporosis—they write a lot about this in *Cosmopolitan,* which I really only read in the supermarket check-out line—propelled me to sign up at the fitness center. I spent the first week trying to pick out the other dykes. Once I gave that up as hopeless, I started to try to figure out how much everybody's trendy little color-coordinated exercise outfits must've cost.

My favorite class is the light aerobics. It's easier to fake it through. The instructor's young and nervous. If she notices me slinking to the drinking fountain midway through with my finger on my neck-pulse, then sliding into the locker room without finishing the class, she's too intimidated to say anything. By the time the other bodies come bursting into the locker room filmed with righteous sweat, I'm soaking in the whirlpool. I realize that Jane Fonda wouldn't do this, but neither would I make a movie in which I wore pointed metal cups over my breasts.

"Make the class shorter," I write with the little pencil. "Jane Fonda's really a wimp." I draw a smile-face, but with the smile turned downward. "Put in a lending library. How about a juice bar? A disco?" I wonder if anybody ever reads these things. It might be the manager, a tall, emaciated woman named Tess, who is dead behind her eyes, with an Egyptian hairdo and penciled brows. Sometimes she smiles, but I think she has it catered. I imagine that at night Tess leans back against the head-rest of her swiveled desk chair in the glass-walled office where you go in to sign up the day you join, where they promise you that all the unsightly flab will come falling off within a week, and that, anyway, the rates go up 200% tomorrow if you don't pay now, reading everything that's on the square little pieces of paper.

She's already singled out the ones with my handwriting, even though I try a different way of writing every time: backhand, block printing, dotting the i's with little hearts like Christie Welsch used to do in grade school—God, what a little snot-ball she was! I know Tess had a personality analyst pick me out from the vast hordes in the light aerobics class, someone who knows body type and pathology and can tell her, "That's the one—with the thickening waist, the slightly sagging breasts, the plump calves. She's your culprit."

Soon they'll come for me while I'm in the shower, standing discreetly outside with their little white coats and the nets tucked unobtrusively under their arms. Of course, they won't get me; I'll have frozen first.

"Why doesn't this center do a benefit for medical research?" I write on the next little piece of paper. I take two classes that day. I seem to have enormous quantities of energy to burn off. Light aerobics alone won't do it. I try a class called stretch-and-flex. This is where you make delicate balletic movements to *Afternoon of a Faun*, then, by the end, whip up to a little *Maple Leaf Rag*. It isn't strenuous but at least prolongs my having to go home where I might have to talk. I can't resist leaving another note on the way out. "Why do nice people have to hurt?"

My lover has dinner ready—Cornish game hen and little roast potatoes. (We are not politically correct.) I refuse it. Her eyes are big and her touch gentle but she says nothing. She keeps on knitting on an afghan she's started. I decide we should take some vitamins and I rummage around in a old drawer until I find a bottle of C about eight years old. I make her take some with a cup of blackberry tea. What's incredible is that she just swallows them without protest. I hate her.

Next day at the fitness center, I try something new—body-ball. This is a totally weird class in which grown women flex a rubber ball around various parts of our bodies, like under chins and between thighs. What purpose it serves, I'm not really sure, except that if you're horny, between the thighs is kind of interesting. I won't make love these days either so it really gets to me.

As I sit in the whirlpool, I think about how my lover and I first began to touch—the softness of her skin, her mouth, the gently rising passion we allowed to claim us. Even now, two years later, I remember the amazing place we entered together—what her body was like and mine—what they were like together—and how each time, now, it's like reading a poem you love over and over, or catching the same phrase of music from a faraway flutist at the end of the day.

No wonder I won't do it. On my way out of the center, I scribble on a paper square. "Why do we have bodies, anyway? How about a class on giving up sex?"

Finally, my lover asks me if I've heard anything about Marya. Since my lover moved here from far away to live with me, she doesn't know all of my old friends. She knows who Marya is, though; other people mention her. The absence of my mention must have been getting pretty suspicious. I have to tell her about the letter—about the cancer and the chemo and how the support group's taking turns driving her, about the special sessions at Marya's house, the chanting, the sound meditations, and the acupuncture and herbs she's doing along with the hospital treatments.

I wait for my lover to ask me if I'm going to call Marya, if I'm going to go to any of the meditations or join the support group. I happen to know that Marya's oldest friends and also her ex-lover are not in the support group, that most of them are younger women who originally didn't know her well or haven't known her that long. They don't know what a bitch Marya can really be, how her eyes just penetrate right through to your backbone.

None of them were with her the night we drove to New York to hear Rhiannon and the window wouldn't roll up in my VW. It was five above zero and we had to tape cardboard over the gaping hole. We ate coconut cream pie in a diner on the Merritt Parkway at 4 A.M. None of them were with her, either, on the Gay Pride March in '79 when my menstrual sponge failed and I just about left a trail of blood all the way to Central Park. And none of them were with me when a particular lover called me from someone else's bed, and Marya rushed over to lie next to me all night singing me obscene limericks and lullabies and offering to call out for pizza.

My lover doesn't ask me anything. She just sits next to me on the couch as close as she can get, knitting her afghan, and later in bed she holds me spoon-style, even though I haven't talked, and she doesn't ask me to have sex.

"Why don't bodies last forever?" I wrote on my paper today.

"Why aren't you lobbying for more funding for cures for things like AIDS and cancer and the heartbreak of psoriasis?"

I skip my light aerobics and go straight to the Stairmaster. I have never used it before. It's kind of like a version of hell where you're stuck on an escalator in Macy's that's broken down and you have to climb all the way to the top, only over and over again. Afterward, I am too wasted to write any more suggestions, think, speak, feel, or exist—which was the idea.

I stop at the discount drugstore and buy a whole lot of vitamins, A, E, stresstabs, zinc. When I get home I start sorting them into little cups for my lover and me to take. I have also brought her a brochure on joining the fitness center.

She tells me that she feels a little peaked today, as it was busy at work, and that a co-worker with the flu breathed all over her at lunch. She lies down on the couch with her unfinished afghan over her and falls asleep. I sit beside her touching her face as she sleeps. I see in the lamplight the little lines of age around the corners of her eyes. A couple of times I imagine her breathing has stopped. I have never felt so scared.

The next day, when she isn't better, I harass her to call a doctor, knowing how much she hates doctors. I storm off in a huff leaving her pinched-faced under the covers, never even bringing her any soup or tea. At the fitness center, I scrawl all over a paper square, "I suggest we call the whole damn thing off. So there! signed ME." I plunge right into the whirlpool, no body-ball, no stretch-and-flex, no Stairmaster, no nothing. I glare at Tess on the way out. "Go eat a hot fudge sundae," I snarl under my breath. "Have a nice day," she says.

Next evening my lover is all better, her fever broken, her stomach settled. She bathes in lavendar-scented herbs, lights a candle in the bedroom, burns sage in a clam shell we found on Plum Island, pulls me to her as gently as rain on spring earth. Her tongue caresses me until my whole body sings. When I enter her, I feel as if I'm going deep, deep into a place that will shelter me forever. When we lie together afterwards, I can't tell whose leg is whose, whose arm.... We are weeping together. Finally I talk—between gulps and sobs and great gusty nose-blowing. Then we sleep, the soup spoon and the tea.

At breakfast, she says, "When are you going over?"

"Early tonight, if she's having a good night. Will you come?"

"You know I will." She has the afghan in a straw tote. "I've been making this for her. I'm starting a new one for us."

"Why do you love me?" I ask.

"Because you make me laugh," she says.

The day after, in light aerobics, I watch the bodies—tall, fat, thin, wide, younger, older, brown, pinky-white, olive-skinned, freckled, ruddy-hued. Marya's body is not like ours anymore. Someday mine will begin to leave me, too. My lover's will leave me and herself. I cannot bear it—but I cannot, now, no longer dance.

Marya has written a letter to go out to all of the friends she's had throughout her life. She showed it to me last night. "Think of me, dear ones," it said, "think of my spirit soaring, coming to you on bright wings, alive with joy."

"You know," she said, as I was leaving, "I always really did hate coconut pie."

As all of us sway and dip and swirl and leap, I see all the colors of the leotards and sweats and gym shorts blending and bouncing. I wrote on my square today, "What is all the pain for?" The music leaps inside my chest. All of the women begin to raise and lower their arms in unison like so many birds taking flight.

Patricia Roth Schwartz was born on Columbus Day in 1946 in Charleston, West Virginia. She holds a B. A. in English Composition from Mount Holyoke College, an M. A. in English Literature from Trinity College and an M. A. in counseling psychology from Antioch/ New England. She works as a psychotherapist in her own private practive.

Schwartz has previously published a volume of poetry, *Hungers* (Blue Spruce Press) as well as poetry, fiction, non-fiction and reviews in such journals as *Plainswoman, Sojourner, Woman of Power, Backbone, Sinister Wisdom, off our backs, Hot Wire* and *The Women's Review of Books.* She writes regularly for *Gay Community News, Belles Lettres* and *Bay Windows.* Her work also appears in the anthologies *Unholy Alliances: New Fiction by Women* (Cleis Press) and *We are Everywhere* (The Crossing Press).

Schwartz lives in Somerville, Massachusetts with her life partner, Suzanna, two cats, Kali and Lilli, a word processor named Ariadne and an abundant garden. She and her partner hope one day to realize their dream of running an herb farm in the country.

Other Titles Available

ound Goddesses: Asphalta to Viscera by Morgan Grey and Julia enelope.($7.95) "All of it's funny and some of it's inspired. I've had ore fun reading it than any book in the last two years."—Joanna Russ

s The Road Curves by Elizabeth Dean ($8.95) Ramsey had it all; a eat job at a prestigious lesbian magazine, and a reputation of never ving to sleep alone. Now she takes off on an adventure of a lifetime.

ll Out by Judith Alguire ($8.95)Winning a gold medal at the Olympics Kay Strachan's all-consuming goal. Kay remains determined, until a udding romance with a policewoman threatens her ability to go all out r the gold.

esbian Stages ($8.95) "Sarah Dreher's play scripts are treasures: good urns firmly centered in a Lesbian perspective, peopled with specific, omplex, often contadictory—just like real people—characters."—Kate cDermott

ray Magic by Sarah Dreher ($8.95) A peaceful vacation with Stoner's iend Stell turns frightening when Stell falls ill with a mysterious disease d Stoner finds herself an unwitting combatant in the great struggle be-een the Hopi Spirits of good and evil.

oner McTavish by Sarah Dreher ($7.95) The original Stoner McTavish ystery introduces psychic Aunt Hermione, practical partner Marylou, d Stoner herself, who goes off to the Grand Tetons to rescue dream ver Gwen.

omething Shady by Sarah Dreher ($8.95) Travel Agent/Detective Ston- McTavish travels to the coast of Maine with her lover Gwen and risks ecoming an inmate in a suspicious rest home to rescue a missing nurse.

organ Calabresé; The Movie by N. Leigh Dunlap ($5.95) Wonderful- funny comic strips. Lesbian and gay politics, relationships, life's chang-, and softball as seen through the eyes of Morgan Calabresé.

ook Under the Hawthorn by Ellen Frye ($7.95) A stonedyke from the ountains of Vermont, Edie Cafferty sets off to search for her long lost ughter and, on the way, meets Anabelle, an unpredictable jazz pianist oking for her birth mother.

unway at Eland Springs by ReBecca Béguin ($7.95) When Anna fly- g supplies and people into the African bush, finds herself in conflict ver her agreement to scout and fly supplies for a game hunter, she rns to Jilu, the woman running a safari camp at Eland Springs, for love d support.

romise of the Rose Stone by Claudia McKay ($7.95) Mountain warrior a goes to the Federation to confront its rulers for her people. She is nished to the women's compound in the living satellite, Olyeve, where e and her lover, Cleothe, plan an escape.